April Storm

Also by Leila Meacham

April Storm

A NOVEL

Leila Meacham

HARPER

An Imprint of HarperCollinsPublishers

This is a work of fiction. Names, characters, places, and incidents are products of the author's imagination or are used fictitiously and are not to be construed as real. Any resemblance to actual events, locales, organizations, or persons, living or dead, is entirely coincidental.

HarperCollins books may be purchased for educational, business, or sales promotional use. For information, please email the Special Markets Department at SPsales@harpercollins.com.

FIRST EDITION

Library of Congress Cataloging-in-Publication Data
Names: Meacham, Leila, 1938–2021, author.
Title: April storm: a novel / Leila Meacham.
Identifiers: LCCN 2024017359 (print) |
LCCN 2024017360 (ebook) | ISBN
9780063323100 (hardcover) | ISBN 9780063323124 (ebook)
Subjects: LCGFT: Detective and mystery fiction. | Novels.
Classification: LCC PS3563.E163 A85 2024 (print) | LCC PS3563.E163
(ebook) | DDC 813/.54—dc23/eng/20240422
LC record available at https://lccn.loc.gov/2024017359
LC ebook record available at https://lccn.loc.gov/2024017360

24 25 26 27 28 LBC 5 4 3 2 1

To Richard and my readers

April is the cruelest month.

—T. S. ELIOT

April Storm

Chapter One

Thursday, April 1, 2010

The watcher sat huddled in his overcoat in the darkness of his SUV, a gloved hand over his mouth to prevent his breath from fogging the windshield. He'd kiss a monkey's butt for a cigarette, but he dared not risk lighting up. The neighborhood's roving security guard had cruised past twice already, the first time beaming his flashlight on the five-day visitor's pass hanging from the rearview mirror. The watcher had ducked out of sight just in time. The pass was a forgery. His vehicle would have been illegally parked had it belonged to a resident. In this exclusive subdivision in the foothills of the ritzy Beaver Creek Resort, homeowners were required to keep their vehicles off the street.

It was the hour before dawn, and any moment, he knew, a jogger would come sprinting out onto the sidewalk from the deeper shadows of the running path. Here in the last grip of winter for Avon, Colorado, only die-hard joggers and walkers used the path at this obscene hour of the morning. The object of his surveillance routinely ran past this point at . . . he checked the face of his luminous watch, for there she was now, wearing the same white running gear and red jacket. He made an entry in his notebook:

6:00 a.m. As usual, she jogged in place to cast a look down both sides of the lamplit street before hitting the crosswalk, blond curls peeking from beneath her white ski cap. It was a nice face, he thought, even without all the makeup.

He capped his pen and stowed the notebook. She was no casual jogger, not at this hour, not in this cold, and not with her form. After observing her for five straight days, he could confidently report to his client that at approximately six every weekday morning, Kathryn Walker could be counted on to appear at this spot. That was his main assignment: to learn the places and times she was likely to show up on a consistent basis, as well as other details of her personal life. In the two months he'd been tailing her, he'd uncovered a reliable source of information, and the rest he had gleaned from observation and newspapers.

Kathryn Walker, a mother in her mid-forties, was a civic leader who had served on a number of charity boards that met monthly. She seemed to be a born leader. She headed everything from the PTA to fundraisers for soliciting college scholarships for underprivileged children to a push for the SPCA to open a fully endowed shelter for homeless animals. She'd also served two terms as president of the homeowners' association of her subdivision—an onerous job, it seemed to him, people and their own selfish welfare being what they are.

According to his source, who had been privy to what went on behind closed doors, Kathryn was everything she appeared to be, an exemplary wife and mother and a fearless advocate for the welfare of her community. But as head of organizations, she had ticked off some folks, and a few had made threats against her—several property developers, the parents of two students she voted to expel from the school district for threatening their teachers, and a couple of homeowners irate that she and the rest of the HOA had thwarted their attempts to bypass building restrictions.

Recently, though, Kathryn had stepped back from several of her charitable activities, and her slower calendar made it easier for him to gather information. There were five activities she still attended—six, actually, but he did not include that last in his notes. Monday mornings every two weeks, she read to a group of pre-schoolers at the public library. When he first tailed her there, he'd thought *Oh no!* as she took her seat among the cluster of wriggly ankle-biters who scrambled in close and called her "Kathwyn." He was not a kid person, especially not with the spoiled, entitled kind they grew in the Beaver Creek area. But in time he had to admit that he found himself looking forward to those Monday mornings browsing nearby shelves in the public library, to the soothing sound of her voice.

She met the first Tuesday morning of the month with her book club at a coffee shop, and on Wednesdays at ten o'clock she joined three other amateur artists for oil painting lessons in an art studio. Thursday, each week, she took a resident of the local retirement home, an elderly woman named Natalie Hunt, out to lunch. One Friday morning per month she kept a standing appointment at the nail salon. And most Sunday mornings, lately alone, she attended services at an Episcopalian church about eleven miles from where she lived, occupying a pew on the left side, four rows from the back.

He grew to enjoy the look of her profile silhouetted by the light from the stained glass window. He wondered what she prayed for when the congregation bowed its collective head. She had no need to ask for anything. She appeared to have it all—a privileged life-style, a successful, handsome husband, and two thriving children, the son an elementary school teacher in Denver and the daughter a senior majoring in business at the University of Colorado in Boulder.

But on the tenth of both February and March, Kathryn had brought flowers to a local cemetery and laid them on a child's grave: ABBY GALE WALKER, DECEMBER 5, 1985–APRIL 10, 1986. It was this last information that the watcher decided to keep to himself.

He filled the report with every other detail, however, having been instructed that nothing was too small: Monday through

Thursday afternoons she spent painting in a cozy room upstairs in her home. Late Friday afternoons seemed to be her favorite time to shop for gourmet items at City Market. (The lady knew her prosciutto from lunch-meat ham, for sure.) He knew she telephoned her children on Sunday afternoons, that she sipped a glass of sauvignon blanc each night while making dinner. He knew the code of the home security system, the shape of the house key hidden in the terra-cotta frog on the front porch, that her housekeeper had been fired three months before, and that the Walkers' best friends had recently divorced. The husband, Frank, lived directly behind them, their back fences facing each other across an alley. Their beloved Sheltie had died last April—"A loss to the family, especially Mrs. Walker," his source had told him. And a relief to *him*, to be sure, to have no dog to notice a private eye sniffing around the property.

Ultimately, the watcher did not care why the client wanted this data, so long as he got his paycheck. He had once been considered among the best in his field—in his more reputable days, he'd been known as the Bloodhound. But then his private investigation firm in Houston, Texas, let him go for double-dealing. Now the majority of clients sought his "research" services in a rented office far from his old posh business address. When he'd been contacted in early February for the Walker job, the caller's voice electronically altered, he assumed he'd best play it straight and agreed to learn all he could about Kathryn. "Time is critical," the voice had made clear. "If you do not provide me with the information I require in sixty days, the deal is off. Is that understood?"

He understood perfectly. A retainer in cash had arrived by courier, along with a burner phone and instructions to text his findings. The majority of his clients left no paper trail, a safeguard that was fine by him, and great for his taxes.

At first he'd assumed the usual, a disillusioned husband looking to dig up photo opportunities to take to court against a cheating spouse. But the longer he shadowed Kathryn Walker, the less he could imagine even an obsessive partner suspecting her of adultery.

Besides, her husband was Dr. Drew Walker, the chief of orthopedics at Winston General Hospital. A brilliant, highly respected surgeon, he was reputed to be a pain in the ass to the business suits that set hospital policies and procedure, his fractious attitude tolerated because he was sought after by professional sports teams, celebrities, and the elite attracted by Beaver Creek. So far, the watcher had discovered nothing to suggest that the man had any reason or desire to divorce his wife, but then he hadn't been paid to investigate him. Dr. Walker could be living a secret life for all he knew, or cared.

Who, then, lurked in the wings with reason and desire to solicit information on the daily activities of Kathryn Walker? Looking back at the list of adversaries from her charity years gave the watcher an idea. If harm came to Kathryn, there would be plenty of suspects without the searchlight turning on his client, whoever that might be.

Chapter Two

Friday, April 2

Kathryn Walker saw the man again as she reached for a wedge of Gruyère in the imported cheese section of City Market and knew with final certainty that it was him. He wore an overcoat with the collar turned up, a bulky scarf, and a golf cap set low over his eyes, but there was no disguising his slightly dropped left shoulder and the faint hump on his back. Today she had first noticed him in the produce section while she was perusing the grapes and he kept looking at her from over a neatly piled mound of grapefruit. In the wine section, while she was choosing a bottle of sauvignon blanc, he was hovering nearby. Now he was here, looking at cheddar. Calmly, Kathryn placed the cheese in her basket, but her heart had begun the beat she'd first felt two weeks before when she realized how often she'd seen the stalker's familiar shape in the places she frequented.

Avon did not have enough business establishments that you could avoid running into the same out-of-towners a few times among the hordes that showed up during ski season. But to see the same man a dozen times, dressed in different weather gear, was far beyond coincidence, especially now that April had begun. The man also didn't look like a winter sports enthusiast. He didn't even seem physically capable of managing a snowboard or pair of skis. He appeared exhausted, as if he subsisted on fast food and alcohol. When she noticed him that first time, she had assumed he was in Avon for some other purpose. It wasn't until this day in the grocery store that the shocking possibility hit her: she had a stalker.

She moved to the breakfast aisle to see if he would follow. When she looked, he had his back to her, pretending an interest in the label on a box of cereal, but she could tell he had her in his sights. For a rash, queasy moment, she thought of confronting him in this public place, where she was safe and well-known. *Who are you? What do you want? Why are you following me?*

But the man could easily cause a scene if he decided to protest his innocence. She imagined the evening news: *Kathryn Walker, prominent civic leader and scientist, today accused a man in a local grocery market of stalking her. The man denied it and is now considering legal action against Mrs. Walker for defamation of character . . .*

Or the man might be deranged and attack her, pull out a gun or knife—who knew what he might do? Willing herself not to panic, Kathryn wheeled her cart toward the butcher's case. Instinct told her that safety lay in not revealing that she was onto him. She would pick up the leg of lamb she'd ordered, check out, and have the bag boy carry her groceries to the car.

Waiting for her turn at the counter, she considered what would happen if he followed her home. She visualized him jumping out of his car as she waited in her drive for the sluggish garage door to rise, holding a weapon on her while she got out of the car, then following her into the house. Should she telephone the police and request that an officer meet her there, or call the retired couple across the street, explain that she was being followed, and ask that they wait for her in front of her house? Kathryn was fairly certain Jim would get his big Uzi-looking rifle that he took to Canada for moose hunting every year, drape himself in ammo, and lie in wait guerilla-style behind their front yard hedge for the man's car to appear. If nothing else, Jim's gun might arrest her stalker's escape and give her a chance to question him.

Kathryn realized she was rubbing her bracelet, her fingers tracing the three charms. It was a habit she had whenever she was nervous or worried about something. The coolness of the diamond-embedded gold chain immediately calmed her, and she landed on a more reasonable idea. She could have her home security company check on her house for a possible burglary, say she was on her way there. She and Drew hadn't been activating the security alarm recently, but now, of course, she'd have to remember more reliably. She would call as soon as she was in her car.

The butcher brightened when he saw Kathryn. "Hi, Mrs. Walker. Come to pick up that leg of lamb?"

"I have, Joe. It's for dinner tonight," she said, forcing a smile and a lightness into her voice.

"Marinated in lemon juice, garlic, olive oil, and sage?"

"You got it," Kathryn said.

"Mrs. Walker is one of my customers who knows what to do with a prime cut of meat." The butcher winked to the customer standing next to her, a local rancher she'd seen a few times, in his western-cut leather jacket, cowboy hat, and boots.

"Sounds like it," the man answered.

"Be right back with that leg," Joe said, and Kathryn sneaked a quick look over her shoulder. Golf Cap was nowhere to be seen. The man could vanish like a puff of smoke, but she had no doubt he was in the vicinity. She could pick up his presence like an odor. The customer beside her cast her a sidelong glance, and she wondered if her jitters, increasing by the minute, were seeping through the layers of her wool-lined raincoat. When Joe returned and handed her the bundle, her hands shook. The rancher reached out to assist her, but she gave him a flickering smile. "A little heavier than I thought," she said, placing the lamb in her basket and wheeling away before remembering to thank Joe for his trouble.

As she neared her white Cadillac, followed by the bag boy, the jitters got the better of her and she dropped her remote key. As she bent to retrieve it from a pool of rainwater, the shoulder strap of her purse slid down her arm straight for the puddle, throwing off her balance as she tried to catch it. Her flesh struck metal as she grabbed the trailer hitch of a Range Rover parked next to the Cadillac, and she yelped.

The bag boy, his arms loaded with groceries and helpless to assist, cried, "Mrs. Walker, are you all right?"

"Thanks, Shawn," Kathryn said, righting herself and ignoring the pain in her wrist. "I am all right. Just a little nervous today. No damage done." She recovered her key and would have dug into her purse for a tip, but Shawn stopped her.

"It's okay, Mrs. Walker. You can catch me another time," he said. "Drive safe."

Once in the car, groceries stowed and the door locked, her hands shaking and wrist throbbing, Kathryn pulled up the number to her home security company.

"This is Kathryn Walker. I'm concerned about a break-in. Could you have a patrol officer meet me at my house? I'm driving home now."

"Certainly, ma'am, we'll send someone over right away."

Kathryn let out a slow controlled breath, like the ones she had practiced in her yoga classes. Pulling out of the parking lot, she felt a small semblance of control.

Chapter Three

Rain had begun to patter. Gripping the steering wheel, Kathryn checked her mirrors as she moved out into the swell of wet rush-hour traffic but saw no golf cap. He would have removed it, and she had no idea what kind of vehicle to look for. A sense of calm purpose had come over her now that she was convinced she had a stalker, like the perverse peace that comes when you hear the dreaded confirmation of a disease.

This was the last thing they needed right now. Drew had become moody and irritable in the past month, and she didn't want to add to his stress. She'd been ignoring his cantankerousness because she understood its source. He had become increasingly dissatisfied with his work environment at Winston General, but now that the new orthopedic hospital was coming to Avon, he was mad at himself that he didn't have the money to buy in as partner, having made an unwise investment a couple of years before. But when she tried to suggest that they cut back on their spending, focus only on urgent house repairs, and stop indulging Lindsay's bank overdrafts at the University of Boulder, he kept brushing her off. And he was adamant that they still make the trip to Europe they had been planning for so long.

Yes, no need to call Drew till she got home. He would be at

the gym, but she could have the front desk page him. Then again, what exactly could she tell him? What could she tell the police? What proof did she have that she was being followed by a stranger? Drew knew better than to think she was imagining things, but he and the police were bound to ask the same questions she'd been asking herself, over and over, every day for the last two weeks. The police would want to know if Golf Cap had approached her in any way, and she would have to say no. He'd been nothing more than a quiet, unexplained presence in the background. In the true crime documentaries she watched, stalkers were pushy people who eventually made physical, sometimes threatening contact with their victims, but this man had made no such move toward her. There had been no telephone calls from heavy breathers, no creepy emails, no mysterious parcels containing cryptic contents left on her front porch.

Her head beginning to pound, Kathryn turned up the windshield wipers. The rain was coming down in sheets now. It was appropriate to this terrible first week of April, she thought bitterly. The month should have heralded a season of rebirth and growth, but for her and Drew, every day was haunted by memories of death and loss. Here in this part of the Rockies, April was an ugly month. The snow melted and sent rivers of mud down the mountainsides into streams and streets. The weather was a prankster, bringing warmth and sun one day, rain and bitter cold the next. Thaws brought out the first buds on the trees, then cold snaps turned them black. For the Walkers, each year waited to dump all its woes on them in April, and it looked as if this year the month had begun right on track.

The rain was still pummeling her windshield by the time she reached home, a huge two-story mountain house with vistas so beautiful that on clear days they could stop the heart. Even after all these years, Kathryn still felt a thrill of disbelief that it was her home. That she owned a home at all, after the way she and Drew had grown up. It was the one extravagance she hadn't resisted when Drew brought her to see the house shortly after he began his practice. They were already in debt, and the mortgage was more than they could afford at the time, but the minute she'd walked into the house's airy, light-filled rooms, she'd felt its arms come around her and known she was home. "Let's buy it!" she'd said immediately to the surprised realtor and her even more surprised husband, and she'd never once regretted it.

Two security vehicles were parked on the street, their lights flashing, and three uniformed men wearing rain slickers were waving flashlights around the front of the house. One broke away to wait patiently while Kathryn's garage door slowly groaned up, then met her on her side of the car. He identified himself as Bill Tyler, head of the security team dispatched to her house, and informed her that they had checked the outside of her doors and windows and found nothing amiss. "Your front door was locked when we got here, so we feel that everything is all right," he said. "Do you want us to make a search inside and see you safely installed before we leave?"

"I would be most grateful," Kathryn said without a pinch of shame for the ruse. It was not unthinkable that Golf Cap or an accomplice could have beaten her here and gotten inside her house.

"We'll leave our slickers in the garage and wear booties on our shoes," the man said with a polite smile. His team was familiar with the protocol for servicing homes in this area. Besides, if there had been a break-in, they did not want to tamper with the crime scene.

While they fanned out through the rooms, Kathryn looked up the telephone number of the Argyle Athletic Club. Her husband practiced what he preached on good bone health and believed in rigorous, consistent exercise. He tried not to allow anything to interfere with his workout sessions on late Monday, Wednesday, and Friday afternoons, and she and his staff, short of an emergency, had been asked to respect the hours he was indisposed.

A young male voice answered, conjuring an image of robust health. "Argyle Athletic Club. Chad speaking."

"Good afternoon, Chad," Kathryn said. "My name is Kathryn Walker, wife of Dr. Drew Walker. Would you please call my husband to the phone? Tell him it is urgent."

There was a mystified pause. "The name again, please?"

"Dr. Drew Walker," she repeated a little impatiently and heard the tap of computer keys. Goodness, besides his being a member of the Argyle for years, Kathryn would have thought Drew's name would be instantly recognizable, given his reputation as a skilled surgeon in the area.

Again there was a small pause, and then the voice, a trifle less peppy, said, "I'm sorry, Mrs. Walker, but we do not have a member listed by that name."

Kathryn stared at the rain lashing the kitchen windows. "Oh, but I'm sure you do. Dr. Drew Walker, chief of orthopedic surgery at Winston General?"

"Ah, Mrs. Walker, I am quite certain Dr. Walker is not a member."

"But he must be. He's been going there for years."

"Mrs. Walker, if you'll just hold the line a minute . . ."

"I certainly will," she said. The young man must be new.

A suave older voice came on the line. Kathryn had the impression her call had been kicked up to an office with deep leather chairs and library paneling. "Mrs. Walker, this is Ralph Lambert, general manager of the Argyle. I'm sorry, but at present your husband is not a member of this club."

"But you must have—"

"Dr. Walker was once a member here, but he has let his membership expire."

Stunned, Kathryn asked in a whisper, "Expire? When?"

"According to our records, six months ago, Mrs. Walker."

Kathryn stammered, at a loss for words. Finally, in a firmer voice, she said, "It must have slipped my mind that my husband has changed his workout venues because of his schedule. I am sure he misses his workouts in your facility. Thank you for your time."

She slowly returned the receiver to its cradle. If Drew wasn't at the Argyle every Monday, Wednesday, and Friday afternoon, where was he? Like clockwork, Drew arrived home on those evenings to unload his workout gear from his gym bag into a special hamper for their exercise clothes. Each Saturday she washed and folded them so that he could repack them the morning of his workout days. It was practically a ritual.

"Mrs. Walker?"

It was the voice of Bill Tyler. Kathryn turned from the phone, and his eyes widened. The eyes of the other two men who had gathered in the kitchen were staring at her as well. She realized that her face must have gone stark white and that she was standing stiff as a pole, as if she'd just heard that a family member had died unexpectedly.

"Really, Mrs. Walker, there is nothing to worry about," Bill assured her. "We've checked your house thoroughly and every room is clear. Nothing appears to be amiss, but if you're still worried, maybe you should call someone to be with you until your husband returns. Or I can leave an officer, if you like."

Kathryn swallowed. She knew she should have gotten one of those new security systems with a camera. "That is kind of you, but I've . . . just put in a call to my husband at his athletic club. He will be on his way home any time now."

"Well, if you're sure . . ." Bill sounded doubtful. He handed her a company card. "If you have any more trouble, just give us a call, and we'll be here in a jiffy. Meanwhile, you might want to follow us out and lock the door behind us."

"Yes, yes, I will do that," Kathryn heard herself say. After seeing them out, she returned to the kitchen in a trance.

At present your husband is not a member of this club . . . She sank into a chair. Her fingers felt icy against her lips as she remembered the flyers that had come to the house this winter, inviting Drew to rejoin the Argyle. A computer mistake, she had thought, and thrown them away as junk mail. Suddenly the full force of the general manager's words hit her like a punch in the stomach, where already her anxiety lay like a ball of iron. The room spun, and nausea rose to her throat. She reached for her phone. Where are you? she typed.

Just before she hit send, she heard the garage door open. Her husband was home.

Chapter Four

The bell of the security system jingled, and Kathryn could hear her husband's footsteps in the hall off the kitchen, as identifiable as his cough, his sneeze, the clearing of his throat. She heard him walk left into the laundry room and unzip his gym bag, and the sound of the hamper lid bumping the wall when he dropped in his workout clothes. She heard him open the door to the utility closet where he stored his gym bag, then draw water, followed a few seconds later by the soft clink of his empty glass on the marble counter in the bathroom. They were the clockwork sounds of his arrival home three afternoons a week.

He hung up his jacket in the hall and entered the kitchen, wearing scrubs. He smelled fresh from a shower and wore the wasted look of someone recently come from a stint of strenuous exercise at the end of a long week. It was his Friday look, the one she'd been familiar with for years. "Hi," he said, giving her a brief smile before turning to look through the mail. "What? No new mail today? Did you forget to bring it in?" It was yesterday's collection of bills, requests for donations, magazines, and catalogs.

When she didn't answer, he gave her another glance, his expression of faint annoyance clearing to concern. "Honey, are you okay? You look a bit . . . out of it."

"Do I?" She realized she was still sitting in a stupefied state. For the last ten minutes, she had been working out how Drew's gym clothes smelled of sweat and felt a little gummy when she emptied the hamper each weekend, and how his muscle tone did not show that he'd taken half a year off from exercising.

Insidiously, Kathryn couldn't help but look at him as she hadn't in a long time, as other women saw him. He was a good-looking man still, tall, lean, and fit, his hair thinning a bit, but even more attractive than when they'd first met. Time and his status as a notable surgeon had added an alluring distinction he didn't have when he was younger. The nurses all adored him. To them, he was charming and considerate; he called them his teammates and left doughnuts at the nurses' station on Mondays.

But something had changed him in the past months. When she first became aware of it, she'd decided they were falling into the snare of many middle-aged married couples who were both busy with their own interests. A distance was growing between them because of the inevitable demands of Drew's work and her deep involvement in charitable causes, but it was more than that. After over thirty years of marriage, they'd stopped putting in the effort to make each other feel special. So, glad for a hiatus from her community commitments, she'd proposed a standing date night at home. They'd silence their cells, take the landline phone off the hook. She'd make a fine meal, and they'd linger over drinks and conversation, get back in touch. Drew had been all for it, suggesting they do this every Friday.

They'd started off fine, but gradually they'd let professional and social obligations interfere, and sometimes Drew would come home too late for the meal she'd prepared or plainly not be in the spirit for the "three S's," as he indelicately put it, grinning wickedly—sip, sup, and screw.

But where had he been, if not at the Argyle? She wouldn't even consider that he was somewhere where he shouldn't be. Recent frustrations aside, she and Drew were one, as interwoven as the warp and weft of the tapestry hanging in the foyer. They practically shared the same heartbeat, and trust in the other's fidelity was as taken for granted as breathing. It was the bedrock of their marriage.

Since they'd agreed to start watching their pennies, had he finally decided that his membership in the athletic club was an expense they couldn't afford right now? Was he making do with jogging at the nearby high school track, or exercising in the hospital's woefully ill-equipped gym, another of his grumps against Winston General? That had to be the explanation, but why hadn't he told her? Their financial slump was no news to her; why keep his withdrawal from the Argyle to himself?

But it would be like her husband to spare her the pain of his selfless sacrifice—and spare himself the embarrassment, since he'd gotten them into their financial straits—in giving up the gym. She knew he loved the place, with its state-of-the-art equipment and its proximity to his office. It would be like him not to mention dropping his membership until he'd figured a way out of the dilemma. That was his way of dealing with obstacles. Although willing to acknowledge his rare screwups, her husband would not admit them until he'd managed a solution. He hadn't wished to worry her, he'd always say, but she had long understood that Drew Walker's main fear was that he might appear weak, somehow unable to handle the normal troubles that got others down. This particular bent to his male pride was the one gap in their marriage she'd never been able to bridge.

But pride or not, he should have told her that he'd canceled his membership in the Argyle. What if she'd needed him—like today?

She couldn't resist asking, "Was the Argyle busy?"

The question caught him off guard. He cast her a startled glance, the look of a stag rearing his head at the cock of a rifle. But then he shrugged. "Same as usual."

She was about to tell him what she knew and ask why he was letting her believe he was somewhere where he wasn't. But years of experience—as a mother and as a scientist—had taught her not to jump to conclusions. There had to be a logical explanation. Instead of prompting a fight when they had a more important problem to face together, she would simply give Drew space to tell her the truth.

I am being stalked, Kathryn wanted to respond to his observation that she looked out of it, but before she could reply, his eye fell upon the butcher-wrapped package on the table. "Kathryn? What's this meat doing out on the table?" He peered at the label. "For sixty-five dollars, it ought to be in the refrigerator. It's leaking blood."

No kiss. No *how was your day?* Kathryn was suddenly nauseated by the sight of the dark-red streak slowly inching its way across the table. "It's the leg of lamb for tonight's dinner. Today's Friday."

"It will have to wait. We've been invited to a get-together this evening. Dr. Camden's having an impromptu birthday party for Barbara Stratton. It's her fortieth, and I promised we'd come. I just heard about it today. Didn't you get my text?"

Kathryn could hear the edge to his tone, stinging as a paper cut across a tender spot. He wouldn't have been in the mood for their date night anyway. Blood rushed to her temples as she got up to clean the mess, but Drew was already at the paper dispenser. With his usual efficiency, he snatched off towels to catch the red trickle before it could drip to the floor. She watched his deft hands wrap the leg in fresh paper towels to store in the refrigerator.

"No, I didn't get your text. Do we have to go?" Her lips felt stiff as wood. "I've had an unusual day, and I was looking forward to a relaxing night together and telling you about it." Barbara Stratton was his surgical nurse, the hospital's mother based on her position. She'd taken Drew under her wing when he first came to Winston General. They were both very fond of her, but why tonight, of all nights?

"I'm sorry, honey," he said in a more mollified tone, "but we do. Barbara would be hurt if we didn't."

"All right," she heard herself say, wondering at her own voice, afraid to ask her husband for the truth of his whereabouts.

He looked at her again. "Did you know you're still in your coat? You must have just gotten in. And where is your bracelet?"

Blankly, Kathryn looked down. Her left wrist was beginning to swell and bruise. Her precious bracelet was missing. Frantically, she pushed up her raincoat sleeve. Not there. Oh, God. It must have come undone when she bumped her arm against the Range Rover. It had probably been pulverized into gold dust by now. "I . . . must have lost it when I fell," she said, her head continuing to throb, beating in time to the rain drumming the windows, the dirge of April.

"Oh, Kath, how many times did I remind you to get the clasp fixed?" Gently he took her hand to examine her wrist. "How did you fall?"

While I was running from my stalker. "I slipped in the parking lot."

He let go of her hand. "Thankfully your wrist isn't broken, but you need to be more careful. You should try calling the market. Hopefully someone's found your bracelet and turned it in. A bracelet like that . . . It can't be replaced, you know."

His voice was soft with dismay, disapproval. To her it wasn't the cost of the bracelet but the sentimental value. It reminded her of their young love, their children, the life that they had built together. And now it was gone. "Yes, Drew, I know," Kathryn said. "You don't have to remind me."

Drew had proposed to her under a rose-covered arbor in full splendor at the Houston Botanical Gardens. He'd said with sorrow in his eyes, "I wish I could give you a ring, but do you need one to tell the world that you are engaged to a man who loves you with all his heart?" Her wedding ring was the plain gold band still on her finger. She'd eschewed the practice of trading it in for the three- and five-carat diamond sparklers that some doctors' wives sported when their husbands began to make money. The bracelet was enough. Drew had presented it to her five years after he'd proposed. He'd bought it with his first substantial paycheck as a resident, spending almost all their money on a down payment that had taken him a year to pay off.

"I saw it and had to get it for you, Kath. It's a reminder of the day we started," he'd said, proudly clasping the chain of tiny rosebuds inlaid with diamond chips around her wrist. The charms were in honor of their three children. Hardly a day had gone by that she had not worn it.

Kathryn picked up the phone to the sound of another vicious slap of rain against the darkened kitchen window. "I'll call City Market now."

"I'll make us a couple of martinis while you do," Drew said. "You look like you could use one."

Chapter Five

They drove in almost total silence the ten miles to Elizabeth Camden's town house, the windshield wipers as hypnotic as a pendulum. Kathryn was stewing more than she should be about the lost bracelet, but it had shaken her. The market had promised to call if anyone turned it in, and there wasn't much to do but prepare for the party. Kathryn knew she did not look her best in her black dress. She'd been dismayed when she asked Drew for his opinion, and he simply looked up from his cuff links, said, "You look nice," and looked back down as he fumbled with his wrists.

"Do you at least have an opinion about my hair?"

"I said you look nice." He smiled. "Hurry up, we don't want to be late."

Drew's dismissiveness didn't help her confidence, and she already felt out of place among the other wives. Susan Jackson and Anne Lawson, young second wives of cardiologists at Winston General, inevitably showed up with designer clothing and the latest procedure from their plastic surgeon. It irked her how much they lit up when Drew was around.

"Who will be at the party?" she asked.

"Only those closest to Barbara, which will eliminate our hospital administrator, the witch from hell Hensley. I don't imagine there will be many. Dr. Camden's work hours haven't allowed her to make many new friends."

Kathryn had barely met Elizabeth Camden, Winston's brightest addition to the orthopedic surgical ward as chief resident, and knew only what she'd learned from Drew. Elizabeth was the only child of an internationally famous heart-transplant surgeon, and she had invited Barbara to move in with her when a kitchen fire made it impossible for her to remain in her condo.

"Have you ever been to Elizabeth's town house?" Kathryn asked.

"Only a couple of times. Drinks after work to discuss business away from Hensley. The walls in the doctors' lounge soak up gossip like sponges."

Their hostess met them at the door. Kathryn had forgotten how beautiful she was. She guessed her to be barely into her late twenties, with hair that framed her face in wispy golden layers that accentuated her small nose and Cupid's bow lips. She, too, was wearing black, but with far more dramatic success. The inevitable strand of pearls highlighted the elegance of her designer sheath, a lustrous opera length that must have cost the equivalent of a year of their daughter's college tuition. Kathryn wondered if she was still dating the handsome ski instructor she'd introduced them to at a Fourth of July picnic last year.

"Dr. and Mrs. Walker," she greeted them warmly. "It's so nice that you could make it on such short notice."

"We wouldn't miss wishing Barbara a happy birthday. You are so kind to do this for her," Drew said and handed over a bottle of wine.

Kathryn saw that the guests were an eclectic mix of nurses, lab techs, and other locals. She caught a glimpse of Elizabeth's ski instructor among the faces. Barbara Stratton was talking excitedly at the center of a circle, wearing a tasteful pantsuit with a dark lipstick that looked good against her short, dark hair. It was a bit odd to see this side of Barbara, all made up with a glass of wine in hand. Every time Kathryn had been with her, she was always in scrubs, with a clean face. As they approached, it became clear that the subject was the orthopedic hospital due to break ground in the summer.

Drew stood quietly listening. One of the doctors said, "I take it you'll be leaving along with the other partners, Drew. It certainly sounds like something you'd enjoy."

A flush stole up Drew's face. Not only was everyone in the room aware of his disenchantment with Winston, but they simply assumed he could afford the $500,000 price tag to buy in as partner. "We'll see," he said.

"What's there to see?" someone asked.

Drew shrugged. "Depends on what they offer."

"How about the state of the art in robotic devices?" another of the doctors remarked, his tone reflecting the others' obvious surprise. "It's what you've been after Winston to install for years."

Kathryn's heart twisted in pity for Drew. It had been his long-time dream to work in a hospital that specialized in his field. His main beef with Winston was their refusal to buy the equipment essential to orthopedic care. Over the years he'd had offers from other bone centers that fit the bill, but acceptance would mean leaving their dream home, their community, the children's schools and friends, and all the reasons they'd moved to the mountains. His plan had been to wait it out at Winston General because, he said, "One of these days, Kath, an orthopedic hospital will come here to the valley of broken bones. It's ripe for one, and I want to be a part of it."

And now it was a bitter pill to swallow to know that he'd have to bypass the opportunity because of his premature investment in the ski resort. He could join the new hospital, but only as a mere member of the staff, with no say in how things were run, a step back from where he was now. Temporarily, he'd have to take a pay cut as well, which their budget could not afford.

In no mood to be sociable, Kathryn wandered away after a few brief greetings to study the magnificent artwork displayed about the room.

"Kathryn, I understand you're an artist—portraits, isn't it?" Elizabeth said, appearing at her side. She had donned a shocking-pink apron to serve the first course. "Drew said you two will be traveling to the art capitals of the world in May."

"I'm afraid that's only partly right," Kathryn said, surprised that Elizabeth knew of her hobby and the trip. "We are going to Europe, but I wouldn't call myself an artist. I'm only a dabbler with a preference for trying to express people's character on canvas, but I like to try my hand at various subjects. I used to be a scientist, so it trained my eye a bit for detail and the human form. You've acquired a beautiful collection."

"Courtesy of my grandfather's estate," Elizabeth said. "He had an art gallery in Santa Fe and left his entire inventory to me. I couldn't bear to part with a piece. Do you like Georgia O'Keeffe?"

"I'm a huge fan. Don't tell me you have one of hers?"

Elizabeth smiled and touched her arm. "Several, as a matter of fact. Go down to the basement. I have a whole wall devoted to her work."

"The basement?" Kathryn said in surprise. "Why down there and not up here?"

"Because that's where I spend most of my time when I'm fortunate enough to be home."

"I see," Kathryn said, liking that about her. The paintings were for her own enjoyment, not to show off. And it was indeed awfully thoughtful of Elizabeth, so dissimilar to Barbara in age and sophistication and position, to have this party for her, a single woman with no family to celebrate her birthday. "I'd love to see the paintings," she said.

Elizabeth turned on the row of wall sconces illuminating the narrow set of stairs to the basement and watched as Kathryn descended, instructing her where to find a light switch at the bottom of the stairs. With the glow of the kitchen behind her, Elizabeth made a glamorous picture in the open door. Kathryn thought, aside from her own daughter, that she'd never seen a woman more beautiful.

"Okay?" Elizabeth called, seeing Kathryn glance back.

"Okay." Kathryn clicked on a bank of lights that bathed the room in an atmospheric glow. Then she gave a small, shocked sound.

"Pretty neat, huh?" Elizabeth called down, smiling.

"Pretty . . . neat," Kathryn agreed in a whisper. But her eyes weren't on the priceless Georgia O'Keeffe paintings. She was looking at a fully equipped exercise gym, gleaming softly under the overhead lights.

Chapter Six

As soon as Elizabeth closed the door quietly, assuming she was leaving her guest to enjoy the art collection undisturbed, Kathryn sank to the bottom step. Fears that an hour earlier she'd ruthlessly banished as beneath consideration suddenly stirred to life. But no—the thought that there could be something more was silly. Elizabeth had her ski instructor. This gym equipment did not prove a thing. As far as Kathryn was aware, Drew knew Elizabeth Camden only professionally. He mentioned her occasionally but only in connection to their work, never anything about her personal life. They were mere colleagues and nothing more.

But then Kathryn recalled the words of her best friend Sandy Danton, twice divorced: *When a married man is having an affair with a coworker, trust me, he will never mention her name. It's his best cover.* Sandy knew of what she spoke. The identity of the woman her first husband left her for had come as a complete surprise.

Kathryn realized she was shaking, and her skin felt clammy when she pressed her hands to her cheeks. She had to get a grip. Her anxiety over the stalker was clouding her judgment. She had only been a part of the group Drew had gotten drinks with a few times after work, he said, and she believed him. She would have her answer soon enough. As soon as they'd left the party, she would tell him she'd called the Argyle Athletic Club and learned that he was no longer a member.

Above her, the door opened. "Honey?" Drew called down softly. "Liz is ready for us."

Liz. Not Elizabeth. After a long minute, Kathryn got heavily to her feet. "Coming," she said, hauling herself up by the railing on legs that felt like lead pipes.

Drew studied her with a worried frown when she finally reached the kitchen. "You're awfully pale, Kathryn. Are you all right? You look like you saw a ghost in Elizabeth's gym."

Kathryn looked at him sharply. "Oh, so you know of Dr. Camden's gym?"

He reared back at the challenge in her tone. "Dr. Camden told me you were in her basement, so I assume from the NordicTrack down there that's what she's turned it into. Now, come on. Everybody's seated and waiting for us." He stepped to the door and closed it quickly, but not before Kathryn had made another discovery. You could not possibly see the NordicTrack from the top of the stairs.

Kathryn was grateful the table conversation did not require her input. Before dessert, Barbara rapped a fork against the side of her glass.

"Okay, everybody, silence for a moment while I make an announcement." From her seat of honor at one end of the table, she smiled fondly down its length at Elizabeth, seated at the other. "We have another occasion to celebrate tonight. Despite all the offers Dr. Camden has received from across the country when she finishes her residency with us at the end of the month, she has decided to stay here at little ol' Winston General."

"Well, that depends on whether my terms are met," Elizabeth said, casting a small smile and meaningful look down the table at Drew. The smile slipped for a fraction of a second as her eye caught a movement from Drew, then flashed fully again. A signal had passed between them, Kathryn was quite certain. An imperceptible shake of Drew's head, a motion of his hand, the bat of an eye, had warned her to remain silent. No one had the lack of taste to ask what those terms were.

A sick suspicion drained through Kathryn. Was Drew staying at Winston General because of Elizabeth? A lack of capital to buy in as partner in the new hospital should not be an issue. He could get the investment money required by selling his shares of the ski resort, or even tap into their savings. She certainly wouldn't object to that—they had enough, especially now that Lindsay was almost out of college. Talk resumed, and Kathryn sat there, smiling when it was appropriate, her stomach in knots with anxiety.

They drove home in the same strained silence that had accompanied them to the party, Kathryn sitting tightly buckled, seized by a fear that thrummed in every part of her body. Finally, she could endure her torture no longer. "What's going on with you, Drew?" The question exploded from her mouth. "You have been . . . not *you* lately. What are you not telling me?"

His hand sought hers in the darkness. "You're right. I haven't been myself. I have something to tell you in the morning, Kathryn, something I dread having to say with all my heart."

Oh, my God, she thought, her hand lying listless in his. She stared rigidly into the wet darkness. "For God's sake, tell me now," she said. "I'm a big girl."

"I know you are. The toughest I know. But I'm dead on my feet tonight, and I want to sleep on it. We'll go out for breakfast in the morning and talk over pancakes. Most bad news is better taken with butter and syrup."

"Bad news?"

"Mistakes. Regrets. Confessions."

The seat belt felt like a band, squeezing the life from her. The weight of his words carried more than just an admission of where he'd been working out lately. "Which of the three is it to be?"

"All of them."

"Just in time for April," Kathryn said, so softly she could barely hear her voice.

Drew breathed a heavy sigh. "Yeah," he said. "Just in time for April."

Drew was asleep later when she came out of the bathroom to get into bed. He'd been reading, and the paperback lay open on his chest, still in his hands, his half-moon reading glasses sliding down the bridge of his nose. Kathryn gently removed the glasses, eased the book from his fingers, and stood looking down at his sleeping face before turning off the bedside light. His features had relaxed, and if she paid no mind to the faint crow's-feet and lines scoring his forehead, the gray at his temples and in the dark thatch exposed in the opening of his pajama top, he still looked like the young medical student she'd fallen in love with one January morning twenty-five years before.

Now, with a rush of fear that was almost blinding, she thought about the decades they'd spent building a life together—all the tears, the laughter, late nights with the children. It wasn't a perfect life, but it was one that she had always dreamed about. *I want to sleep on it*, he'd said. What did that mean—that by morning he could change his mind? That they wouldn't have to cross the point of no return?

It was irrational thinking. All her instincts rebelled against the idea of Drew having an affair with Elizabeth Camden, or anybody else, for that matter. He loved his wife. The suspicion was like a scorpion that was hard to kill. She would not tell him about her stalker until she heard what he had to say to her. Her pride would not allow it. Something was going on with Drew, something deep and dark that he had been desperately guarding.

She pulled the throat of her flannel pajamas tight and crawled into bed. The new nightgown she'd bought hung in her closet, its silken folds limp and empty.

Memory immediately began its assault. They were young again, Drew twenty-three, in his second year of medical school at the University of Houston, and Kathryn twenty-one, in her last undergraduate year at Rice University in Houston.

Chapter Seven

The year was 1985. Stopped at an intersection that early January morning, Kathryn saw a man behind the wheel of a truck tearing up the street from the opposite direction and realized in horror that he was going to run the red light and broadside a Ford Fiesta in his path. Seconds later there was a terrifying explosion of metal colliding with metal, glass breaking, tires screeching, and the long, insistent blowing of a car horn locked in position. Shaking badly, frightened at what she would find behind the wheel of the Fiesta, Kathryn got out of her secondhand Volkswagen at the same time the driver in her rearview mirror jumped out of his early-model compact. He was young, tall, and supple-limbed, and she could remember how he rushed past her, feet barely skimming the ground, and jerked open the victim's door. "Ma'am?" she heard him say to the woman driver in a calm voice contrary to the urgency of his sprint. "I'm a medical student. Let me see what I can do."

The front seat was a mess. The airbag had not deployed, and the steering wheel had driven into the driver's body, slicing flesh and crushing bone. As Kathryn rushed up, he ordered over his shoulder, "Somebody call an ambulance!" in a voice born to be obeyed.

They stayed with the woman until it arrived, Drew talking

soothingly to her the whole time while he staunched the blood with his shirt and gently explored the bone damage with long, competent fingers. Out of earshot of the crash victim, he told the EMS attendants, "She's in bad shape. Looks like the humerus, clavicle, and pelvic girdle took a hit."

"You a doctor?" she asked.

"Trying to be."

They exchanged names while they waited to give the police their statements, finally able to take each other's measure. No wedding rings, cheap haircuts, faded jeans. He had an interestingly handsome face—good features a bit irregularly arranged—and Kathryn liked his deep-sable-brown eyes and slender cheeks. But all Drew said was, "You have a pleasant accent."

"And you have a pleasant bedside manner," Kathryn said. "Very calm." She'd recently treated herself to art lessons, and she thought of the colors, the scene she'd paint to capture his serenity on canvas. "Like a bed of clear spring water on a summer day," she added with a smile.

They gave their phone numbers to the police officers, Kathryn hoping he would make a note of hers, but she did not see him again until they were summoned a few weeks later as witnesses in the criminal trial.

Drew had slid next to her on one of the uncomfortable courtroom benches. "We really must keep meeting like this," he whispered in her ear during the hearing.

"Fine by me," she whispered back, going loose in the knees at the slow crack of his smile.

On their very first date, they walked by a bookstore featuring a bestseller titled *How to Recognize the Trophy in Catastrophe* in its window display. This was after they'd sat four hours in the booth of a TGI Fridays nursing two beers and an artichoke dip while they discovered they'd walked similar paths to get to where they were now. Drew had grown up in a sleazy trailer camp as the unwanted third child in a family tagged as "trailer trash." She had been raised in a foster home. By the time they met, each carried the unshakable conviction that they could put their trust in no one but themselves.

Haltingly, painfully, as if it had to be dragged out of a rusted underground storage tank, Drew told of his miserable years growing up in a sordid caravan park in a town outside Dallas. His parents were alcoholics who hung out with a lowlife crowd in pool halls and honky-tonks, and his two brothers, nine and seven years older than he, were constantly in and out of trouble with the law. No one in the family had interest in a kid who, almost from the time he was old enough to run around in bare feet and dirty diapers, exhibited a sharp curiosity and thirst for knowledge as well as an aversion to filth and ignorance.

Listening to Drew, Kathryn imagined him as a rare, exotic plant blooming in hostile ground. He had graduated at the top of his high school class and taken off on a scholastic scholarship to attend the University of Houston, with a plan to enter its College of Medicine after his undergraduate work.

Kathryn had a kindred story to tell. Born in Birmingham, Alabama, the only child of only children, she had been an accident, her parents a professional couple absorbed in each other and in their careers. She was still a toddler when her father was arrested and jailed for embezzlement of company funds, then killed shortly afterward in a prison altercation. Not long after his death, her mother, driving home drunk one night, died in a three-car pileup later determined to be her fault. Her nanny was let go, and her paternal grandparents took her in at the age of four, until her grandmother succumbed to cancer and her grandfather contracted Alzheimer's disease—all before Kathryn's sixth birthday. After a year under the protective wing of the Alabama Child Welfare Agency, she was placed in a foster home. Harry and Gloria Harrison were not cruel, but neither were they particularly kind. In their house, she learned to live alone, never forgetting that she was a foster child and that the other two girls the couple took in were not her foster sisters but fellow travelers on the journey to get out of care and to make for themselves a better life.

By the time Kathryn graduated from high school, she was seasoned in the ways to protect and defend what little she could call her own—her side of the bed, her apportioned time in the bathroom, her share of meat, her body and dignity. She was luckier than most of the other displaced children she knew. Her exceptionally high IQ, along with her diligent studies and her status as a ward of the state, netted her a full academic scholarship to Rice University.

Foster parents and foster siblings parted after high school and lost touch after a few years' exchange of Christmas cards. The only thing that kept Kathryn going was her friendship with Natalie Hunt, the social care worker long ago assigned to her by the child welfare service. Natalie, childless, unmarried, was her guardian angel from the day Kathryn was turned over to the care of the Harrisons. Natalie was the business card she always carried in her pocket, the telephone number she knew by heart to this day, the one person who remembered her birthday, the surrogate relative who showed up for her award ceremonies and band concerts and made sure she had a dress for the prom.

That night in TGI Fridays, Kathryn had glimpsed in Drew a deeply buried pride. He told her he'd decided to become an orthopedic surgeon when he realized he was never going to get a football scholarship, seeing it as a good way to make a lot of money and still keep him close to the sports he loved. Kathryn confided that in her high school science classes she'd felt drawn toward a profession that would allow her to make inventions that might help improve health care. She'd been inspired by the story of Charles Lindbergh, who in the 1920s created an artificial heart-like device to keep organs alive when removed from the body.

"Charles Lindbergh!" Drew exclaimed. "The one who flew across the Atlantic?"

"The same," Kathryn said. "He was also a successful inventor and eventually teamed up with a scientist, Alexis Carrel, who won the Nobel Prize for organ transplantation. I want to do something like that. I'm going to get my doctorate."

Across the table, Drew had looked at her admiringly. "Do you suppose that . . . you and I meeting as we did . . . is the trophy in the catastrophe we witnessed?"

They'd both recognized the timing as disastrous. Neither could afford even to consider marriage. Kathryn's application to bypass a master's degree and jump into a three-year doctoral program at Rice looked as if it were going to be approved, Drew had his medical degree to complete, and each had student loans to repay, despite the generous grants they'd received. But fight it though they did, they couldn't go a day without seeing each other, and one morning Kathryn woke up nauseated and vomited up her breakfast.

She was not going to tell him. First, she refused to interfere with his career path, and second, she couldn't have borne him telling her that he couldn't—he wouldn't—give up the pursuit of his dream to marry her, or suggesting an abortion. It was not the end of her dream. She would have the baby and somehow continue her education.

One night in her small kitchen, Kathryn saw him slide the business card of her obstetrician out from under the telephone where she'd hidden it. He studied it before slipping it back, the ridge of his jawbone hardening. That was that, she thought. She'd never see him again after that night.

But he called again the next day, and a week later, he said, "You're pregnant, aren't you?"

"Yes," Kathryn said, "but it's not your problem. It's mine. I'll handle it by myself."

"Like hell you will."

"You mean you'll help me?"

"I mean . . ." He pulled his lip between his teeth. "I mean I'll marry you."

If Kathryn had not witnessed that brief nibble, her elation would have overcome her common sense. "No, I won't let you give up your dreams, your goals."

"Who says I'm giving them up?"

"The road will be harder with a wife and child."

"I'm used to hard roads."

"And you'll be poorer, longer."

"There's poverty, and then there's poverty, Kathryn. No matter how rich I plan to become, I'd be poor all my life without you and our child. Besides, I love you."

They were married in the office of an Episcopalian minister less than a month later. Natalie Hunt was their witness. Drew was scared. No doubt about it. His voice wavered when he said "I do," but he held her hand hard when they left his office and said in a voice of awe, "A family. Now I have a family."

Chapter Eight

The year passed, those difficult but blissful months of domestic life. Their grants and Kathryn's tutoring job provided them barely enough to meet expenses, but Drew was able to go to school full-time, and Kathryn to begin her doctoral program with a concentration in biomedicine, and to their minds, at the end of the day, their bare little apartment near the University of Houston College of Medicine was as appealing as the finest home in River Oaks, the city's most expensive neighborhood. Its walls comprised the first true home either of them had ever known. Here they experienced the joys of loving and being loved, of being supported and accepted as they were, but most of all, for the first time in their lives, they learned the exquisite release of placing their total trust in another human being. Despite conflicting schedules, meager funds, long, dogged hours poring over their studies, their constant fatigue, and Kathryn's prolonged morning sickness, their love buoyed them up rather than dragging them down. They had found the trophy in what could have been a catastrophe.

In December, Kathryn gave birth to a beautiful baby girl they named Abby Gale. She was the bright morning star in their sky, both she and Drew vying to hold her when they returned at the end of the day. Reluctantly, but gratefully, Kathryn left the baby in Natalie's care.

Natalie had relocated to Houston a few years earlier, after Kathryn notified her of an opening in its child welfare department, and they had continued the close and devoted relationship that had made all the difference to Kathryn while living in her foster home in Alabama. Natalie's recent retirement had coincided with the birth of Abby Gale, a sweet child Natalie doted on like her own grandchild.

And then one April night, it happened. April 10. She'd never forget the sound. A deep male cry from the nursery startled Kathryn from sleep. She bolted upright to see Drew in the doorway, clutching their baby in her pink blanket. "She's gone," he gasped, shattered, the lean contours of his face streaked with tears. "Dead."

Sudden infant death syndrome. The odds against marriages surviving such a tragedy were staggeringly high, but Kathryn and Drew beat them. She would always credit their unwavering love for each other as the ballast that kept them afloat. They took turns holding one another up when the other would have fallen. If love was their life raft, Drew's determination to become an orthopedic surgeon and Kathryn's to earn her doctorate in bioengineering was their lighthouse on the hill. They both agreed that tiny Abby Gale wouldn't have wanted her parents to give up their dreams.

And so they persevered blindingly, achingly, hand in hand, until one day in that year a light shone through the gloom. Kathryn learned she was pregnant again. This unplanned new pregnancy meant greater debt, increased academic straits, more sleep-deprived nights, but Drew laid his head on her stomach and sobbed in gratitude. After the birth of their son, Bobby, their flame-haired daughter Lindsay followed twenty months later. Through all the disruptions, the midnight feedings, their son's terrible twos, and the poverty that reduced them to applying for food stamps, they plowed on.

Through it all, though, they grew to dread the fourth month of the year. An April never arrived without a roll of misfortune in some form of domestic calamity. April seemed to herald illnesses, accidents, car problems, and unexpected expenses that wiped out the family budget. The most devastating blow fell in the April of the final year of Kathryn's doctorate, when her seventy-page dissertation was rejected. The doctoral committee's consensus that her hypothesis was "unsupportable" meant a denial of the degree essential to the job waiting for her as a biomedical engineer at a manufacturing firm of medical implant devices in Houston.

"Your project is not clearly defined, based on your research, nor are the links between it and its execution well explained," her faculty adviser explained. "At the moment, the committee agrees that your hypothesis borders on science fiction. I'm sorry, but I suggest you go back to the drawing board with your concept and supportive arguments. In other words, begin again."

Kathryn felt the committee's judgment drop like a hammer on her financial plans. She hadn't the time or money to start over on another proposal. They were out of grant money. She had no choice but to find a job to support two children and a husband in medical school. Now, rather than being employed as a biomedical engineer, she would have to take a job as a lab assistant, a glorified name for a gofer. The difference in her salary would mean eating tuna from a can rather than from a butcher's case.

Bereft, Kathryn delivered the news to Drew. "It doesn't matter," he said. "I can earn a little working a few hours as an orderly at St. Joseph's. We'll make it work."

Drew plowed on through medical school and a residency in his specialized field, and finally, at the age of twenty-nine, he received his license to practice orthopedic surgery. On the day he graduated, clutching his diploma under one arm, he'd encircled her and the children with the other. "Right here," he'd said. "Right here, I have it all."

Kathryn rolled over to study the sleeping face of her husband. She'd been wrong to think he had emerged from his childhood with no emotional gap longing to be filled. Drew had craved a home and family to love as much as she had. It was absurd to even consider, after all their marriage had survived, that he could be unfaithful to her, deceive their children, shatter their happy home—not her trusted Drew, beloved father, adored husband. Her anxiety and sleep deprivation over her stalker had affected her clear thinking. It was so unjust to suspect him of having an affair with Elizabeth Camden just because the woman had gym equipment in her basement. That look they flashed at the dinner table could have meant anything; it was probably professionally motivated. Tomorrow they would go out to breakfast as planned, and Drew would put her heart to rest. He would explain where he'd been three afternoons a week, and she would tell him about her stalker, and they would decide what to do about Golf Cap.

Chapter Nine

Saturday, April 3

They awoke the next morning to rainy skies and dissolving snow. Kathryn had dozed off toward morning and fallen into a deep, insensible sleep. Drew was already shaved and dressed in a flannel shirt and corduroys and had made coffee by the time she blearily shuffled into the kitchen in her robe and gown.

Drew stood with his face raised to the calendar clock on the wall. Was he remembering, as she was, the beginning of that terrible April twenty-four years ago, or was he asking of the clock, as if it were an oracle, what evil the month had in store for them this year? Or, given what he'd said the night before in the car, did he already know?

"Good morning," she said.

He turned, and his somber face lightened a bit. "Well, good morning. I decided not to wake you. You looked dead to the world."

"It's too nasty to go out. How about I make banana pecan pancakes, and we can stay here, together?

He handed her a cup of coffee. "I don't want you going to the trouble," he said. "It will be nice to go out to someplace steamy and cozy in this weather. The Columbine, maybe? Do you mind if we leave as soon as you get dressed? I have to go to the office after we finish breakfast. Besides"—he gave her a fleeting glimpse of his old smile—"you may want me out of the house after we talk."

Not so long ago, he would have welcomed her offer to stay in and eat her pancakes. Perhaps he couldn't endure sitting at the table with her, alone in the married confines of the kitchen, the rain sluicing down the windowpanes, weeping at whatever he had to confess to her, ushering in another April of heartbreak.

"Now why would I ever want you out of the house?" She reached out for him, her hand sliding down his arm, hoping for reassurance. "You don't have to go into the office today, do you?"

"My desk is a mess, and I'm drowning in paperwork. I won't be able to get to it next week. We'll have a nice breakfast together, and then I'll head into the office. I promise it won't be for too long."

An hour later, Kathryn played with a packet of sugar at one of the shiny oak tables that dotted the eating area of the Columbine Café. The sweet smell of breakfast pastries mixed with the warm, earthy scent of coffee.

After the waitress had come to take their orders, Drew cleared his throat and caught her eye. He was ready for his confession.

"I am so sorry, Kathryn. But . . . we will have to cancel our trip to Europe."

It was a few moments before she could process what he was saying. "*That's* what you had to tell me?" she asked, her voice an incredulous croak.

"Well, what in the world did you think it was?" He reached his hand across the table, a gesture of hope. But Kathryn, confused, untrusting, slipped her hands below the table, holding them together tightly on her lap.

"Well . . . I . . ." Her mouth refused to work properly. When she didn't answer, Drew continued.

"I've been approached to conduct knee surgery on two Denver

Nuggets players during the three weeks we are supposed to be in Europe."

"Why can't we change the dates of our trip? We can go after the surgeries."

"They expect me to be around for the post-op and to monitor the players' rehabilitation. They have to do it during their offseason this summer."

"Can we go before the surgeries?"

Drew shook his head. "And cancel all my other surgeries? These are high-profile. If it goes well, this will almost certainly guarantee that I'll be selected as the team's orthopedic surgeon when Davis retires next year. It could mean an invitation to join the new hospital with clout, Kath. I wouldn't have to buy in as partner. I'll have as much voice as if I put up the five hundred grand. I'm sorry about the trip more than I can possibly say, but I can't turn this down. And, frankly, we can use the money. Medicare is cutting fees, as you know, and with the economy so bad, people are putting off knee and hip and shoulder replacements. And malpractice insurance is going up. The hospital is taking a financial hit, and Hensley has talked about cutting staff salaries." He sat in front of her, looking dejected and truly sorry. "I know you're shocked and disappointed." He offered his hand, palm up, across the table. "I wouldn't blame you for throwing the syrup pitcher at me, but, Kathryn, you've got to believe this is for the best."

Slowly, she laid her fingers in his open palm. "The trip is a disappointment, Drew, but that's not what I'm most worried about, we can reschedule someday. But are you sure you can't find a better way to buy in to the new hospital? Why can't you sell our interest in the ski resort?"

He withdrew his hand as though she'd given him an electrical shock. "I signed a contract."

"So did the company. According to the terms, weren't they to have had a certain number of rooms built by now? And they haven't.

If that's considered a breach of contract, couldn't the delay legally give you license to withdraw our investment money?"

Drew turned his concentration to the range of syrup selections. "They wouldn't just let me out of the contract. We'd have to hire lawyers; we'd be tied up in litigation for months, and be no better off than we are now."

"Well, then," she said, "I suppose you have to make a choice between what dream you want to come true—being part owner of a ski resort or a player in an orthopedic hospital. And you also need to bear in mind there's no guarantee you'll be selected as the Nuggets' team physician. You could end up still stuck at Winston."

He dropped her hands as the waitress brought them their food. "Thanks for your vote of confidence, Kath."

She was not going to allow him to turn this on her. "You know I have every confidence in your abilities, Drew. It's other people's confidence in your abilities you can't be certain of. You've got a bird in the hand here. Why risk it?"

"Why risk losing the chance to have both?" he countered. "Look, Kathryn, we could go on and on about this. Believe me, I have had many more than second thoughts about investing in the ski resort, and if I'd known an orthopedic hospital was on the way, I wouldn't have, but if I get the job with the Nuggets, and there's no reason to believe that I won't, it's a washout."

Kathryn dropped the argument and played with the coffee creamer on the table. To be fair, it's not as if Drew had gone out on this limb alone. Kathryn had reluctantly agreed, a couple of years ago, to the investment. The developers had made a strong case for the property and the potential for a handsome return.

But as usual, her husband had been working on an alternative plan—a rabbit to pull out of the hat of his poor judgment. Kathryn had known their financial situation would come to this. She wondered if Drew remembered their disputes in the early days, when the money started coming in. He'd wanted to begin making up for all the material deprivations of their childhoods and the long, grueling road to his achievement "while we're young enough to enjoy them." She'd argued that they'd find greater satisfaction in becoming debt-free and knowing that extra was being put aside to pay for unexpected expenses, the children's education, and their retirement.

In the end they had compromised. "Let's take the first five years and buy anything for us and the kids we want," he'd suggested. "After that, Kath, we can start saving for college educations and retirement and pay off the mortgage ahead of time."

But they'd been kidding themselves. It was impossible to go back to hamburger after tasting filet mignon. And it had been hard to deny Drew. She'd known he wanted things—a fine home, luxury car, membership in the country club, good clothes—not to flaunt his new wealth but simply not to feel inferior. "I don't want money to lord it over anybody," he explained to her once. "I want it so nobody can lord it over me."

That was the crux of Drew's hang-up. He was always having to prove to himself that he belonged among his colleagues. No matter how Kathryn tried to reassure Drew that she loved him for the man he was, not the rich man he aspired to be, she still wondered if it wasn't enough. More importantly, if *she* wasn't enough.

"I've already accepted the job to do the surgeries. It's too big an opportunity to pass up. I'm sorry it's cost us our trip to Europe. I know how much you were looking forward to it, and it hurts like hell to have to disappoint you, but those art museums aren't going anywhere, and . . . maybe we can make the trip another time."

Her ear had picked up the uncertain *maybe*. "Is that all you were going to confess to me?"

"Well, good heavens, Kathryn, isn't it enough?" He squinted a puzzled eye at her. "Why would you ask me that?"

"You've been so . . . withdrawn lately," Kathryn answered him. "I wondered if there was more that you weren't telling me."

Their pancakes arrived. "No more than the usual gripes with Winston that have gotten me down," he said, briskly spreading butter over the crisp-edged mound on his plate. "What else could there be? I must say you're taking it better than I expected. Maybe it hasn't sunk in yet, and you'll throw a pan at me later." Knife halted, head canted sideways, he asked uncertainly, "Are *you* all right?"

She looked at him. *What else could there be?* She had always respected Drew for his honesty and integrity, but he still hadn't mentioned the Argyle. Now, for the first time, he seemed to be actively hiding something from her. She could feel her respect for her husband eroding.

"Yes," she said after her moment's reflection. "Pass me the blueberry syrup, please. I don't want the maple."

"But you like maple syrup."

"Not today."

Drew slipped her the blueberry syrup and said, "Look, Kath, if you really, really have your heart set on going, we'll go. You're right that I might not get the job with the Nuggets."

"Really, it's all right, Drew. You're right. We need the money, and we really can't afford the trip right now, not while Lindsay's still in college."

Drew laid his knife down. "You've pointed out that I have not been myself over the last few months, but I have noticed that you haven't been yourself over the last few days. You've looked like you were in pain . . . or grieving. Is there something wrong? Is it the kids?"

"No," she said. "Nothing to do with them."

"Then what is it, for God's sake. What's been bothering you?"

Kathryn looked him in the eye. "Someone has been following me."

Chapter Ten

Drew stared at her. "What?"

"I'm being followed," she repeated

Drew's mouth hung open. "How do you know? Have they threatened you?"

Kathryn told him about the grocery store, and her realization that a man had been following her for weeks. "He's not from around here. I would have known, in a town this size."

Drew briefly squeezed shut his eyes, his way of concentrating. "So, he hasn't threatened you at all?"

"No, we haven't talked." Kathryn sipped at her coffee. "I know there are a million reasons why a woman can be stalked, but I can't help but wonder if it might have something to do with one of your past patients. Someone who is upset about a surgery gone wrong."

"I can't think of anyone who would be that upset with me." Drew took a large swig of his coffee. "What does this guy look like?"

"Caucasian, medium height—older than you, I'd guess, but not by much. I never saw his entire face, but I would think it . . . worn, like his body appears to be. He certainly doesn't seem physically fit." Kathryn described his dropped shoulder and slightly humped back, adding, "I notice things like that."

"I know. Your painter's eye." He flashed her a wry smile. "You've never seen him before—at a meeting, maybe?"

"Never. He's a perfect stranger to me, which is so odd, because women are usually stalked by people they know. At least, that's what I found when I looked it up online. You believe me, don't you?"

"Oh, honey . . ." Drew slipped his palm across the table again. "Of course I believe you. You'd never make up something like this. You're the most levelheaded person I know. But we can't go to the police, not yet. They won't do anything until you have been threatened, unfortunately. In the meantime, I want you to keep your cell phone with you at all times, and keep it charged."

Kathryn nodded. "Good thing I've never really used social media. We should probably change all our passwords, though."

"I agree, and you need to vary your routines. Don't take the same route twice, if you can." Drew sighed. "I'll call our travel agent from the office to cancel the trip, so you don't have to deal with it," he said, as if the issue were settled and there was nothing more to say.

The rain had gone and the sun had come out when they left the restaurant, leaving the air fresh and clean, the skies clear and blue. Drew lifted his face toward the sun's warmth, closed his eyes, and breathed in deeply. "Let's hope this turn in the day is a good omen," he said. "I could sure use one."

"So could I," Kathryn said.

Chapter Eleven

Kathryn thought she recognized the voice on the other side of the phone after Drew dropped her off at home. "Excuse me, is this Kathryn Walker?"

"Yes. How may I help you?" she asked cautiously.

"My name's Mike McCoy. We spoke briefly the other day at the market."

"Are you the gentleman at the meat counter yesterday afternoon when I was—"

"Picking up the leg of lamb you'd ordered?" Mike finished. "Yes, ma'am. When I saw the bracelet in the parking lot, I recognized it as the one you were wearing when Joe handed you the package of lamb."

"I recognized your voice."

"Recognition is a good thing." Was that a subtle warning she'd heard in the man's voice, or had she imagined it? What a strange thing to say. *Recognition is a good thing . . .*

"I hope you don't mind that I called you, but I thought you might be missing your bracelet. Diamond?" Mike continued.

She felt a rush of relief. "With three charms? Yes, that's mine."

"Near my Range Rover, in the parking lot of City Market."

"Thank goodness," Kathryn said.

"I'm afraid the clasp is broken."

"Yes, I'd been meaning to get that fixed. Where and when may I bother you to pick it up?"

"Would the Mountain Bar and Grill at the Park Hyatt Hotel be convenient for you, say, this afternoon, about five o'clock?"

"Perfect," Kathryn said, thinking the time and place would be a good spot in Drew's day to meet her and the rancher. She and Drew could stay for a nice dinner afterward, and hopefully she'd be able to get an answer from him about the Argyle, figure out what he was hiding.

"Very well then. See you there."

Kathryn quickly texted Drew to let him know that her bracelet wasn't lost after all.

Kathryn arrived at the Park Hyatt ten minutes early, and selected a table rather than a booth so that she would be more visible. Frustratingly, Drew had yet to respond to her text. She was contemplating calling her husband when she saw Mike McCoy through the large glass window, walking toward the restaurant. She waved at him from the table, glad they were in a public place, since Drew wasn't here with her.

The rancher answered with a small smile and headed over, dressed in the western gear of his trade, as he'd been at City Market. He looked the real deal. No urban cowboy about him.

"Mrs. Walker," he said.

"Kathryn, please." She offered him her hand.

"Well, in that case, it's Mike." After releasing her hand, Mike took a seat, withdrew a small gold-embossed box from his pocket, and slipped it across the table. "I imagine you're ready to lay your eyes on that," he said handing over a gold box. "I figured something like this needed a special container."

Kathryn lifted the lid immediately, and a childlike glow flooded her face. "This is it," she said as she removed the bracelet and slipped it around her wrist. "I can hardly believe it. I never expected to see it again."

"I repaired the clasp for you."

"I see that." She was studying it in surprise. "I don't know how I could ever thank you enough, but I'd be happy to pay you a reward . . ."

"Don't even think it. I'm just glad I found it," Mike said, taking his assessment of Kathryn Walker. She was the epitome of class, he thought, in her yellow sweater and cream wool slacks, a Burberry raincoat hanging from her shoulders. "Besides its monetary worth," he continued, "I am sure it has great sentimental value to you. The three charms are for your children?"

"Yes," she said, her voice faltering. Her clear blue eyes briefly lost their spark as her fingers moved gingerly over the charms.

Pain, Mike thought. He had seen a look like that far too often.

"And you?" she asked.

"I am a widower, and no—no children," Mike answered. He was thankful when his favorite bar attendant appeared at the table.

"Your usual, Mike?" she said.

"Please, Shelly. How about you, Mrs. Walker?"

"Thank you, but no. I can't convey how grateful I am to you, but I really can't stay." Kathryn reached for the strap of the handbag hanging on her chair back. "I need to be getting home."

Mike put his hand on the table between them, a gentle gesture to recapture her attention. "You were being followed," he said, lowering his voice. "When I saw you at the grocery store the other day, there was a man tailing you."

She stiffened. "Excuse me?"

"A man with a slouch. I couldn't help but notice him following you around the grocery store."

Kathryn dropped her purse with a thunk. "How do you know that?"

"Because I know a private investigator when I see one."

Chapter Twelve

Kathryn held Mike's gaze. There was a decency about him. She remembered his warning from the phone call. *Recognition is a good thing. Take care, Mrs. Walker.* He knew something. He was not a tall or big man, but he had the confidence and hardness of a man who had been forged by experience. She trusted him, despite herself. And besides, Drew might come through the door at any minute. Early diners were strolling in, the bar getting busy. No matter what, she was safe in this public place.

"How do you know that?" she asked tensely.

"I don't mean to frighten you, but when I watched him trail you around the City Market, I was pretty sure that you were under surveillance."

"Under surveillance?"

"Close observation."

"I know what it means," Kathryn said sharply. "But that term applies to a criminal, which I most certainly am not. A better word to describe the man's behavior is *stalking*."

"No, Mrs. Walker, it is not. That's why I am glad of this chance to meet. You're not being stalked. The man's a private investigator, somebody who's been hired to follow and record your movements. He'll disappear now that he knows you've made him—"

Kathryn drew back from the table in surprise just as the bar waitress reappeared with a scotch and water for Mike.

"Thank you, Shelly." He raised an eyebrow at Kathryn. "Perhaps Mrs. Walker would be ready for some white wine?"

Kathryn recovered her breath. "Sauvignon blanc."

"A glass of your best, then," Mike said to Shelly, smiling.

When Shelly was gone, Kathryn leaned forward. "Who are you? How do I know that you know what you're talking about?"

"I was trained in surveillance techniques in the army."

"I've seen you around town off and on for years. I took you for a local rancher."

"I *am* a rancher. I own a small cattle operation not far from Avon. Avon is my hometown, and I retired here after twenty-six years in the military."

"I'm sorry, but I'm finding this all rather hard to believe. Do you have some ID or any other proof?"

Mike obliged by removing his military identification card from his wallet and handing it over. "I went straight from my high school graduation to the army recruiter's office. Ended up in a counterterrorist organization called Delta Force. I fully intended on staying in the service forever, but when . . . when my pregnant wife . . . died, well, everything changed. I got out as soon as I could."

"Oh, Mr. McCoy, I'm so sorry." Tears sprang to Kathryn's eyes. She couldn't imagine losing a partner on top of the too-familiar pain of losing a baby. She glanced down at the laminated card. "You were a colonel?"

"That's right."

She couldn't buy this man's story too soon. Anybody could forge a military ID card. He could be in cahoots with Golf Cap, and this could be some kind of crazy game they were playing. "There is nothing here to indicate that you were a member of an organization that does . . . secret things for the government."

Mike suppressed a smile. Apparently, Kathryn Walker's vocabulary lacked *covert operations*. "No US military identification card includes the specific organization of a member of the armed forces, so I'm afraid you'll have to take my word for it." He hoped she wouldn't feel the need to go looking for more, because there was nothing more to find.

The more Mike worked with Delta Force, the more his records became redacted. So much so that if anyone ever requested his files it would be nothing more than a piece of paper covered in thick black bars. It would take an act of Congress to uncover the truth behind all his missions. And as far as his work with the Central Intelligence Agency was concerned, it didn't exist. Those missions were conveniently left off his records.

Looking unconvinced, Kathryn asked, "How is it that you happened to be in all the right places at the right time to observe my so-called investigator . . . surveilling me?"

"As I said, I am a resident here. I'm often in the library to check out and return books for my foreman, who lives at the ranch, and I've been a regular at the Columbine for years. As for City Market . . . do you know any other place in Avon to shop for groceries?"

Kathryn handed Mike his card. "Okay, so let's say that I believe you. Why would you go out of your way to share all this with me?"

Now, Mike thought, was the point where he should follow Lonnie's advice. *Mrs. Walker*, he should say as he got up to leave, *I care about you as one human being to another. Whether you believe what I have told you or not is up to you. I have given you the benefit of my observation and experience, and you may do with the information as you wish.* But instead he said, "My wife was murdered. She was pregnant with our first child. I was unable to save her, but maybe my information will help save you from danger."

Shelly returned with the wine. "You said the best, Mike, so"— she turned to Kathryn—"it's Pape Clement sauvignon blanc for you, m'dear."

Mike smiled. "Thank you, Shelly."

"You want me to run a tab?"

"I'll let you know," Mike said, eyes on Kathryn. Her cheek-bones were washed of color, and her stare was locked in a zone between doubt and trust.

"Have you shared your stalker theory with your husband?" he asked when Shelly had moved away.

Kathryn took a quick sip of the wine, pierced by a coldness that left her numb. "Yes," she said. "He says that it's too soon to do anything rash. In the meantime he has had me change all our passwords, not take the same route home, that sort of thing."

"You should have invited him to join us."

"I did. He was supposed to meet me here, but . . . he's a doctor, you see, an orthopedic surgeon. Some emergency must have flared up. . . ."

"What will he think once he finds out your stalker is a private investigator?"

"I don't know. Who would want to investigate me?"

"Tell me about your enemies."

Kathryn attempted a wry smile. "I've ruffled feathers in the civic organizations in which I've served, but anybody trying to dig up dirt on me would have a hard time finding any. I've lived an open-book life, Mr. McCoy, both in my public and private life."

"What about relatives, somebody from your past?"

Kathryn took another sip of wine. "I have no relatives. I can't imagine there's anyone from my past who'd have the slightest reason to have me investigated."

It could be, Mike thought, that the husband suspected her of cheating and had hired the investigator to follow her movements, but she apparently did not suspect him. She didn't seem the type of woman to cheat. Against his own wisdom and Lonnie's warning, he said, "You have my phone number if you'd like to contact me again, Mrs. Walker."

Kathryn set down her wineglass and unhooked her handbag from her chair. "This is excellent wine, and I'm sorry that I can't stay to finish it. I will leave the gift box with you in case you have a future need of it." She adjusted her Burberry around her shoulders and rose, managing a smile as Mike got to his feet. "Thank you again for the bracelet, Mr. McCoy. As I've said, I am more grateful than I can possibly express."

Mike took the hand she offered, the bracelet sparkling on her wrist. He could see she was having trouble making up her mind about him. She might even be thinking that this could all be a ruse designed to seduce her. She was wise to be dubious, but he trusted she would not ignore his warning. She was too smart for that. "Goodbye, Mrs. Walker, and be careful."

Kathryn said, "I will consider your advice. Goodbye, Mr. Mc-Coy. I am sincerely sorry for your losses."

Chapter Thirteen

In a nightmarish daze, Kathryn checked the message machine when she returned home, just in case Drew couldn't call her cell phone for some reason. Nothing. Where in God's name was he? When he walked through the kitchen door, her husband had better have an excuse bigger than the state of Texas. She'd needed him to be sitting at the table with her in the Park Hyatt to fully grasp that chilling meeting with Mike McCoy.

Frankly, she thought Drew might have been a little more concerned about her meeting a strange man about the bracelet. She didn't need a savior, but he still could have made an effort to go to the meeting with Mike. At the very least check in on her. A simple text would have sufficed.

Even if Mike's ranch and place of residence checked out, the guy could be a mental case with a sharp eye and a penchant for true crime. What if . . . this April, with the kids gone from the nest, no civic responsibilities to keep her occupied, and her husband always busy with work, Kathryn had finally snapped?

Her fear swelling to anger, tears of frustration gathering, she drew a glass of water and stared across the alley to the kitchen window where once she would have seen her best friend, Sandy Danton, preparing dinner. They used to communicate through their windows like schoolgirls, holding up their coffee cups to each other in the mornings, and in the evenings, glasses of wine. But now no lights shone there. A year before, Sandy had divorced her second husband, Drew's best friend Frank, and moved back to her hometown of Houston. Kathryn had always told Sandy everything, from problems with the sprinklers to some childhood stories she hadn't even shared with Drew. Sandy would have tagged along with Kathryn for her meeting with Mike. Except, of course, Sandy had abandoned her, just like her husband.

Kathryn poured a glass of sauvignon blanc and debated whether to call the children. What if there was something to Mike's theory? What if her son and daughter were being followed as well? What if they were in danger?

Drew would be furious if she called and frightened them, but so what? They could handle it. If she was imagining Golf Cap's attention, and Mike McCoy was simply spinning tales, then they had nothing to worry about. But if she wasn't wrong, then they needed to be warned. Whoever hired the man trailing her could have also hired someone to trail her children. She had no idea what his motive or end goals might be. Kathryn couldn't live with herself if she didn't know for certain that her children were safe.

She dialed Lindsay first, hoping to catch her before she left for a night out. She and Drew marveled at how their daughter could maintain top grades and enjoy such an unremitting social life. Lindsay was her father's daughter—proud, determined, brilliant, confident. She was premed, just like her father, and had no intention of compromising on anything, ever. She had entered this world fully aware of who she was and what she wanted.

"It's my mother. Can you turn the volume down?" Kathryn could hear Lindsay saying as she picked up, probably to her roommate. "Hey Mom, what's up?"

"I hope I didn't catch you on your way out," Kathryn said. "Do you have a few minutes?"

"What's up? You usually call on Sundays. Did Dad tell you to get me to go easy on the credit card?"

"We will discuss that at another time," Kathryn said. "I'm calling for another reason, darling." She'd rehearsed how to subtly alert her daughter to the problem without scaring her, but now that she had Lindsay on the line, her mind had gone blank. Too emotionally drained and worried to mince words, she came right out with it. "Have you by any chance noticed anyone following you around campus recently?"

In the silence Kathryn could hear Lindsay's unspoken *Mom, what kind of crazy question is that?*

"It's important, Lindsay."

"Why?"

"I'll tell you when I know more."

"No, I haven't. What's going on? Have you been watching too many crime shows?"

Her daughter had answered too quickly to have really thought about the question. "Concentrate now, honey," Kathryn said. "Think back to the places you've been in the past month and try to remember if you've seen the same unfamiliar face show up, someone who doesn't seem to belong."

"You're freaking me out, Mom." Kathryn could picture her daughter's brow furrowing, just like it had when she was little.

"Please, Lindsay."

"I'm thinking. I promise, I haven't seen anyone unfamiliar, and I would have remembered once you mentioned it. Mom . . ." A worried note crept into Lindsay's voice. "Are you okay?"

"I'm fine, darling. Better now, actually. For now, could you trust me on that without asking for further details? It would mean a lot to me if you did."

"I . . . trust you, Mom. Is Dad okay?"

"He's fine, also. Working too hard, as usual."

"Well, the trip to Europe should fix that up."

Kathryn hesitated.

"Mom?"

"We're not going to Europe after all," Kathryn said. "Something's come up, and we'll have to cancel. So, kiddo, now would be a good time to call off the weekend parties at the house that your mother's sixth sense tells her you had planned."

Kathryn expected vehement denials that her daughter had even *thought* of inviting the Chi Omegas over for weekend blowouts, but Lindsay surprised her. "You're not going?" she burst out, indignation in her voice. "But you've been looking forward to that trip for years!"

Kathryn heard genuine sympathy in her wail. Maybe her little girl was growing up, thinking of her mother for a change. "Now is not a good time, honey. I'll explain another day."

"This doesn't have to do with money, does it?"

"No, and I don't want you worrying about our finances. Your only job is to do well at school. The cancellation is work-related. Your dad was offered a job he couldn't pass up."

There was an extended silence, then Lindsay said, "What a bummer. I'm sorry, Mom. And . . . if it helps, I'll watch the credit card."

"Thank you. Now, I'm going to call your brother. Anything you want me to tell him?"

"Are you going to ask him the same question you asked me?"

"Well, yes, among other things."

"Bobby's going to hate it that you're not going to Europe."

"What, did he have a party planned here too?" When Lindsay didn't laugh, Kathryn added, "We'll keep the news between us girls for the time being, okay?"

"All right . . . ," Lindsay said reluctantly. "Tell my big bro that I've got a date lined up for him if he's interested."

"Will do, but you know what he'll say to *that*."

"Uh-huh, but what are sisters for if not to *attempt* to look after the love lives of their clueless brothers?" There was a second's silence. "I should go—my date's here. The sun was out today. I hope it shone there, too."

Kathryn did not miss the innuendo. Lindsay knew why her mother hated April. On some preternatural level, her daughter missed and mourned the big sister she never knew.

"It did, brilliantly," Kathryn said. "Talk to you next Sunday. Be safe. I love you."

"You too." The connection broke, but Kathryn felt better. Her daughter would now be on her guard.

Chapter Fourteen

After hanging up with her daughter, Kathryn immediately called Bobby. She knew he would be home, in his small apartment cozily decorated with furniture from his parents' early marriage. Her only son was a homebody. Kathryn was sure she'd caught him with his feet up on the ottoman in front of his fireplace, marking up homework from his fourth-grade students—on a Saturday, when other young men his age would be going out with their friends.

"Hey, Mom. This is a surprise. You usually call on Sundays." She could hear classical music softly playing in the background. "To what do I owe the pleasure?"

As usual, hearing Bobby's voice lightened Kathryn's heart. His birth had been the balm for their wounds, their oasis in the desert, after losing Abby Gale. Drew loved him with a fierceness that made her heart ache, though Bobby would have preferred his father's respect and approval. Their son had been a concern to Drew from grade school on. Slender and fine-boned, Bobby spent his time playing video games or *Magic: The Gathering* instead of sports, as Drew had done.

His choice of profession had also been a disappointment to Drew. "The kid's brilliant. He can go into any field he chooses," he'd moaned. "Why teaching, for God's sake? He'll never have two dimes to rub together."

"He wants to make a difference," Kathryn said.

"He can make a difference in another profession."

"Without teachers, there would be no other professions," she argued.

"He could at least had been a college professor instead of spending his days wiping noses," Drew had grumbled.

"Mom?" Bobby's voice brought Kathryn to the present.

"I just finished talking to your sister, who wants me to relay that she has a girl on the hook for you."

"Well, she can let her go. I prefer to cast my own lures."

Kathryn chuckled, then broached the purpose of her call. "Have you noticed anyone out of the ordinary following you?"

"No, Mom. Why do you ask? What's going on? You sound strained."

"I do?" But of course she did. Bobby could always pick up on her moods. "It's probably nothing, sweetie, really. It's just that I . . . well, I've seen the same man frequently in the places I've been these past few weeks, and I was wondering if . . . you've seen anyone near your apartment or school there in Denver."

"You're thinking he's a *stalker* of some kind?"

There was no use beating around the bush with Bobby. Lindsay called her brother "the direct-line kid."

"We're not sure. He hasn't made any threats or anything, so we are just being careful."

"What do you think?"

"Well, I have to admit I've had an uneasy feeling about him. He doesn't look like he's from around here."

"He could be looking to move to the area. The neighborhood is always changing."

"That could be right. But . . . you'll keep an eye out, won't you, for any strangers?"

"Mom, you're worrying me."

"I know I am, honey, but indulge me, will you? Your dad wouldn't want me to worry you, but it's better to be safe than sorry. He doesn't think there's even a reason to call the police yet."

"Trust your instincts, Mom. If something doesn't feel right, call the police, no matter what Dad says."

"Promise me you'll give me a call if you see anyone suspicious?"

"I promise, but only if you promise to keep me posted."

"A deal. And for all I know, I won't ever see the man again," Kathryn said, remembering Mike McCoy's prediction.

"Well, if you do, just walk up to him and ask what he's doing in Avon."

Her direct-line kid. "Ha, why didn't I think of that approach?"

"I'm serious. If you see him again, and there are people around, do it, Mom. Catch him off guard. That will tell you a lot about his intent."

"Thanks, darling," Kathryn said.

Drew arrived ten minutes later. Kathryn glanced at the clock when she heard the groan of the garage door open, surprised it was only 6:30. She felt she'd lived a lifetime in the last nightmarish twenty-four hours.

Drew hurried in without stopping in the hall to hang up his jacket. "Thank God you're here, Kathryn," he said, sounding as if he'd run the distance to the house. "I was worried when I didn't find you at the restaurant."

"You would have had no reason to worry if you'd shown up on time as promised," Kathryn said, ice in her tone. "Where were you?"

Drew threw his ring of keys on the kitchen desk, the household's collection point. "By the side of the road after being pulled over for speeding by a cop out to prove himself. If he weren't new to the force, I'd have a word with the police chief about him. Rude jerk. He gave me a ticket." Drew handed the ticket to Kathryn. VIOLATION SUMMONS AND COMPLAINT, it read.

Kathryn asked slowly, "Why were you speeding?"

Drew heaved a sigh and took the wineglass from her hand. He took a sip, then handed it back. "Because I was late leaving the office. I got an SOS from the hospital. Some fool kid who thinks he's Evel Knievel thought he'd get in the last of the season's skiing on a slippery slope and broke his leg in four nasty places. Dr. Camden paged me to see if I'd come by and take a look at the X-rays for Dr. Jenson. I ended up assisting, so I was later leaving for the restaurant than I'd planned. I guess I did press a little heavy on the pedal. Why didn't you stay?"

"Why didn't you call to let me know you'd be late?" Kathryn countered.

"When Elizabeth paged me, I left the office in a hurry. I meant to call you on my cell from the car, and then discovered it was out of juice."

"You couldn't have called from the hospital?"

"Why the grilling, Kathryn? I didn't have time when I got there. You know what it's like in an emergency, and the boy was in so much pain. I was looking forward to our having dinner together. Why did you leave?"

"I wanted to come home." Kathryn decided not to relate her conversation with Mike McCoy. She was in no frame of mind for Drew's reaction.

"Well, I see you got back your bracelet," Drew said.

"I thought you were concerned about my being in the company of a strange man."

"Well, I was, honey, but I figured you'd be okay in a busy restaurant at that time of day." Drew frowned. "The man didn't give you reason to wish I'd been there, did he?"

Kathryn felt a jab of the unease the rancher's information had stirred. "He was a perfect gentleman."

"Okay, then. We can still go out." He motioned to the glass of wine. "Got any more of that?"

Kathryn placed the violation slip on the counter. "In the fridge," she said softly. Drew's set of keys was spread apart like an open fan.

She noticed an extra key on the ring, and written on it in black was a small letter E. Her stomach lurched. *The key to Elizabeth's town house.*

"Drew? What's this extra key doing on your key chain?"

Drew withdrew a bottle of wine from the refrigerator. "Oh, that belongs to Dr. Camden's town house. She gave it to me today in case of emergency. She knew no one else she could trust with it, since Barbara now lives with her, and they'd probably be out of the house at the same time."

"Oh," Kathryn said, letting another chance to confront Drew slip through her fingers. Did she give a damn at this point? The more important problem was whether her life was in danger, and she was on her own to figure it out. She had to be proactive.

She sat down at the desk in her office. It was time to make a couple of lists—one of the people she'd crossed paths with in recent years who might have a motive to kill her, and another of those from her past. Something might bubble to the surface once she cast her mind back. Some silhouette might emerge from the shadows that she recognized.

She wrote down four general headings under "Motive for Murder"— "Money," "Hate," "Love," "Power"—and stared at them, already feeling a sense of futility.

She wrote down the names of the public organizations where she'd voted against petitioners' requests. There was jealousy and in-fighting when she worked with the charities, but certainly nothing that would push someone toward killing her. She could think of no parents she'd tangled with while serving on the Board of Education. Still, where your kids were involved, you never knew. She wrote down the names of two couples.

Kathryn made another set of headings for her own history: "Early Childhood," up to the age of five; "Foster Care," from six to seventeen; "College," from seventeen to twenty-one; and "Early Marriage and Graduate School," from twenty-one to twenty-four. She stared at the heading "Early Childhood." What did she really know about those years? She never actually knew her parents, nothing of her maternal and little of her paternal grandparents. Their past lives were a blank to her. Her parents had had no siblings, but what about her grandparents? Kathryn had never seen pictures or heard mention of great-aunts and great-uncles, but were there cousins roaming about out there somewhere? Kathryn knew that her mother's father died while his daughter was in college, his wife a few years later. Kathryn had presumed that her paternal grandparents were her father's only family, but could there be some long-lost relative who saw her as a threat to a possible inheritance?

Now that she thought about it, what happened to the grand house where her parents had lived, and to the money that had supported their lifestyle? And what about the money from the sale of her paternal grandparents' more modest home? Kathryn recalled no will, no lawyer's visit. She had gone into foster care empty-handed. But that was odd, now that she thought about it. Who had disposed of her family's properties and received the money for them and the assets they might have possessed? Had the money gone to pay creditors, attorneys, medical bills? Was money or scandal somehow behind this nightmare?

Chapter Fifteen

Sunday, April 4

Drew was still asleep on Sunday morning when Kathryn dressed quietly for services at the Episcopal Church of the Transfiguration. Usually, she'd never have let him sleep in on Easter Sunday, but today she had something she had to accomplish alone. If her stalker was in church, Kathryn intended to confront him, as Bobby had suggested.

But Golf Cap did not appear. She kept scanning the pews, but there were only the usual worshippers, dressed in ski jackets, anxious to get in the last bit of skiing for the season.

When the service was over, Kathryn made a point of asking the archdeacon about the man who had been tailing her, hoping that the minister had spoken to him.

"No, Kathryn," Father Joseph said. "I noticed him, but he never went through the greeting line. He must have gone out the side door every Sunday."

"Perhaps he filled out a visitor's card?"

Father Joseph shook his head. "I intentionally checked. If ever I saw a man in need of God's grace, it was he, but the two times he visited us, he left no information. May I ask why you're interested in him?"

"I've reason to believe he possesses information about someone I know, and I'd hoped to have a word with him."

"Then I'm sorry I couldn't be of help."

Kathryn drove out of the church parking lot inclined to believe that Mike McCoy was right, and she'd probably seen the last of Golf Cap. She would know for sure once she located the place where the man was staying. The choices were many, but they were upper-scale and would seem, going by his overall appearance, beyond the man's reach. She would begin with the budget motels first.

At her second stop, the desk clerk, a balding man with shifty eyes, admitted, "You're the second person who's asked about that guy. A man was in here yesterday."

"Oh?" Kathryn said. "Did you get his name?"

"No. Didn't ask."

"Could you describe him for me?"

"For that information, you'll have to make it worth my while."

Kathryn opened her purse. Fifteen minutes later, she left the motel with the information she'd paid for, if doubtful of some of its validity. Mike had gotten here first, asking questions, and likely received the same information. The clerk had given her Golf Cap's license number, under the name Tim Grayson, with an address and telephone number listed in Little Rock, Arkansas. *Little Rock?* Surely this was a fake ID. In any case, he had checked out on Friday. A different matter was Mike McCoy. To Kathryn's question of whether the clerk had the impression that the rancher was acquainted with Golf Cap, he'd replied, "Why would he ask his name if he knew him?" So at least they weren't in league together. Maybe the man really had been a visitor from Little Rock, in Avon simply to look over property to buy.

Kathryn strove for emotional calm as she turned toward home, but it was useless. The sun was shining, drying the final moisture from the rain, and she turned off the heater and lowered the window to let in a draft of the fresh mountain wind shaking showers from the aspens. Instantly cold air swept into the car, up her coat sleeves, chilling her flesh, but she felt nothing. It was such a beautiful day, a gift to be treasured in this unpredictable season, but to appreciate it, you had to feel alive, and to feel alive, you had to be at ease in body and spirit.

That Golf Cap was no longer a danger was a relief, but if Mike McCoy was right that her stalker was an investigator, who had hired him and why? For what purpose? Once again, an ache spread in her chest. It hurt to remember that her husband had left her alone to work her way through this maze. She was used to tackling problems under her own steam, but over the long years of marriage she'd come to rely on Drew's understanding and encouragement, so much that she wasn't sure where she began and he ended. A devoted mother and wife, she had become used to putting her needs last.

In her early years she had been convinced that she could depend on no one but herself for protection and emotional stability, and, more importantly, that she needed no one. But sometimes a tree interweaves with another, and they grow as one, partners wrapped in a perennial dance. Lumbermen maintain that the intertwining of two different species of trees weakens one of them. That was what Kathryn felt like now, she realized: a tree whose life was slowly being cut off by an invading species.

When she was Lindsay's age, she'd thought ruthlessly that acquiring a college degree and having a career would be the only way she could gain happiness. But then she fell in love with Drew, and then her children. Her world grew bigger, and she allowed her academic career to slip. Her pursuits were always in her heart, but the needs of her family engulfed her own dreams.

"*I'm* not depending on any man for *my* happiness," her daughter said once. Just a simple declaration as she helped her mother clear the dishes from the table after a family dinner.

What the child didn't know.

Her daughter did not know what it was like to love someone

enough to put their interests above her own. She had no knowledge of the bond created by her parents' neglected childhoods and the struggles of their early marriage. The children knew of their sister's sudden death. But they had been told nothing of their parents' backgrounds and their years of poverty, while their father labored to earn his medical degree and their mother to pay for it.

"Why don't we ever have tuna in the house?" Lindsay had once demanded. "All my friends' mothers make their kids tuna fish sandwiches."

"Because your dad and I ate an awful lot of canned tuna around the time you were born and for a number of years afterward."

"So what?"

There were times Kathryn had wanted to answer that *So what?* To give their daughter an explanation of all that they had suffered. But Drew had been opposed. The children, especially Lindsay, saw their father as rich, suave, and important, an image he didn't want destroyed. Their children had grown up among friends with pedigrees far more impressive than that of a man who had overcome nearly impossible conditions to achieve success. Never, he said, did he want his children to know of the losers who had conceived him and the squalor in which he'd been born.

Truthfully, Kathryn was equally reluctant to discuss her early years, not out of pride but because of the pain their memories evoked, and she'd been grateful that their children had simply accepted that both sets of grandparents had died long before they were born. To this day, Kathryn felt the sting of her parents' indifference, the shame of her father's imprisonment and her mother's inebriation.

But now, for the first time in a long time, Kathryn found herself wondering: Had her marriage destroyed her dream of a doctorate? Sure, dreams change, but while other children dreamed of being rock stars, she had dreamed of getting her PhD in biomedicine and saving lives. If she could do that, perhaps another little girl wouldn't have to grow up without a family.

For thirty years she and Drew had traveled side by side along the same road, sharing similar likes and interests, goals, table, and bed, experiencing the good and bad times together. What was marriage if it wasn't a mutual blending of strengths and needs and tastes so that individuals became one?

Against her will, Kathryn pictured those intertwined trees in the forest and herself manning the logger's saw, primed and ready.

She drew the scene so vividly in her mind that she ran a stop sign.

Chapter Sixteen

The smell of frying bacon greeted Kathryn when she let herself into the hall from the garage. Entering the kitchen, she found Drew with his head poked into the refrigerator. "I heard you drive in," he said as he emerged, holding aloft two glasses with leafy celery stalks showing above the rims. "Voila! Bloody Marys for the cleansed soul—" He stopped in midsentence, the cheer in his voice turning to concern. "Honey, what's wrong? You're shivering."

He set down the glasses and quickly wrapped her in his arms, the warm flesh of his neck against her cold cheek. "No wonder. You're freezing!" he exclaimed. "Wasn't the heater working in the car?"

"I turned it off and put the window down."

"Why?"

"I wanted to feel the wind."

He searched her face with the same worried intensity she'd caught in his gaze yesterday afternoon. "Whatever tunes your engine, I guess. Why are you so late? I thought church service would have been over more than an hour ago."

"I went looking for the motel where my stalker stayed, and I found it. He checked out Friday."

Drew's brows shot up, but his tone made it sound as if that settled the matter. "Well, there you go. Now I hope you are satisfied that he's no threat. Take this. It will warm you up." He handed her a Bloody Mary and turned the bacon slices with a fork. "Brunch in ten," he said. "I've made a batch of pecan and banana pancakes to make up for the ones you didn't eat yesterday."

Unwilling to let the subject drop, Kathryn said, "I got the guy's name and address and license plate number. He lives in Little Rock, Arkansas. I think the information is worth my asking someone from the police department to run a check on him."

Drew looked at her and let out an exasperated sigh. "Kathryn, let it go. The man's gone. We'll keep an eye out, but I doubt he'll be a threat anymore."

"Yes, you're probably right," Kathryn said, relenting.

"I didn't hear you leave this morning. Why didn't you wake me?"

"I didn't want to disturb the sugar plums dancing in your head."

"Don't I *wish*! God, what terrible dreams—all brought on by guilt, I'm sure."

"Guilt?"

"For not taking you to Europe, especially since I'm going to have to leave you."

The news caught Kathryn as she was swallowing, making her cough violently. She set down her drink and gasped, "You're going to leave me?"

Drew plucked a paper napkin from its holder and handed it to her. "In early May, when I have to go to Denver to do the operations. I'll stay in quarters at the hospital for the first week of the players' recovery."

Kathryn wiped her mouth.

"You look surprised. Didn't I mention that the surgeries were to be done at UC Health University, not at Winston General? The players don't want to be away from their families."

"No, you didn't mention it," Kathryn said. "Will anybody else be tagging along from Winston General?"

"Only Dr. Camden, to observe the surgeries. The experience will be good for her."

"Naturally," Kathryn said. "How long will you be gone?"

"A few weeks at most."

"I don't suppose you'd want company?"

"Thanks, if that's an offer, but what would you do? I'll be tied up most days—you'll be bored. Look at it this way, Kath, it will be a good time for you to do what you want to do without me underfoot. No cooking, no washing my gym clothes, no worrying if I've put the right shirt with the right pants. Freedom!" Drew held up his Bloody Mary to touch glasses.

They clinked rims. The tomato-vodka mixture tasted bitter on her tongue. Was that what she'd become to her husband? Only someone to cook his meals, wash his clothes, select his wardrobe? "Freedom," she said, but she heard only the whir of the logger's saw.

Chapter Seventeen

Monday, April 5

Ever since Mike met Kathryn at the restaurant, he hadn't been able to get her out of his head. She reminded him of his wife, the way she would play absentmindedly with whatever was on the table—a sugar packet, creamer, even the silverware—in an effort to keep her hands busy. His wife had been a pianist—not professionally, but she'd always kept a piano in their home just for the sheer joy of it. He kept wondering if perhaps Kathryn was an artist of some sort.

In the end, though, Mike couldn't escape the thought that Kathryn needed someone to help her. There wasn't anything the police could do about Reggie Morris, the private investigator. He hadn't made any threats, and there was too much red tape in the civilian world with too little action. The people who truly needed help, people like Kathryn Walker, they were left on their own. Only when something terrible happened did people say, *Oh, if we had only done something*. But when the next woman who needed help came around, they forgot, and the cycle was repeated.

Not this time.

Mike decided to take it upon himself to do something. He flew to Houston early Monday morning, and headed straight for the Reggie Morris Detective Agency. In the rental car, his cell rang. The caller was Lonnie.

"Where are you?"

"Houston," Mike said.

"Uh-oh," Lonnie said. "Couldn't let it go, could you?"

"I feel a responsibility, Lonnie. Can't shake it. It's like knowing that a store is about to be robbed without warning the owner. If I'm wrong, I'm wrong, but at least I'll have peace of mind about it."

"I have a feeling you aren't coming home with peace of mind, boss."

"Me neither."

Mike parked across the street from the detective agency at a 7–Eleven with bars on the windows, in a parking lot littered with fast-food wrappers. Midmorning, he saw a black Dodge SUV pull into the narrow drive to the detective agency's carport, and the driver let himself into the side entrance of the small building. Lights came on inside. After a few minutes, Mike walked across the street to introduce himself to Reggie Morris.

A bell hanging over the door signaled Mike's entrance. There was a reception area but no receptionist. The desk looked as if it was a space to dump drawer files and newspapers, and the chair behind it was missing.

"Be right there!" a male voice called from an inner office. "Make yourself at home!"

Mike heard movement in the other room and eventually caught the acrid smell of instant coffee. He waited, standing, until the agency's owner appeared, stirring his coffee. "What can I do for . . ." He halted in his speech when he saw Mike, as if something had caught in his throat.

Mike held out his hand. "Mr. Morris, name's Mike McCoy."

"From the grocery store in Avon." After a hard swallow, Reggie Morris hesitantly shook Mike's hand. "You might as well come on in," he said with a motion of his coffee mug. He paused behind his cluttered desk and, without sitting down, asked, "Like I started to say, what can I do for you?"

Mike remained standing as well. "You can tell me why you were tailing Kathryn Walker."

"Want some coffee? It's instant, but it's all I got." Mike shook his head, and Reggie pulled out his desk chair and waved for Mike to take the chair before it, a wooden ladderback with a frayed cushion.

"Damned if I know, and that's God's honest truth. Don't think about beating the crap out of me for information I don't have. I wouldn't if I were you. Understood?"

Mike inclined his head in agreement as Reggie continued. "And before I tell you what I do know, I want you to tell me why you are here. Didn't seem to me that you and Mrs. Walker knew each other."

"Perhaps you don't know everything," Mike said. "What our relationship is, is none of your business. I pinned you as a private eye for some time before she got on to you, but the poor woman thinks you are a stalker."

"Well, she would, wouldn't she? I let myself be hard to miss. What about you? You're not the average local rancher."

"Military." Mike sat down. "I warned her about who you are, but she can't recall anyone who would want to investigate her, any more than she can figure out why she'd be the target of a stalker."

"Mrs. Walker underestimates herself." Reggie scrutinized Mike, his eyes scanning him from his short hair, the same cut he had when he first signed up for the military, to the way he sat. Poised to jump up at any moment. "You look like you could be a colonel. Can I call you Colonel?" When Mike didn't respond Reggie continued, "So, Colonel, you're here to find out what I know? Well, I can't help you there, and I sincerely wish I could. I've never met the person who hired me. Whoever it is calls from an untraceable phone using an electronically altered voice and has left no trail that I've been able to follow. I can tell you that the security code of the house and a duplicate key to the one under the terra-cotta frog on the Walkers' front porch are now in the hands of my client, so you might warn Mrs. Walker to have both changed."

"You wouldn't happen to have any sources you could share with me?" Mike asked.

Reggie thought a moment, then hiked his shoulders in a *what does it matter?* shrug. "If I were you, I would have a chat with Rosalie Deemer. She was the Walkers' old housekeeper. Worked for them for several years before she was fired out of the blue."

Mike made a note of that. "What's your professional opinion about the husband?"

"That he's in the clear. He'd know the information my client hired me to get, and if he suspects her of fooling around, or of anything else, why me? Colorado doesn't have detective agencies?"

"Unless it was a deliberate move to cover his tracks," Mike said, but it was a point to be considered, he thought. It suggested that Reggie Morris's client lived in Texas.

"I wasn't hired to investigate him. Handsome surgeons attract women like flies, so it's possible the doc could be seeing someone on the side." Reggie shrugged regretfully. "I wish I could offer more assistance, Colonel, but I'm afraid I can't. With all her work in the community, I would look at some of the people she might have offended. I'm sure there are a lot more of them than Kathryn is letting on."

"Anything else?"

Reggie rubbed his chin. "Not that I can think of."

Mike got to his feet. He believed the detective was telling all that he knew, other than the name of his source, and he had convinced Mike that his instincts were right. Whoever the person in the shadows who had hired Reggie Morris was, they meant nothing good for Kathryn Walker.

Reggie stood also. Neither man offered a hand to the other. "Like I say, I sincerely wish I could be of more help, and I'm relieved you've taken an interest. You might be able to help her dodge a bullet, literally. I'd have liked to warn her myself, but . . ." He gave a lopsided smile. "Got to watch my own six, you know?"

Mike nodded and turned to go.

"Mr. McCoy?" Reggie called when he was at the door. "Why are you here, really?"

Mike paused. "Someone I loved very much was killed because of my lack of due diligence."

"And you're making up for it now."

"You could say that," Mike said, and walked out.

Chapter Eighteen

"Would it be too much bother to have Frank come over for dinner tonight to watch the NCAA championship game?" Drew asked Kathryn Monday morning as he prepared to leave for his office. If he noticed she wasn't in her running gear, he did not comment. Kathryn had decided to follow advice and change her routines. "You've got that leg of lamb to roast," Drew said. "Rain is forecast, making today even drearier for him."

Well, who does he have to thank for that? Kathryn could have said, but it would only have started an argument. Frank Danton was Drew's best friend. A year before, in April, his wife, Sandy, had filed for divorce. *Irreconcilable differences.* In their case, the charge was right. How could anybody as different as Frank and Sandy live together? Kathryn detested the man, but she tolerated him because he loved Drew and adored her children. Drew and Frank shared a history together that had forged the kind of friendship that Kathryn knew she'd never understand. Frank idolized Drew, and Drew accepted Frank as he was, warts and all, which most people found untenable.

The two had been best buddies since the first grade. Frank's parents had all but adopted Drew during their youth, giving him a surrogate home and family. The boys had been roommates in college, had served as one another's best man in their weddings, and Frank had been godfather to Abby Gale. Kathryn had always thought it ironic that the senior Dantons' examples of generosity and grace hadn't taken with their only son. After many years of marriage Sandy had finally had enough of Frank's controlling, tight-fisted ways and left him.

"Tell him seven o'clock," Kathryn said. "That should give you enough time to get home from the Argyle, don't you think?"

Drawing on his coat in the hallway, face turned away from her, Drew said, "I'll cut my workout short. I know that Frank will really appreciate a home-cooked meal. The game will keep him out of your hair for the evening. You'll be at the library reading to the kiddos this morning?"

"As usual. Don't forget your gym bag."

He didn't take her bait.

When he had gone, Kathryn drank her coffee while gazing across the alley into the Dantons' kitchen window. Frank ate all his meals out, including breakfast, now that Sandy was gone. Frank was the main influence luring Drew to move their family to Avon. Drew had fallen in love with the Rockies when Frank's family invited him to spend his summer vacation with them in their second home in Vail, when the boys were in high school. After college, Frank moved to Avon and set up a prosperous insurance agency. From the start, Kathryn had known that once Drew finished his residency, he would be looking for a position in an area that offered the variety of four seasons and the pleasures of mountain sports. When Frank had learned of an opening for an orthopedic surgeon in the regional hospital, he let Drew know about it, and the rest was history.

From the moment she'd met him, Kathryn had felt Frank's dislike for her. Apologetically, Sandy had explained, "In some areas, Frank is a snob, and he has never felt that you were good enough for Drew."

The two men's dispositions could not be more at odds. Frank

was a sour man, a pessimist who mistrusted the world around him. Drew, on the other hand, was disposed to find the trophy in catastrophe. Frank also had boorish manners. "Sometimes I wonder if you and Frank were switched at birth," Kathryn once admitted to Drew, who gave her a half-hearted laugh.

Kathryn considered Frank's only saving grace to be his surprising fondness for children. She had once overheard a discussion between him and Drew about Bobby.

"He's too into his fantasy world," she once heard Drew say. "All he does is talk about *Lord of the Rings* or *Doctor Who*. I'm afraid he's too concerned with playing elf or whatever to experience life in the real world."

"The world ain't gonna get a bite out of that kid. You ought to be proud of him. If anything, those stories teach him to have courage, and really, that's what you need for survival. I would be proud of him if he were my kid. Hell, I'd even go to one of his conventions with him."

After that, Kathryn had been able to abide Frank Danton.

The phone rang so suddenly she almost dropped her coffee cup. Lord, but she was jumpy today. The call was from the librarian at the Eagle County Library. "Kathryn, you don't need to come in this morning," she said. "Janet is taking her car in for servicing and can open up the library. Also, most parents are extending the Easter holiday through today, so you won't have many customers at reading hour. Why don't you take the full day off? Janet can read to the few who will show up."

Janet Foster was the other volunteer with whom Kathryn worked. On Mondays each week, they gave the librarian a break. Kathryn was sorry to miss the children today, but it was another routine she knew it was wise to change up. When she opened, she was often alone in the library until nine, getting the cranky radiators going and the place tidied up.

With the extra time this morning, Kathryn decided to get started marinating the lamb. As she peeled the garlic, she tried not to think of Mike and their disturbing conversation. She couldn't think of anyone who hated her enough to hire a private investigator. Usually, that was the realm of jealous spouses. If anything, these days Drew was nowhere near being the jealous sort. She didn't even know where he was most days anymore, if he wasn't at the Argyle.

Maybe I should have him followed, she mused.

When the phone rang again from the librarian's number, she hoped it meant they needed her to come on in after all.

The woman's tone was panicked. "Kathryn, have you heard the news?"

"What news?"

"Oh, dear. It's been on television all morning. I'm sorry to be the one to tell you, but Janet was struck by a hit-and-run driver in the street right in front of the library this morning as she was arriving for her shift. She's at Winston General, and thanks to your husband, looks as if she'll pull through, but Dr. Walker has his work cut out for him in the months ahead. I know that Janet will want to see you as soon as she's stable enough."

Shocked, Kathryn listened to the few details—how a motorist had found Janet Foster lying in a pool of blood in the street, her blond hair matted, her legs at a crazy angle, her Burberry raincoat marked with mud from the vehicle. "Whoever hit her did it intentionally, according to the police," the librarian said, her voice quivering with outrage. "It was a deliberate act of malice. We can only hope that the police find something in the surveillance cameras."

Kathryn hung up the phone, imagining the slight figure of Janet Foster flung into the air, the sickening impact of her body hitting the pavement, the excruciating pain and brief awareness of what had happened before losing consciousness. Sweet, innocent Janet Foster, who everyone secretly referred to as Kathryn's clone. Who in Avon would be capable of committing such an act of hate against a young wife and mother of two small children? And why hadn't Drew called to tell her the news himself?

That evening Drew arrived home an hour before his usual time on gym days. He looked tired and drained. "God, I need a drink," he said, coming into the kitchen where Kathryn was finishing the last preparations for dinner. While he poured and mixed, he related the gruesome details of Janet Foster's injury. She was lucky to be alive—"Or not," he said grimly, explaining that her whole body structure had been compromised, so that she would probably live with pain for the rest of her life. "She reminded me so much of you, Kath, her hairstyle and Burberry, and the fact that she was struck before the library . . . I couldn't help but think that it might have been you lying on that operating table, God forbid." Drew closed his eyes and took a deep swallow of his martini.

Kathryn paused with her lips poised at the rim of her glass of sauvignon blanc, struck by the horror of the same thought.

"Kathryn, this is absolutely delicious," Drew said.

"Pretty decent, Kath," Frank agreed, helping himself to another slice of roasted lamb. "You don't happen to have mint *sauce*, do you? I prefer it to this mint jelly."

"I'm afraid we're fresh out," Kathryn said, pasting on a smile. She resented hearing her nickname in Frank's mouth. Only Drew had the license to call her Kath. "You boys want to eat your dessert while watching the game?"

"What is it?" Frank inquired.

"Strawberry shortcake. Will that do for you?"

"I guess, as long as you don't put Cool Whip on it. I like the real stuff."

"I just happen to have whipping cream." Kathryn kept her smile glued on while she threw a glance down the table to Drew, its message plain, and he answered back with an apologetic shrug and roll of his eyes.

"How about if we take a few minutes for you and me to discuss a couple of your insurance policies, Drew," Frank said. "The term policy on Kathryn's life is about to expire at the end of the month. By adding the cost of her premiums to the disability policy you have now, you can increase the benefits you'd receive if you become unable to work."

"Sounds like a good idea," Drew said, "but let's talk about it over lunch this week. Kathryn is upset over her friend, you know, that victim of the hit-and-run all over the news today."

"Well, she doesn't have to be a part of the conversation, and I thought this was as good a time as any."

Typical of Frank, the consummate male chauvinist, Kathryn thought, to cut her out of the conversation by speaking directly to Drew, as if she weren't at the table and her opinion on the subject did not matter.

Twenty years before, when the kids were babies and they were penniless, Frank had sold them—rightfully so—on the idea of taking out a $5 million term policy on her and Drew's lives. They had balked at the amount for hers. Why would Drew need $5 million upon her death? Frank had pointed out that she was the breadwinner, whose financial support Drew counted on to complete his medical degree. Should she die, nannies and housekeepers didn't come cheap, especially over a long period of time, and funerals didn't either. Ultimately, the policy gave Kathryn peace of mind to know that her family would be cared for financially if something should happen to her. At the time, twenty years seemed like an eternity, but now that period was coming to an end. Where had the years gone?

"Don't let me interfere with a male-only discussion, Frank," Kathryn said dryly, getting up from the table. "Drew can fill me in later."

Frank handed her his plate over his shoulder as Drew pushed back his chair to help Kathryn clear the dishes. "Not bad," he said.

"Thanks for the compliment." Kathryn patted his shoulder. "Don't bother getting up," she said when he didn't stir. "Drew and I can manage."

Kathryn was pretending sleep when Drew finally came to bed. The game had gone into overtime, and he and Frank had lingered over brandy, talking long into the night. Usually after an emotional day—after the loss of a patient or any tragedy that made them glad they had each other—her husband would nuzzle her awake when he came to bed, take her in his arms, and tell her how much he loved and needed her, and often they'd end up having sex. But not tonight. Within minutes of his pulling up the covers, Kathryn rose on an elbow in injured surprise to look at him. He lay on his back, mouth slightly open, emitting the snore of the deeply exhausted.

Chapter Nineteen

Tuesday, April 6

"So you're going to warn her?" Lonnie asked Mike the next morning after he had returned from his trip to visit Reggie Morris.

"Yeah, I'm driving straight to the coffee shop from here. According to Reggie, that's where she meets her book club the first Tuesday of the month."

"After yesterday's tragedy, she might not be there." Lonnie gestured toward the news report on the television. "There was a hit-and-run in front of the county library. Somebody mowed down a young mother in the early morning hours, right in the street." A picture of the victim flashed on the screen, and Mike stepped forth for a closer look. The picture was of the blond volunteer he'd frequently seen sorting books at the library. She often wore her Burberry because of the faulty heating system, a raincoat much like Kathryn's.

"Dear God," Mike said. "She needs to know that whoever hired Reggie Morris has a key to her house and knows the code to her security system."

Lonnie crossed himself. "Let's hope she's at the coffee shop."

The coffee shop was bustling with the last of the season's skiers.

Soon Avon would be left to the "townies" until summer, when another group surged in from the Southwest and South to get out of the heat. Among the vehicles in the parking lot, Mike saw no sign of a white Cadillac, but he had arrived early.

Mike took a seat at the counter and kept an eye on the glass-walled conference room as the Tuesday book club began to file in, the subject of yesterday's hit-and-run incident on everyone's tongue. By ten o'clock the group had assembled and taken their places, but Kathryn Walker was not among them. Perhaps she was late, Mike hoped. By his fourth cup of coffee he gave her up as a no-show.

What should he do now? If he left a recording of his notes on her answering machine, who knew when she'd hear it, and Dr. Walker might listen to the message. Going to her husband with his notes was out of the question. Despite what Reggie had said, Mike wasn't ready yet to rule him out. If Mike appeared at her house unannounced, she might not open the door to him, but there was still hope that he could reach her in time. The person who wanted her dead would have to regroup now that his first attempt on her life had failed, so there was a short window of opportunity to warn her. Tomorrow morning at ten o'clock, he'd plant himself at the door of the art studio where she took oil painting lessons and hand his notes off to her personally.

"Not taking your morning jog?" Drew asked when he entered the kitchen wearing his surgical scrubs to find Kathryn still in her robe and gown.

"I'm not running today, and I'm not going to stay home today," she said. "I need to talk to you, Drew. It's urgent."

He glanced at his watch. "Well, you'll have to be quick about it. I've got to check on Janet Foster and Evel Knievel before my first appointment."

Kathryn pulled out a chair. "Sit down. If you love your wife, this is even more important."

Drew's brows hiked. "What's going on?"

"Drew, I think somebody is trying to kill me." There! She'd said it out loud. "I am convinced that yesterday's hit-and-run was meant for me. Think about it. You said yourself that Janet looks enough like me—in height and size, the color and style of her hair, her raincoat—to have been mistaken for me in the morning fog. I was the target, not Janet."

Drew sat down. He took a deep breath and reached for her hands to draw her toward him. "Kath, there must be a dozen women in Avon with raincoats similar to yours. Honey, you've let this stalker get to you, and he's gone. Yesterday's tragedy was the result of someone driving recklessly. The police will get him, and then you'll see."

Kathryn yanked her hands away and spun angrily to pour a cup of coffee. "I think Mike McCoy was right, and Golf Cap was an investigator hired by someone to follow my movements, to know where I'd be at certain times. I know you said that we have no reason to be alarmed and that it is pointless to go to the police, but now I think we have something."

Looking completely confused, Drew said, "*Golf Cap*? And are you talking about the guy who found your bracelet?"

"Golf Cap is the guy I thought was a stalker, and yes, Mike McCoy is the one who found my bracelet. He had a pretty compelling theory about what's going on. You might want to hear what he has to say. I have his contact numbers."

"Kathryn, the man's a rancher." Drew sounded bewildered. "What does he know about these things?"

"He wasn't always. Mr. McCoy—*Colonel* McCoy—was military, in special services. He's retired now, but he served in a secret organization called Delta Force."

"You mean . . . like the counterterrorist organization featured in the *The Unit*?"

"That's right. He's trained in surveillance, and he recognized the man as a private investigator and warned me that my life could be in danger. I know it all sounds far-fetched, Drew, but you've got to believe me. Every instinct in me tells me he's right, especially after what's happened to Janet Foster."

"Kath, honey . . ." Drew rose from his chair and took the coffee cup from her hand, carefully setting it down. "We need to think about this logically. It does us no good to overreact. This is all pretty heavy stuff, and we still need proof. All we have is your hunch. As good as your instincts may be, they mean nothing in a court of law. If we go to the police with this, nothing will happen."

Hands on her shoulders, he drew back to gaze into her face. "Janet should be lucid enough today. Maybe she'll give us something to go on," he continued in a more mollifying tone. "I'll ask a few questions myself after she talks to the police. For instance, does she think the hit-and-run driver saw her face when she got out of her car?"

When Kathryn didn't say anything, Drew continued, "What does Janet drive?"

"A dark-blue BMW." It was at the shop, she wanted to add. But Drew was clearly not ready to hear her.

"Well, that is definitely different from our car." Drew touched his lips to her forehead. He looked at his watch. "Look, honey, I'm sorry but I've got to run. I'm glad you are staying home today; you can get some much-needed rest. Maybe you can change the password to the security alarm again? I'll call you to let you know when you can see Janet. Okay?"

No, it was not okay, but Kathryn was out of energy. "All right," she said, watching Drew hurriedly pull on his jacket. Kathryn resented that Drew was right; if she brought this all to the police, they would make a report and that would be it. While searching the internet, she'd come across an article that said that there was a backlog of over three thousand untested rape kits in Colorado. She resented that as a woman she had to curtail her own life just to stay out of danger.

As she watched Drew prepare to leave, she couldn't help but wonder why he didn't do more. Here she was worrying about her safety, and Drew was treating it like any other day. The thought infuriated her. It was as if he didn't even care.

"Drew? Do you still love me?" she asked.

He paused in adjusting his jacket collar. "What kind of question is that?"

"One that requires only a yes or no answer."

He caressed her shoulders. "Don't make me say it. Look, I know I've been preoccupied lately and haven't given you the attention you deserve—"

She threw off his hands. "So you believe, as the police would, that I am making this up to get your *attention*? If you entertain so much as an inkling of that possibility, Drew Walker, then you don't know me at all!" She turned her back on him. "Go to work, Dr. Walker, and don't worry a second about your wife. She'll be fine. She knows how to take care of herself. She's just out of practice."

"Kath, honey . . . ," Drew called, his voice desperate. "What do you expect me to *do*?"

But Kathryn had left the kitchen.

Chapter Twenty

The only person who might be able to give her answers was Natalie Hunt. Kathryn would surprise her with a visit at her assisted living facility. Her old social case worker from Alabama would be out of her room, having coffee with her cronies on the front porch. She had no cell phone; Kathryn and Drew had offered to buy her one, but she'd refused. "I'd just forget where I left it, and you and Drew do enough for me," she'd said.

Kathryn found Natalie on the porch in her usual rocking chair, surrounded by her neighbors, wheelchairs and walkers everywhere. Everyone brightened when they recognized Kathryn coming up the walk. She had stopped by a doughnut shop to pick up an assortment of their favorites, as well as cups of coffee and cocoa that earned exclamations of delight.

Natalie, sharp as ever to Kathryn's signals, excused herself to take her visitor inside to a secluded corner of the lounge. "What's up that couldn't wait until Thursday lunch, Katy Wonky?" Concern showed through the screen of love in her eyes.

Now approaching eighty, Natalie had moved to the assisted living home in Avon when it became apparent that she could no longer look after herself. Kathryn would always be grateful that Drew had agreed without a peep to pay the part of the bill that Natalie's social security wouldn't cover. She appreciated, too, that he never said a word about the extras Kathryn provided to add more quality to Natalie's life—clothes, cable television, phone, beauty shop treatments. The expenses put more strain on their budget, but Drew knew what Natalie Hunt meant to Kathryn, how much she owed the woman.

"Natalie, can you tell me any details about my parents' financial situation at the time of their deaths? For instance, where did the money go from the sale of their house? From my father's life insurance policy? I assume he had one, and I know the house was sold, because my mother and I lived in an apartment when Dad went to prison."

Natalie frowned regretfully. "There was very little life insurance money. Along with the money from the sale of the house, it went to pay back the funds your father . . . *took* from the company he worked for. The house was your parents' only asset of any value."

"What about my grandparents' house? Where did the money go from that sale?"

"Your grandparents remortgaged their house to pay your father's astronomical legal bills and for your mother's funeral," Natalie said gently. "Then your grandmother fell ill with cancer, and your grandfather with Alzheimer's. Home health care costs and medical bills stripped them of their last penny. The bank foreclosed on the house after your grandfather's death. All this information was in your file."

"Good God," Kathryn said. How much wreckage her parents had left in their lives. "And you know of no extra property somewhere that could be coming to me as an heir?"

"That information would not have been in the file." Natalie's gaze narrowed. "What is this all about, Katy Wonky? Why are you asking these questions now?"

Kathryn shrugged. "Oh, I don't know. Curiosity, I guess. I'd have never given it a thought if Drew and I weren't thinking of revising some insurance policies and updating our wills." She bit into a maple bar and closed her eyes in pretended enjoyment. Chewing, she said, "I see you've got fried chicken on the menu today. I hope the doughnuts haven't spoiled your appetite for it."

Natalie sniffed. "They have no idea how to fry chicken in this state. You've got to go to Alabama for the real thing."

Kathryn chuckled to herself. Natalie was very particular about her food. On Thursdays, the dining room served meatloaf—"An abomination," Natalie called it, the reason Kathryn treated her to lunch on that day—and on Fridays, kokanee salmon, which Natalie considered "atonement."

Kathryn stayed for lunch—Natalie was right about the chicken—and turned on her cell as she was leaving in the early afternoon. It rang almost immediately. "Where the hell have you been?" Drew demanded. "I've called the house several times to get no answer, and your cell must have been turned off. I almost called Jim Kittredge to go check on you!"

Kathryn almost laughed, thinking of the neighbor the street had dubbed "the great white hunter." "I've been visiting Natalie. It's too sweet a day to stay inside. I'm heading home now."

"Just keep your cell phone with you if you're in your studio. I'll call you this afternoon." He didn't apologize for their fight this morning, and neither did she.

Back home, locked in, Kathryn looked at her lists. For the time being, she could cross off "Early Childhood," depressing as this new information had turned out to be, but she'd lost the desire to think through the other headings. In her frame of mind, it was a good day to work in her studio. She was partway through a portrait of Father Joseph that his wife hoped to hang in the church vestibule.

As she entered the light-filled corner room on the top floor of her house, Kathryn felt her shoulders begin to relax. Up here where the mountains met the skies, she could think with a cooler head, and she could see how Drew, who approached problems logically, might be skeptical of her allegations.

A clearer vision, a different perspective, were what this room gave her. It was an inner sanctum for her alone, a space for her dreams and thoughts and memories, paints and canvases. Drew and the kids rarely visited here. There was no electronic connection to the outside world except her cell phone, almost a sacrilege in this place of tranquility. There was not even a calendar or clock, only a couple of easy chairs and a gas-burning fireplace for heat in the winter and an overhead fan to assist the mountain breezes in summer. At her canvas on weekday afternoons with a view of the mountains and sky, Kathryn felt at peace.

It was cold in the room today, though. Kathryn turned on the gas logs, remembering to rotate the hanging brass sign to read DAMPER OPEN.

Chapter Twenty-One

Driving by the Walkers' residence on his way home from work late that afternoon, Frank Danton saw a squad car parked in front and decided to find out what in blazes was going on. As he pulled in the drive, the officer on the porch and an older man that he recognized as the Walkers' neighbor from across the street, Jim Kittredge, looked over at him.

The policeman waited for Frank's approach. "Who are you?"

"The Walkers are my best friends," Frank answered. "Is everything okay here?"

"Your name, please?" the patrolman asked, snapping open his notebook.

"Frank Danton. Like I said, I'm a friend of the Walkers. Jim, here"—he nodded to the neighbor—"knows me. I live a street over. What's going on?"

"May I see some identification, Mr. Danton?"

"Well, I guess," Frank said, reaching inside his suit coat, "but why are you here? Has there been a robbery?" He handed over his wallet, open to his driver's license.

"He says not," Jim said.

"Could you please remove your license, sir?"

"Oh, for Christ's sake." Frank wormed the stuck license out of its plastic holder and thrust it up close to the officer's eyes. "There," he said. "Now will you please tell me what the holy hell is going on?"

The officer ignored him, comparing the license to a note he had written on his pad. Frank felt his scalp tingle. Had something happened to Drew or Kathryn? "Please, Officer," he said. "Are the Walkers okay?"

"I am not sure. Dr. Walker can't reach his wife and has asked me to perform a wellness check. She's supposed to be home, but she's not answering the bell."

Frank snatched back his driver's license and brushed by the officer to pound his fist on the front door. "*Kathryn! Answer the goddamn door!*" he yelled, and then glued his finger to the bell. When there was no response, he looked back at the officer. "Are you sure she's home?"

"We never saw her go out," Jim said. "My wife knits by the front window."

"Her husband said she was going straight home when he last talked with her at two o'clock today," the policeman said. "She was expecting a call from him about a friend who recently underwent surgery. He says this time of day, she's usually in her art studio."

"My wife can testify to that," Jim said. "Drew must have been worried to call you."

"The captain says he sure sounded like it."

Jim left Frank and the policeman to run around to the side of the house and peer up at the windows of Kathryn's studio. "There's a light on up there," he yelled as he rushed back to the front door. "We've got to go in."

The officer picked up a rock and prepared to lob it through the window. "What in hell are you doing?" Frank cried, horrified.

"I'm going to break the window."

"No, you're not; there is no need to destroy property. There's a key right here." He grabbed up a terra-cotta frog from a planter by the door and released a hidden cavity on its back. "See?" he said, holding up proof of his claim.

The officer snatched the key from his fingers, inserted it into the lock, and threw the door open. "*Mrs. Walker!*" he yelled. He threw a look at Frank over his shoulder as he ran toward the stairs. "Where's the studio?"

"Top floor, at the end of the hall," Frank said, he and Jim following the tall, lanky form of the officer who had drawn his gun.

❋

Awaking to the sound of whispering above her head, Kathryn fought her way through a fog. Finally she could make out the faces of Drew, Barbara Stratton, and another nurse peering at her as if she were a rare specimen in a fish tank.

"She's opening her eyes," Barbara said.

"Thank God," Drew whispered. He wiggled Kathryn's chin. "Honey? Hello in there."

"What happened?" Kathryn asked, staring up into his brown eyes. "Where am I?"

"In the hospital," Barbara said softly from the other side of the bed, and Kathryn felt her cool fingers stroke her arm. "You were overcome by carbon monoxide gas."

"What?" Groggily, Kathryn attempted to sit up.

"No, honey, lie still, or you'll have one doozy of a headache." Drew smoothed her brow. "You'll be all right, thank God. Your blood work shows no permanent damage, but we may have to do a cardiovascular workup later."

"How would I get monoxide poisoning?" Kathryn asked.

"In your studio, honey. You must have forgotten to turn the damper sign properly the last time you lit the fireplace," Drew explained. "You thought you'd opened the vent when you actually closed it."

Dreamily, Kathryn objected, "No, I didn't . . ."

"You must have, honey. But it's okay. Next time you'll know to be more careful."

"What sign are we talking about?" Barbara asked.

"Kathryn bought signs for each of the fireplaces, to tell us when the vents are open or closed."

"I'll have to get one of those," Barbara said. "Elizabeth left the flue open last time, and a bird flew down the chimney." She smiled.

The door opened, and Frank Danton stepped inside. With barely a glance at Kathryn, he addressed Drew. "That Dirty Harry wannabe, Officer Harmon, is still here, hanging about in the hall. He insists on questioning her. Want me to tell him to get lost?"

"Dirty Harry wannabe?" Kathryn asked.

Barbara patted Kathryn's shoulder. "I'll stop by later, Mrs. Walker. We'll take good care of you."

Drew groaned. "That's the cop who pulled me over and gave me a ticket the other day. Tell him Kathryn's not up to answering questions right now. He can go home or wait. If he decides to wait, take him down for his supper in the cafeteria on my tab."

"Right-o," Frank said. "I'll keep the receipt." He looked at Kathryn. "You should be more careful, Kath. We don't want to give Drew reason to collect that life insurance policy."

Kathryn gave him a small smile. "I'll . . . keep that in mind."

When he'd gone, Kathryn grinned thinly. "What a guy."

Drew grinned. "Just so you know, he and Jim saved your life."

"Tell me what . . . happened," Kathryn said.

Chapter Twenty-Two

Drew explained that when he telephoned first their home number, then her cell, and there was no answer, he'd become worried. "I was scared, honey. The way we left things this morning . . . I didn't know what to expect . . ."

"You mean you . . . actually thought I might have . . . done something to myself?"

"Of course not! I thought someone might have done something to *you*. That's why I called the police. I left the hospital as soon as I could. The EMS had already arrived and secured you to a stretcher. Frank used the key in the frog. Jim was convinced something was amiss, and sure enough, he and the patrolman found you unconscious in your studio. If they had been a half hour later . . ." Drew's eyes closed briefly. "I can't bear to think it. We're going to have to install one of those carbon monoxide detectors to keep this from happening again."

Kathryn forced breath into her windpipe. "I didn't . . . forget to turn the sign correctly, Drew."

"It's okay, honey. Don't try to talk. We all make mistakes."

"This wasn't . . . one of them. The last time I was . . . in that room was Thursday. I didn't . . . stay because the rain made it too . . . dark to paint. If the damper . . . had been open, I would have heard . . . rain falling down the chimney. There would have been puddles on the hearth."

"Are you sure you would have noticed?"

"You know that . . . I'm the one in the family that . . . always checks for open windows. I want you to . . . remove the key from the . . . frog. Promise me, Drew."

Drew replaced the oxygen mask over her face. "Okay, I'll remove it. Now, shush, not another word. It's too much of an effort. We'll discuss this in the morning. You're staying here tonight."

She had made no mistake, Kathryn thought, closing her eyes. She knew the damper was closed on Thursday when she left the room. Somebody had deliberately opened the vent, knowing that she would close it before lighting the gas. In her mind's eye she retraced her steps, the night before. She remembered how odd it was to find cake crumbs when she got home from the retirement center. The counter was clean when she left the house. The bastard had helped himself to a slice of cake.

A crowd seemed to have gathered in Kathryn's hospital room. Barbara Stratton had stopped by again to check on her, as had several nurses of whom she was fond, and Officer Harmon was back after his meal in the cafeteria, pad in hand. Drew had brought up a sandwich to eat for dinner at Kathryn's bedside. Frank had gone, but returned to give Drew a ride home, since he had ridden with her in the ambulance.

All visitors but Drew and Frank scattered when the policeman cleared his throat. "My name is Cal Harmon, Mrs. Walker. I'd like to ask you a few questions."

Before he could continue, Frank said, "We thought you were a goner—"

Harmon opened his notebook. "I need to speak with Mrs. Walker, alone."

"Alone! Why do you need that?" Frank demanded.

The police looked from Frank to Drew. "I think it would be better if she and I speak alone, please."

"It's fine," Kathryn said. "You can leave."

Drew planted a kiss on her forehead. "We'll be right outside the door if you need us."

"I promise you, it was an accident."

"I didn't say one way or the other what I think, Mrs. Walker, but when I was filing my report, I saw that your security company had filed a report with our department. Would you like to tell me what that was about?"

"I didn't know they would file a report with the police," Kathryn said.

"Sometimes they file a report with us in cases of robbery, arrest, or suspicious activity."

Kathryn reached for her water. Her mouth had gone dry. She took a full swallow and answered, "Yes, I called them. I . . . had reason to believe a man was stalking me and that he'd beaten me home and . . . would accost me when I drove into the drive."

"A stalker?" Cal Harmon repeated.

"Yes, but he . . . did not materialize."

"Did you report this man to the police?

"No. I had no proof. It . . . was just a feeling I had, since I'd seen him in more than a number of places I frequent, too often to be a coincidence."

"In these places, did the man make any kind of threatening move toward you?"

"No," Kathryn said.

"Regardless of the situation, we recommend that you always report a stalker." Officer Harmon let his eyes roam over the hospital room. "If you want, I can file a report."

"No, that's not necessary. He's harmless." When Officer Harmon raised his eyebrows, Kathryn continued, "I found out he is a private investigator. There is nothing to worry about."

"Not necessarily, Mrs. Walker. There was an incident once where a private investigator killed a woman's cat and left it for her to find. He did it because he wanted her to know that she was being followed. The same could happen to you. I can't force you to do it, but if I were in your position, I would have the police look into it. We can investigate the man and make sure he is properly licensed."

"And if he is licensed?"

"Then there is nothing we could do to stop him unless we have proof that he has harmed you."

"And I would be back to where I am now." Kathryn leaned back against her pillows, her head reeling with all that the officer had told her.

There was a knock at the door, and a large bouquet of pink-and-white lilies barged into the room. Elizabeth's smiling face poked out from behind the flowers. "Hello, I know you are a bit busy, but I just wanted to drop off these flowers for our special girl."

"We're finished here anyway," Officer Harmon said, putting his notebook away. "Please think about what I said."

"I will." Kathryn watched him leave as Drew entered the room.

"I don't know about you," Elizabeth said cheerfully, "but flowers always do wonders for my psyche."

"How kind of you," Kathryn said as she watched Elizabeth set the large vase on the nightstand.

"Everything okay?" Drew asked.

"Yes." Kathryn closed her eyes, feeling very tired.

"Barbara and I are going to a concert tonight," said Elizabeth. "If you're released before I see you tomorrow, Kathryn, please know I wish you all the best. I am sure you'll be right as rain in no time, though I have never been sure what that phrase alludes to."

"Especially in April in Avon, Colorado," Kathryn said.

"Well, I mean it to say that you'll be fit and well in no time." Elizabeth smiled. "I just wanted to drop off the flowers before the concert. Feel better soon."

It was as if a rainbow had appeared and suddenly vanished when the door closed behind her. Frank exclaimed, "My God, who was *that*?"

"Dr. Elizabeth Camden, a resident here," Drew said.

"Why have you kept her from me, your best friend? I didn't see a ring on her finger," Frank persisted.

"She's not married."

"Well, then, I'm going to depend on you for a proper introduction, as in setting us up on a double date with you and Kathryn."

"You're out of luck, buddy," Kathryn's husband said. "She's already spoken for."

In her bed, Kathryn felt the need to replace her oxygen mask.

Chapter Twenty-Three

Wednesday, April 7

The next morning, Kathryn dressed and slipped from her room before the nurse came to take her vital signs. She didn't want to bother with formal release procedures, but she needed to visit Janet Foster. She found the young woman swaddled in various forms of traction gear, her jaw bandaged, needles taped to her arms to feed fluids into her veins.

Kathryn had to stifle a cry, but the visible part of the patient's face brightened when she saw her. "Oh, you're here! Thank you so much for coming."

Kathryn placed Elizabeth's container of flowers beside Janet's bed. If Elizabeth recognized them, let her think whatever she pleased. She took a seat by Janet's bedside and, careful of the IV, covered her hand with her own. "Tell me what happened."

"It came out of nowhere, Kathryn. I'd barely stepped off the curb before it came barreling toward me."

"Did you see what kind of car it was?"

"Dark-green or blue Jeep, I think." Janet sniffled. "I left my car at the garage before they opened to be serviced and walked to the library. It was so scary." Tears began to trickle from the corners of her eyes, and Kathryn leaped up to grab a tissue. As she dabbed at Janet's tears, she couldn't help but think that the driver would not have seen Janet get out of her vehicle. It was a point she'd be sure to mention to Drew.

"The police think it was a joyrider," Janet said. "But I don't know how this could have happened. Who goes joyriding so early in the morning?"

"You're right, Janet. I'm sure the police will get to the bottom of this."

Kathryn decided to call a taxi, estimating that Drew would be on his way to the hospital by the time the driver deposited her at home. She needed the time alone to figure out what to do next, even if her house wasn't the safest place to do it.

At home, she was relieved to find that the key in the frog's cavity was gone. The private investigator could have slipped up the stairs and opened the damper in her studio fireplace. The private investigator must have known about the frog, but that also meant that he knew the house code, even though she had changed it. A cold chill ran down her spine. He could have made a duplicate house key. She swallowed hard.

The quiet street was lined with large houses and tall oak trees that swayed in the breeze. Terror paralyzed her for a moment, adding to the physical weakness from her ordeal, but the image of Janet Foster in traction and rage at the perpetrator who had put her there gave her strength. As her eyes roamed the street, she realized that there was only one woman she needed to talk to—Tessie Kittredge, who daily knitted before her front window, acting as a one-woman neighborhood watch.

As soon as Tessie opened the front door, she engulfed Kathryn in a bear hug. "I am so happy to see you up and about! When did you get back from the hospital? Is Drew with you?"

"No, I didn't want to bother him," Kathryn said. "But I wanted to ask you—have you seen anyone unfamiliar come to our house in the last week or two?"

"No, darling, I can't say that I have. Why do you ask? Did it have anything to do with the security folks that came by last Friday?"

"No, I was just expecting a package."

"Oh, I am sorry, I didn't see anything. You have to be careful—there are a lot of package thieves around. Hopefully they didn't take it. Do you want any coffee?"

"No, thank you," Kathryn said, stepping back toward the door. "I'm going to go home and rest in my own bed."

Wrapped in a thick terry robe, on her third cup of tea, Kathryn sat curled up in fear. Somebody out there had access to her house, and they meant to kill her. She would have Drew call to change the locks, but it didn't feel like that was enough. What if she took the drastic measure of moving out of the house, putting distance between her and Avon? But that just felt like running from her problems, not getting any closer to an answer.

Who else knew about the hidden house key and the code to the security system? The only other person with knowledge of the key was Rosalie Deemer, their fired housekeeper, but Kathryn didn't think she could be responsible for these threats to her life. The woman was seventy years old and arthritic, owned no car, and had ridden the city bus to work—though Lord knew, she had left the Walkers' house with no love for them. "You'll be sorry for this!" she'd said.

It was back when Drew first raised the alarm on their finances. "We need to trim some corners" was all that he had said, as if firing the cleaner and the gardener would make that much of a difference. When Kathryn started to tell Rosalie that they would no longer be able to employ her, she became indignant. "I've worked for you for years, and this is how you repay me? How am I supposed to take care of myself?"

When Kathryn couldn't provide an answer, the woman had simply said, "You're all alike. You're just another spoiled rich girl, with no care for other people who can barely afford to eat."

"I'm sorry," was all Kathryn could say, too embarrassed to admit that they could barely afford to eat either.

Rosalie Deemer was definitely worth considering as the leak. The woman had been so bitter about her dismissal, she would have had no qualms spilling all she knew of the Walkers to someone willing to pay her for the information, especially if she did not know what Golf Cap meant to do with it.

Kathryn would have to wait until tomorrow morning to pay a visit to her old housekeeper, though. She still wasn't steady on her feet, and she couldn't hold down food. Besides, Drew was bound to call, and if she didn't answer, he might send the police again, or ask the Kittredges to check on her.

She wouldn't tell him of her mission, of course. He would only object, and she was through arguing with him.

Kathryn lay back in her chair, assailed again by the old desolation. Once more she was on her own, with no one to protect and defend her. It was a feeling that had been creeping in even before the appearance of Golf Cap, she realized.

From far away, a long-ago memory drifted into her consciousness.

"Kathryn?" Miss Hunt's gentle voice addressed her from the chipped doorway of the playroom in the Alabama Child Welfare Service Center. "Come here, child."

Obediently, she left her crayons and coloring book. She was six years old, slight for her age, her eyes too big for her face, as they were described. "Yes, ma'am?"

"You'll be leaving us, Kathryn. You're going to a foster home. This is Mr. and Mrs. Harrison. I've packed your things. You have only to get your coat."

Kathryn stared at Mr. and Mrs. Harrison in the doorway and instinctively stepped back. They loomed large and threatening, like the sinister night shadows in the hall where she dared not step after lights were out. Harry and Gloria Harrison smiled and frightened her more. The man rumpled her hair. "You'll be happy with us, Kathryn. Come along now."

"I have to get Buddy."

"No, Kathryn," Miss Hunt said in her kind manner. "You can't take Buddy. He'll have to stay here. I will take care of him."

"Leave Buddy here? But I can't. He's my dog."

"We don't take dogs," Gloria Harrison said firmly.

She began to cry and backed away when Mr. Harrison reached for her hand. "No, I'm not going. I want to stay here with Miss Hunt and Buddy."

"Let her at least say goodbye to her dog," Miss Hunt said. "They've been together since they were both babies."

"Well, make it snappy," Mr. Harrison said. "Our other kids will be home from school soon."

Kathryn shook her head to banish the memory of that shattering separation from the woman and dog who had given her the only love and protection she'd ever really known. Now she felt the same swamp of forlornness, the same shaft of separation as then, this time from the husband she loved and the house where she'd once felt safe, secure, and protected.

Chapter Twenty-Four

Thursday, April 8

On Thursday morning, Kathryn waited for Drew to leave for the hospital before she got up. The afternoon before, he had rushed through the door, wrapping her in his arms.

"What was that about?" she'd asked as he let her go.

"I was worried about you," he responded, taking a step back. "You left the hospital without waiting to be discharged. The nurse on duty called me as soon as they realized you were gone. You gave us all a fright! Why didn't you wait for me?"

"I didn't want to bother you," she said, avoiding his eyes.

He sat on the ottoman opposite her. "Is that why you didn't tell me that you called the security company last week?"

Kathryn gulped. "Did Officer Harmon tell you?"

"No, the Kittredges did."

"I thought my stalker might follow me home and . . . do what stalkers do. I needed some form of protection."

He put his hands on her knees. "Then you made a smart move, if you were worried for your safety. I wondered what had made all those heavy tire tracks in front of our house last Friday. I only wish you had told me."

All evening he'd been solicitous, preparing them a salad and omelet for dinner and falling asleep with her cuddled in the curve of his body. "It will be all right," he had mumbled sleepily. "Everything is going to be all right," leaving Kathryn to wonder exactly what he meant would be all right.

Now, despite not feeling fully herself yet, she dressed as soon as he'd left and drove out to meet Rosalie Deemer.

Rosalie lived in a quiet mobile home park in the old part of Avon between the highway and the train tracks, built when the town belonged to farmers and ranchers, before the quiet burg had transformed into an international skiing mecca.

Kathryn was prepared for anything when she walked up the warped porch steps and rang the doorbell. She waited patiently among the dead plants that curled in on themselves in their dirty pots. After a few minutes, she peered through one of the windows into a room void of any indication of life.

"She's not home," said a crusty voice behind her.

Kathryn turned to find an elderly man standing on the sidewalk, leaning on a cane, a small dog at his side. "Good morning," she said. "Do you know when she'll be back?"

"Can't say. Maybe never, from the way she took off."

"Took off?"

"Like a scalded cat, all nervous and jittery." He looked Kathryn up and down. "She said something about heading out of state to visit her sister."

Kathryn's heart began to thump. "Do you know why the sudden departure?"

"Who's asking?"

"Kathryn Walker. Mrs. Deemer was my former housekeeper. I . . . came to have a word with her."

"Ahh, her description wasn't that far off." He sucked a tooth as he regarded Kathryn. "She only said she didn't want to live in Avon anymore, after I told her about that hit-and-run. I have no idea what got into her."

"Would you happen to know the sister's address?"

"Nope. And don't think I should tell you much more."

Kathryn thought fast. Considering the threats Rosalie had made upon her dismissal, Kathryn had no doubt as to why she had run away. She must have fed the investigator details about the house and Kathryn's schedule to pass on to his client.

Pierced by the chill of this conviction, Kathryn realized the man was staring at her as if she'd been struck by lightning. "Are you all right?" he asked.

"No. No, I'm not," she said, pulling her coat tighter and hurrying past him to her car.

Trembling behind the wheel, the door locked, Kathryn watched the man shuffle off, shaking his head. *Crazy woman*, she read from the motion, but Kathryn knew she wasn't crazy. She wasn't imagining the danger to herself. Rosalie Deemer's sudden, desperate departure was not a coincidence. She'd had reason to be frightened. The woman had not lacked for intelligence, and she'd figured the person who wanted her former employer dead might not wish to leave any trail. Now Kathryn had to convince Drew that if he wouldn't believe that there had been two attempts on her life, she might not survive a third.

Afraid to go home, Kathryn put the Cadillac in gear and headed for Drew's office. He always ate a salad or sandwich from the hospital cafeteria and worked through lunch at his desk, so she was sure she'd find him there. It was time to go to the police.

She parked next to Elizabeth's Mercedes in the rear parking lot and punched in the code for the private entrance. She could hear Drew's voice through the paper-thin walls of his office down the hall. There was also a sound of subdued crying. Kathryn paused. Was that Elizabeth's voice?

Slowly, Kathryn approached, listening. Drew was speaking soothingly to his chief resident. "It will be all right, Elizabeth. You just have to be patient and give the situation a little more time. She's not used to change."

There was the sound of more quiet sobbing, and Kathryn heard the squeak of Drew's desk chair. She could tell that he had risen to take Elizabeth into his arms.

"I just want a commitment, one way or another," she said.

"I know you do, Elizabeth, and I want it, too, but now is not the time to tell her, not until she's sorted out this latest problem. Why don't we wait till the end of April, and then—"

"And then what? There's no guarantee that she is going to agree. You said it yourself—she isn't good with change."

"Have you tried to talk to her?"

"What's the point? She's always distracted." Elizabeth's voice hardened. "I don't want to leave you, Drew, but I can't continue to live as we do. I want to get married."

"I understand."

"Until the end of April, then."

"Until the end of April."

Kathryn backed away and retreated down the carpeted hall to the exit as fast she could walk. She closed the outside door quietly and made her way blindly to her car. He had been speaking to Elizabeth, and he had until the end of April to make good his promise to marry her.

Chapter Twenty-Five

Eyes burning with tears, breath heaving as if she'd surfaced from being held long underwater, Kathryn drove out of the hospital parking lot without direction. Her safe places were lost to her. She could not go back home; her killer might be waiting for her in the living room. She could not retreat to her husband's arms.

Betrayal, hot and heavy, swept through her. She simply could not wrap her mind around the reality that her trustworthy husband of twenty-five years planned to divorce her to marry someone else. Drew was no actor. How had he fooled her? If not for that phone call to the Argyle, regardless of the distance that had grown between them, she would never have suspected.

Suddenly, with a need so great it seared her throat, she wanted to be with her children. Forgoing her usual careful planning, she decided to drive the three hours to Boulder and take whatever time Lindsay could give her that night and the next day. She knew the timing wasn't great, since Lindsay was preparing for her finals before spring break, but she'd feel better if she was there to take care of her daughter. Friday she would drive to Denver and spend the rest of the weekend with her son. To see her children's faces and know they were safe was the only thing in the world she wanted.

Leaving meant she would have to cancel her luncheon date with

Natalie and forgo her visit to Abby Gale's grave on Saturday, even though it was the anniversary of her death. But perhaps Abby Gale would understand this one time, since she visited on the tenth of every month without fail. *You are not forgotten. You are loved, our angel*, was the message she believed her visits and flowers conveyed to her daughter, who she visualized as fully grown, smiling down upon her from heaven.

Drew preferred to remember Abby Gale sleeping in her crib, swathed in pink, than think of her in a cold casket underground. He only visited once a year, on the anniversary of her death. He would think Kathryn had lost her mind completely when he learned she planned to miss the anniversary. But she didn't give a damn. She'd call his office and leave word of her intentions with one of his staff. She would not speak directly to Drew, whose words to Elizabeth were a deafening roar in her ears.

After her visit with Bobby, she would take a flight to Houston to see Sandy for the week. Sandy would put her up, and Kathryn would tell her best friend everything. At least there, she would be safe. They would talk into the night, and in her aggressive but practical way, Sandy would help her to decide what on earth to do as her life crumbled around her.

She was ten minutes away from Lindsay's dorm before she noticed the dark-green Jeep behind her, right on her tail. Its windows were too darkly tinted to see anything but the shape of a baseball cap. *How could it be? He was supposed to have been gone.* She'd been too tangled in the web of her distraught thoughts through the whole drive, and too distracted by the persistent ringing of her cell phone—calls from Drew that she was stubbornly ignoring—to pay attention to her surroundings. Now, though, what else could account for the madman right on her tail, when traffic was so light?

Multiple possibilities ran through her mind. If she could manage a 911 call with her eyes glued to the highway, she could ask for police assistance. But as she reached for the phone, her shaking hand accidentally bumped it, sending it tumbling to the floor of the passenger side. Her only chance was an exit that led to a gas station or restaurant, anyplace where there were people and safety. The Jeep was staying right behind her, despite Kathryn's foot heavy on the gas. The outline of the driver's cap had not moved. It was as if his eyes were boring straight into the back of her head.

The opportunity Kathryn hoped for came two minutes later. Driving over a bridge, she saw a truck stop where there were parked not one but *two* county police cars! Without signaling, she wheeled onto the exit ramp. The Jeep did the same. Now Kathryn felt herself trembling uncontrollably. Her right leg cramped as she accelerated, laying on her horn to let the motorists on the access road know they better yield or suffer the consequences. The truck stop was but a couple hundred yards away. Again without signaling, Kathryn made a sharp right into the parking lot, the Jeep staying right behind her until a truck on its way out blocked its path. At the screech of the Cadillac slamming to a halt, heads turned at the tables by the restaurant's plateglass windows. She grabbed her purse and jumped out, leaving the Cadillac running and the door open.

By the time she'd flung open the door to the restaurant, all eyes were upon her, including those of the two officers seated at the counter, who were beginning to recognize that a crisis was underway. Kathryn rushed toward them as they slid from their barstools.

"Please help me," she begged her, trying to calm her voice to avoid sounding hysterical. "There's a man in a Jeep out there who's been stalking me. He wants to kill me. I—I know I'm not making sense, but please, please believe me. He's right there." She thrust a finger in the direction of the window as the Jeep careened into a space marked HANDICAPPED.

"Okay, ma'am, just take it easy," the one with a sheriff armband said. The door of the Jeep flew open, and Kathryn gasped in dismay as a young woman in a baseball cap jumped out, ponytail swinging through the hat's ventilation hole.

Collective breaths were held, and then, amid murmurs of surprise, Kathryn watched, horrified, as the girl slung a large flowered bag over her shoulder and straightened, holding a baby out at arm's length.

The officers immediately stepped back, and the sheriff hurried to open the door of the restaurant and point to the restrooms that were thankfully at its entrance. All faces turned toward Kathryn, some customers shaking their heads, and she felt her cheeks begin to burn. The waitress nearby murmured, "You need to get some help, honey."

Kathryn leaned against the counter and watched apologetically as the police officers returned, the older grim-faced, the younger fighting a grin. They accompanied her outside to the open door of her Cadillac, which was still running. The young officer reached in and turned off the ignition while the grim-faced one said, "Ma'am, I'm afraid you misunderstood that situation. That young mother was not trying to kill you."

Kathryn's felt her head go light. She braced herself against the Cadillac for support, surprised that her purse was still hanging from her shoulder. "Officer, I am so sorry. I feel so ashamed, but a vehicle like hers ran down a good friend of mine a week ago because she looked like me. She was a volunteer at the library, and then there was an attempt on my life in my own home. Somebody got into the house and tampered with our fireplace to try to asphyxiate me. The killer has the combination to our security system and a key to the house. I'm afraid to go home . . ." She stopped when she realized that she was babbling and not making a dent in their skeptical expressions.

"Where are you from, ma'am?" the sheriff asked.

"Avon."

"Have you filed a police report on these attempted assaults?"

"Actually, no. I—my husband—I don't have proof yet."

"Uh-huh. Well, I'm afraid we can't let you get behind the wheel of a car right now. My deputy here is going to take charge of your keys and drive your vehicle over there out of the way, and then we can call somebody to come get you. Your car can be picked up later. You have somebody to call?"

Kathryn closed her eyes and pressed the heel of her hand to her forehead, mindful but uncaring of the stares she was still drawing from the plateglass windows. She would have to call her daughter. Kathryn could visualize Lindsay's stunned surprise to find her mother practically in the custody of two county police officers, her car keys confiscated. . . . She'd think her mother was as crazy as her father seemed inclined to believe.

"My daughter," she said. "She's a student at the University of Colorado. She'll come get me."

"Well, my deputy will stay with you until she does, but I'd appreciate your understanding that he can't be tied up long. If your daughter is unavailable, you'll have to call a taxi, and you can pick up your car keys at the sheriff's office as long as you have a driver with you with a current driver's license. Understood?"

Kathryn nodded.

"Okay with you, David?"

"If you say so, Sheriff," the deputy said, clearly not okay with the order.

The young mother came out of the restaurant, the baby now freshly diapered and wrapped in a blanket. The woman glanced in curiosity at the cluster of Kathryn, the sheriff, and his deputy, then drove off, blissfully unaware of the drama she had caused.

Chapter Twenty-Six

It was Kathryn, however, who got the surprise when Lindsay arrived. She'd been hard to reach. Conscious of the deputy's growing impatience, the increasing cold, and the state of her own nerves, Kathryn's hand had shaken as she punched in her daughter's number. She left a voicemail, the deputy's eyebrow perking when she explained that she was having car trouble and needed a ride. Next, she tried Lindsay's roommate's number and breathed a sigh of relief when Tiffany picked up. By now the deputy had moved the Cadillac to the air pump station beside an overloaded dumpster. A motorist had taken his German shepherd to the yellowing clumps of grass nearby for a bathroom break, and the foul smell from the dumpster and odor of fresh fecal matter wafted to Kathryn as Tiffany said, "Mrs. W! What a surprise!" A short pause and then, "Is anything wrong?"

Kathryn held her nose and gave a little laugh, shivering in her wool blazer. Afternoon shadows were creeping over the parking lot, and the temperature had continued to drop. She hoped to keep her voice even and teeth from chattering when she answered, "Well, yes, there is a bit wrong. I'm having car trouble and am stranded at a place just inside the city limits. I need Lindsay to come pick me up when she's out of class. I hope it's not an inconvenience, but could you possibly get word to her that I am at a truck stop and restaurant off Highway 70 coming from Avon. It's called"—Kathryn glanced at the sign designating the establishment—"Barton's Truck Stop. 'Eat here. Get gas,' the sign reads. She won't be able to miss it."

Kathryn heard a chuckle. "Oh, my God. It really says that? 'Eat here. Get gas'? Well, you can't say customers aren't warned. Sure, Mrs. W. I am through for the day. I'll catch Lindsay when class lets out. Was . . . she expecting you? She didn't mention it to me."

"Uh, no, it was on the spur of the moment that I decided to come. Do you know how long it will be?" At the question, Kathryn noticed the deputy glance tellingly at his watch.

"Her class is about out. Twenty, thirty minutes?"

"Twenty, thirty minutes it is," Kathryn repeated for the benefit of the deputy, who immediately headed for his squad car, her ignition keys in hand, before she thought to ask him to pop her trunk for a blanket. At least she'd thrown a spring raincoat, this one a pale yellow, into the back of her car. She doubted she'd ever wear her Burberry again. After hanging up with Tiffany, Kathryn slipped limply into the coat and then into the driver's seat, trembling from the morning's emotional drain, her fright, the cold, and now the humiliation of finding herself in this situation. Would the deputy leave it to her to explain to her daughter what happened, or would he blurt out the full details?

Lindsay arrived in her silver-blue Camry, a gift her father had insisted on buying for her rather than have her drive "somebody else's castoff." Kathryn was relieved to see that Tiffany had accompanied her. Lindsay's roommate could drive the Camry back to campus, and Lindsay the Cadillac. As her daughter pulled into the parking lot, Kathryn got out of the car and waved, a signal that quickly drew the deputy from behind the wheel of his vehicle, visibly ready to get this over with.

Lindsay spotted Kathryn immediately. She got out hurriedly, tall and leggy in jeans and a sweater, reddish hair long and streaming, high cheekbones rosy, azure-blue eyes bright and clear, even lovelier than the last time Kathryn had seen her.

"Mom!" she cried, hurrying toward Kathryn and pulling her into a tight embrace. "What a dismal place to be stranded! Were you scared being out here all alone?"

"Uh, well, there was a police presence here, so I figured I was okay." Kathryn nodded toward the approaching uniformed figure.

The deputy had made haste while popping on his western hat, Kathryn's car keys in hand, ready to pass on, until Lindsay turned to face him. He drew up so abruptly that he almost rocked back on his boot heels.

"This is my daughter, Deputy," Kathryn announced. "She can take over now."

"Well, not so fast," the deputy said, his eyes glued to Lindsay as he tucked the keys back into his jacket pocket and drew out a notepad. "I'll need to know who I am handing you off to, Mrs. Walker."

Lindsay looked confused. "She just said. I'm her daughter."

"Yes, but I need a name and address, please, also a phone number. It isn't that your mother is having car trouble," the deputy explained. "It's that she's not allowed to drive her vehicle in her condition. That's why she called you." He clicked the ballpoint pen.

Lindsay turned toward her mother. "Condition? What condition?"

"I'll explain later, dear," Kathryn said.

"Your mother ran into some trouble a while ago. She'll tell you all about it in her own way." The deputy shot Kathryn a look. His pen poised over the notepad, he said, "So now let's have name and address and phone number, please, miss."

Lindsay, still looking confused, gave him the information.

After asking for a few details Kathryn was sure were unnecessary for his report, the young man said, "Mrs. Walker, we'll want to check on you later to make sure you're okay and able to drive. How long will you be in town, and where will you be staying?"

"I was thinking of spending the night here in Boulder, at a motel, then driving on to Denver to see my son tomorrow afternoon," Kathryn had begun when Lindsay interrupted her with a look of astonishment.

"Why?"

"Not to worry, Miss Walker," the deputy said. "You mother isn't driving anywhere until I check on her to make sure she's okay to get behind the wheel of a car. So, Mrs. Walker, where will you be staying tonight?"

"Oh, well, I am not sure—" Kathryn began. Lindsay's room had no couch.

"She's staying with me at the Chi Omega House, Officer," Lindsay informed him decisively. "She's not going to any motel."

By now Tiffany had joined them and said, when Kathryn began to protest, "No problem, Mrs. W. Celia next door left this morning. She's through with finals and won't mind my using her room."

The deputy made a note. "Good idea. So then, I'll be dropping by the campus. Chi Omega House. Right?"

"Yes." Lindsay verified the address distractedly. She handed Tiffany her car keys and placed her arm around Kathryn's shoulders, beginning to guide her back to the car. "Thank you for your concern, Deputy," she said in dismissal.

"My pleasure," he said, tipping his hat. "Wait a moment. Your mother's keys." Without taking a step, he removed them from his jacket and jangled them at her, forcing Lindsay to turn back. As Lindsay reached to take them, the deputy took her hand and laid the set in her palm as if it were a precious stone she might let drop. The intimate and unprofessional gesture prompted a roll of eyes from Tiffany, but again Lindsay didn't seem to notice. "Now, if you'll just sign your name as the responsible party to whom I've returned the keys . . . ," he said, holding up the pen and notepad.

Lindsay dropped the arm around Kathryn and resignedly took the pad. "Now, may we go? My mother is freezing. I need to get her out of this wind."

"Of course," the deputy said, but irritatingly, to prolong the moment, he added to Kathryn, "You take care, Mrs. Walker, and if you need anything, you can give the department a call and ask for me. David Dearborn." He took another minute to take his wallet from his back pocket and withdraw a card.

"Thank you," Kathryn said, sticking it in her raincoat pocket without looking at it.

"Come on, Mom," Lindsay urged, turning Kathryn toward the Cadillac. "Let's get you into the car before you catch pneumonia, and I'll get a blanket from the trunk to warm you up."

After Kathryn was tucked in, she saw through her side mirror that the deputy remained at his spot, as if awaiting some farewell, but he was long gone from Lindsay's mind. Instead, Lindsay asked, "What's this trouble you ran into, Mom? "

"I know I caught both of you at an inconvenient time and should have called," Kathryn said. "Frankly, I don't know what got into me. I just felt an overwhelming need to see my children—you know how hard this time of year is for me. Here you are in the middle of finals, and Bobby probably has plans for Friday night."

Lindsay cut her off gently. "Forget about interfering with my finals, and Bobby will be thrilled to see you. We've both been worried about you. It's just that I wouldn't have expected you this weekend, since it's April tenth." She pressed her point by giving her mother's arm a tender squeeze, tone and gesture unexpected. "In any case, I'm so glad you came."

Kathryn turned her face away to gain control of the bottled-up panic and hopelessness that surged through her. Adding to her anguish and mortification was her inability to come up with a story that Lindsay would buy. Why indeed *had* she come? What had she expected from her children in this April storm?

"I'll try to explain the idiocy of my actions over a cup of coffee once we're away from this place," Kathryn said. "That's what I need, a strong cup of coffee."

"No, you need more than caffeine," Lindsay said, "and a desire to see your children is not idiocy. I am taking you to a place with a roaring fireplace, quiet booths, and stiff drinks. No matter what's going on, I'm here for you, Mom. You can count on me. We'll work it out together, okay?" She drew over to the side of the road leading to the highway and motioned for Tiffany to pull alongside her. After telling her roommate to take the Camry to the sorority house and that she would not be returning for a while, Lindsay drove on, and Kathryn, still feeling the gentle pressure on her arm where her daughter's hand had been, studied her in wonder. She recalled the amaryllis that she'd struggled to force from its rigid bulb. She'd given it everything it needed to bloom, but it seemed stuck in its inert, dormant state. Then one morning, bathed in early sunlight streaming through the kitchen window, she saw that a shoot of which she'd been unaware had emerged and flowered into a beautiful blossom. Just like the gorgeous, thoughtful daughter here beside her.

"Sounds good," Kathryn said.

Chapter Twenty-Seven

Friday, April 9

The next morning, Mike arrived in his jogging suit at the main crosswalk of the subdivision, the same spot where Kathryn Walker usually appeared at six o'clock. He jogged in place, checking both directions for an oncoming car. To anyone watching from the nearby dark-blue Jeep Wrangler, Mike would be simply a careful man who habitually glanced both ways before crossing. The Jeep was parked on the wrong side of the street, facing the crosswalk, a few yards beyond the glow of the streetlight. Mike had no doubt that it belonged to Kathryn's would-be killer. The victim of the hit-and-run had described her assailant as driving a dark, square-bodied vehicle. Its location would give the driver full opportunity to rev up and mow Kathryn down in the crosswalk.

He jogged on without giving a second glance at the Jeep Wrangler, but even so he noticed the absence of a visitor's pass and a small dent on the right front bumper. The driver was taking the chance he would do his business and be gone before even the security detail was likely to be about on this cold, wintry morning.

Mike ran several yards down the densely bordered path, then circled back to a screen of thick forest growth close to the street, from which he could keep an eye on both the crosswalk and the Jeep. Its windows were darkly tinted, making it impossible to see anything inside, not even the glow of a cigarette. He took out a .45 from the holster under his jacket, as well as a blinding flashlight used for self-defense. The minute the woman appeared, if he heard the Jeep's ignition, before the vehicle moved, he would blind the driver with the light and shoot out the tires.

Mike was an hour early. He was accustomed to standing for long periods while on surveillance, but as six o'clock came and went, then another thirty minutes passed, then another fifteen, he understood that Kathryn was not going to appear. The driver of the Jeep must have thought so, too. As the first streak of dawn lightened the sky, Mike heard the turn of the ignition and the Jeep's quiet pull away from the sidewalk. Mike knew the number of the license plate would be false or too muddied to make out, so he concentrated on the face behind the tinted window in the brief flash from a streetlight. All he could tell was that the driver's profile was a man's.

Exasperated, out of all options to notify Kathryn of her danger but one, Mike hurried back to his Range Rover. There was one place he was sure she'd turn up. Tomorrow morning he would waylay Kathryn at the cemetery where her daughter was buried.

Kathryn woke Friday morning in Tiffany's borrowed bed, with the sun peeking around the edges of drawn blinds. The memory of yesterday's exchange between Drew and Elizabeth and the feelings of hurt, anger, and betrayal overcame her the moment she opened her eyes, but miraculously, she had slept through the night.

She'd finally accepted a call from Drew as she was getting ready for bed. By then, as she replayed over and over the conversation she'd overheard, Kathryn had rigorously examined his reason for waiting until the end of April to ask her for a divorce. Was Drew buying time to change his mind about leaving her? Was that the impetus behind the voice in her head that persisted in advising her to wait? Was it because Kathryn knew that if he could not bring himself to abandon the wife and home and life they'd made together, she would forgive him? She loved him. Their marriage would not be the same, of course, but she was sure it was still worth fighting for. But what she didn't understand was why he didn't seem able to take seriously the threat to her life.

"Kathryn, honey . . . ," Drew had begun, and she'd heard his struggle to keep his voice calm. "What are you doing visiting Lindsay during her exams, and why the hell didn't you answer your phone? I've been worried sick about you."

"The house wasn't safe for me to return to, and Lindsay and I have been busy," she answered coldly.

"The house isn't safe?"

Kathryn explained that the person who wanted to kill her had learned the location of the house key from Mrs. Deemer. A stranger had free access to the house, she warned him, so it would be wise for Drew to find someplace else to stay.

"Mrs. Deemer!" Drew exclaimed, cutting her off before she could give further details. "How would the guy even know about her?"

"Through the private investigator," Kathryn had responded dryly. "I'll be staying with the kids for a while." Then she'd hung up the phone.

One light pierced the darkness of her turmoil. She and her daughter had *bonded*. Between the Christmas holidays and now, her daughter had become a woman, full of wisdom and understanding that Kathryn had never expected after Lindsay's difficult teenage years.

Yesterday afternoon in a neighborhood tavern, Lindsay had put the most pressing question to her first. "Mom, tell me the truth. Are you ill?"

"No, sweetheart. You can put that worry aside. Why? Do I look ill?"

"Well, you don't look your usual perky self. You've lost weight, and the color in your cheeks is gone."

So that was how she saw her mother . . . perky and self-possessed, the way Kathryn had thought of herself less than a month ago. "Well, I promise I'm healthy," she assured Lindsay. "I had a complete physical in January."

Lindsay had studied her closely, and then, without sounding convinced, said, "Okay, but something serious is going on. Bobby and I have been worried about you. Did that stalker have anything to do with how you happened to end up in the arms of the law today?"

Kathryn couldn't resist chuckling. "Which is where that deputy wants you to end up—in his arms."

Lindsay laughed. "He was pretty obvious about it, wasn't he?"

"Oh, so you *did* notice?"

"Who could have missed it? Now back to you. What is going on?"

Chapter Twenty-Eight

The gin had kicked in, and Kathryn had ended up telling Lindsay just enough to explain why she could have mistaken the woman driving the Jeep as her suspected stalker, including the parts about Janet Foster's hit-and-run and the carbon monoxide poisoning. The only thing Kathryn left out was her husband's affair. Lindsay worshipped Drew, and it would be shattering for her to hear about her father's faults.

"I couldn't see through the tinted windows, you see, except for the baseball cap, and the driver was right on my tail," Kathryn said. "When it turned out to be a woman with a dripping baby, you can imagine how I looked to the policemen and the customers. No wonder the sheriff thought I wasn't fit to drive."

Lindsay looked as if she would have laughed at the scene had it not involved her mother. Instead, she asked suddenly, "Does Dad know you are here?"

"I . . . left word with one of the nurses before I left. If we'd spoken, your father would only have tried to talk me out of coming."

"Mom, you are doing the right thing by getting away for a little bit."

Kathryn gratitude swelled. "Thank you, honey. I thought that after I see Bobby, I might catch a flight to Houston to visit Sandy for a while. It's been too long."

"And did you leave word with the nurse of those plans, also?" Lindsay had asked, the question implying that her father would be displeased to hear the news secondhand.

"No, because I'm not sure of my plans," Kathryn said. "I might change my mind. If I go, I'll call him from Bobby's and let him know. He'll understand that a little trip to see my kids and best friend will give me a break, and he won't feel so guilty about not being able to spend time with me, especially since we had to cancel our trip to Europe."

It was a plausible story, but Kathryn could tell Lindsay wondered how much her mother wasn't saying.

As they'd expected, the deputy appeared in person before midmorning to give Kathryn his official okay to drive, his uniform sharply pressed, leather and metal gleaming. Lindsay sweetly thanked him, saying that she and her mother must be on their way to run errands, but as the deputy returned to his squad car, Kathryn suddenly remembered something she'd wanted to do.

"Excuse me, Officer!" She hurried down and caught him as he reached the curb. It was worth a shot, and she was desperate.

"Deputy Dearborn," she said, taking a slip of paper from her pocket on which she'd recorded the license plate number of the investigator's SUV and the name and address under which Golf Cap had registered. "Would it be inappropriate of me to ask that you check out the name and address connected to this license plate number? Supposedly he lives in Little Rock, Arkansas, and I have reason to believe he's the man who has been following me. I was told by another officer that you could check to see if he is a legitimate private investigator. I've included my cell phone number for you to contact me."

Deputy Dearborn tucked the slip of paper into his shirt pocket. "I'll see what I can find out," he said.

"What was that all about?" Lindsay asked when Kathryn returned.

"I was just thanking him for his understanding of my embarrassment, and for not making me out to be a crazy person to my daughter," she said. "I'm sure law enforcement officials have a thankless job."

"That was sweet of you, Mom."

In her haste to get out of Avon, Kathryn had left with only the clothes on her back, cosmetic essentials in her purse. Lindsay had not questioned her mother's neglect to pack a weekend bag, but Kathryn knew it was another mysterious issue of concern to her.

When the mall opened that morning, Kathryn suggested they do a little shopping. Later they grabbed a sandwich and coffee at a student hangout, where Lindsay introduced her mother proudly to several of her friends. Then mother and daughter spent the afternoon on a campus bench talking, Lindsay sharing with her for the first time her plans after graduation. She was going to get a master's degree before applying to medical school, since one of her professors said it would look better for her applications. Tiffany planned to go for her master's as well, and they already had an apartment lined up and would share expenses, so her dad was off the hook for paying her bills. Kathryn was thrilled at the news, not least because it meant that her daughter would remain local for at least another year.

The hours passed too quickly, the brief silences between them thick with questions. Kathryn was grateful for Lindsay's restraint, another sign of her new regard for her mother. But at five o'clock, Kathryn's purchases stowed in the Cadillac, car keys in hand, Lindsay finally blurted out, "Mom, you and Dad are okay, aren't you? Nothing's going on that I should know about?"

The question had come too suddenly for Kathryn to assume an amused expression at such an absurd idea. Her face was never good at concealing the truth anyway, and her daughter was too adept at detecting it. "That's it, isn't it?" Lindsay said. "This other thing"—she waved aside the issue of the man with the slanted shoulder—"is not your only worry."

Kathryn stared into Lindsay's eyes with all the sincerity she could manage. "Your father and I are just fine, sweetheart. Every marriage has these periods when a husband and wife need a break from each other. Distance does make us appreciate each other more. Like I said, I needed some time to remind myself what truly matters." She cupped her daughter's cheek.

As she turned the ignition, before she closed the door, Lindsay said, "Remember that I am here for you, Mom, no matter what."

Kathryn left her with a smile and drove away with a sad understanding of what Lindsay had meant by "no matter what." Maturity had its drawbacks, Kathryn thought with a sigh. With a woman's instincts, Lindsay had come close to divining the real truth behind her mother's escape from Avon. Driving away, Kathryn felt proud of the woman Lindsay was becoming.

Chapter Twenty-Nine

After knocking on her son's door with no answer, Kathryn let herself into his apartment with her duplicate key. Just before she arrived, Bobby had texted her: Went to the store for your favorite wine. Make yourself at home, I'll be back soon. I love you.

Kathryn could tell that her son must have rushed home after school to ready things for her arrival before striking out again to buy her wine and a few necessities for the fridge and pantry. The stamp-size second bedroom that usually served as a collection bin for anything too much bother to put away was neat and orderly, the sofa bed made, and fancy towels kept on hand for visitors hung in the bathroom, which had also been tidied. Kathryn could smell cleaning fluids. What a sweet boy.

After slipping off her shoulder bag and setting down her packages, she sat down on one of Bobby's vintage upholstered chairs. Bobby and Kathryn had always believed that guests should be made to feel comfortable throughout their stay, while Drew believed that visitors, like fish, began to smell after three days and shouldn't feel too much at home. Their son was much like his mother in so many ways, and now she was beginning to think that it had been a mistake—a worry to Bobby—for her to come. She could trust Lindsay to mention nothing of the truck stop occurrence to her brother.

They would keep that between mother and daughter, but her son would ask why the sudden trip to see him, during a weekend when she would usually be visiting his sister's grave. What reason could Kathryn give him that he'd be willing to accept?

Her cell phone rang, and Kathryn dug in her purse to locate it before the caller, probably Drew, disconnected. Or it could be Lindsay, calling to see if she'd arrived safely. But the identification screen listed neither. The caller was Deputy David Dearborn. Kathryn decided to let the message go to voicemail to avoid a conversation with him. She'd listen to it later, for now, she just wanted to spend some time with Bobby without the stress of her problems creeping in.

Dearborn's message stated that no number or address for a Tim Grayson existed in Little Rock, Arkansas, and his driver's license number was bogus. He asked that she come into the station to make a formal restraining order.

Kathryn blew out a breath. It was as she'd expected. Golf Cap would not have registered by his real name and address. But her gut said that was not the case with the local rancher, Mike McCoy. She had googled Delta Force, her eyes widening. Delta Force—or Special Forces Operational Detachment–Delta—was indeed an ultra-secret counterterrorist force of "shadow warriors" that operated on the fringe of military legality. They were an elite group that worked wherever their services were required and for whomever needed them—the FBI, CIA, or the military services. They answered only to one person—the president of the United States.

Had Kathryn spurned the one person who believed her and who could render professional advice on her next move? Kathryn unzipped a compartment of her purse where she had slipped the notepaper on which she'd written Mike McCoy's contact numbers.

She was studying the numbers, recalling the calm, sensible man she had met, when she heard her son unlock his door, paper sacks rattling, and the voice call out that had warmed her heart every time she heard it after school. "MOM! You here? I'm home!"

"I'm here, Bobby," she answered, the gray space inside her brightening.

Helping Bobby unload and put away the groceries, she said, "Thank you for letting me come on such short notice, son. I hope I've not thrown your weekend for a loop." She looked at him tenderly and laid a hand on his cheek. The sacks contained mostly items mindful of her dietary preferences, such as almond milk, and he'd remembered that on Saturday mornings she treated herself to Rice Krispies and bananas for breakfast (Monday, Wednesday, and Friday mornings were for egg white and vegetable omelets, the other days interspersed with oatmeal and fresh fruit). Two packets of pancake mix were included as well, a hint for her to consider stirring them up for his favorite Sunday breakfast, and there were two bottles of her favorite sauvignon blanc.

His puzzled, but delighted, surprise at her unexpected visit had been written all over his face when he'd greeted her. Kathryn could feel the question of why she'd chosen now to show up on his doorstep like a draft in the room, but she knew he would not press.

"Actually, your timing is perfect, Mom, so thank *you* for coming."

"Well, that's nice for a mother to hear. And why is my timing perfect?"

"Because my apartment lease is up at the end of the month, and I've found a house to rent that I want you to take a look at. I want a place I can make more of a home, a house with a fenced-in yard, and I've found a rental that suits me perfectly. Also . . ."

Kathryn watched a grin spread across his face, and he looked more boyish and lovable than ever. "Another reason I'm glad you're here is that I want to introduce you to my new roommate."

"Roommate?"

"A corgi that I have made plans to adopt. He's the reason I need a place with a yard. I've made an appointment at the Humane Society for tomorrow afternoon to pick him up, and I need you along to keep me from walking away with half the dogs in the pound." He added somberly, "I miss having a Billy in my life."

Billy was the name of the Walkers' Sheltie when the children were growing up. He had died just short of his twentieth birthday. "Is it okay if I bring my new little guy home for spring break?" Bobby asked. "I don't want to leave him at the Humane Society until I get back. He'll think I've abandoned him, and none of my friends are available to take him."

Kathryn smiled. "Of course you can bring him. Can you imagine your sister's reaction if she didn't get to meet him?" *Spring break.* She only hoped that home would be safe enough for the children by then.

"But what about tonight? Are you sure you want your mother tagging along? Did you warn your friends that I'm crashing the bash?" Bobby had described an evening of playing board games and drinking a selection of craft beers.

"I am absolutely sure. You'll fit right in as you always do. The guys' dates will be there, and when everybody meets you, they'll be glad you joined the party."

So it was settled, and for the first time since her frantic getaway from Avon, even at the Chi Omega House with Lindsay, Kathryn felt herself start to relax. In Boulder, she had been constantly looking over her shoulder. Here she felt safe, at least for the next forty-eight hours. She had yet to follow up with Sandy about staying a few nights at her place, but she could take care of that tomorrow.

Meanwhile, her time with Lindsay had reignited her drive to build a different future, with or without Drew. She wanted a job. The academic atmosphere had her thinking she could freshen up her college résumé by taking a few courses in her field before trying to complete her doctorate in bioengineering. She could do it right at the university in Boulder and be near her daughter.

Chapter Thirty

Later Friday evening, Kathryn finally returned Drew's call, trying not to think about where he might be. Drew had answered tentatively, "How's it going with the kids?" A slight edge in his voice betrayed that he was still hurt about her leaving without telling him.

Kathryn had cut right to the chase. "I'm not coming back until you have the locks changed, Drew," she said. "While you are at it, have the garage doors fixed as well. As they are now, an army could swoop in before those doors closed. I'm serious, Drew. Those requirements are nonnegotiable if you want me to come home." When he was silent, Kathryn added, "That is, if you want me to come home."

Drew let out a frustrated sigh. "Why would you say such a thing? Of course I want you to come home. It's just that your behavior is worrying me."

"Good," Kathryn snapped. "At least you're worried about something other than work."

"That's not fair," Drew said. His voice was unusually quiet. "I have to work so much to make sure our family is taken care of. I've come too far to become like my parents. And while yes, I am concerned about this stalker, there is no proof that he is out to murder you. We have to think logically about this."

There it was—Drew always had to be logical about everything. When she met him, she found it so comforting to have someone who thought things through, who was steady. But now it felt more like a curse that haunted their marriage.

"That hit-and-run was meant for me," Kathryn insisted. "I did not leave the fireplace damper open in my studio. Somebody has a key to our house and knows how to get past our security system. Just look at what they did to Rosalie Deemer."

"Okay, let's discuss why you are sure of that," Drew said in an even tone.

"Rosalie left in a hurry early one morning and gave a neighbor the impression she was too scared to stay in Avon and wouldn't be back. Her house is as vacant as a cadaver's skull."

A brief silence followed. "Of furniture?"

"Of *life*," Kathryn bit off, knowing the usual logical direction Drew was going with his thinking. "It looked like something out of a creepy horror film."

"How do you know this?"

"I went by her house to question her. When I didn't find her home, I spoke with a neighbor. He said it wasn't at all like her to up and leave like she did. I am guessing she figured it out when Janet Foster was almost killed. Rosalie knew my daily schedule."

"It's been months since we let her go. How could your schedule be tracked?"

"Drew, I haven't changed my schedule in years." When she admitted that, her heart sank. It was true; her schedule had not changed since the kids went to college. She'd turned into one of those predictable housewives that she'd dreaded becoming in her youth. "Rosalie must have assumed that whoever was after me would be after her next, in order to leave behind no trail."

"Did Mrs. Deemer tell the neighbor where she was going?"

"To her sister's. Drew, Rosalie doesn't have a sister."

"Just because she doesn't talk about her sister doesn't necessarily mean she doesn't have one. I don't talk about my brothers."

"You don't even talk to your brothers."

"Exactly, because I like to pretend they don't exist. Every family situation is different. Just because she worked for us doesn't mean we know everything that goes on in her personal life."

"Well, sister or no sister, it takes money to go off and leave your house. Where do you think she got the money for that?"

"She won the lottery?" Drew's attempt at a joke did not land.

"The investigator *paid* her for the information, Drew. You don't think she offered it for free." Kathryn sighed. "I know what I know." It was the first time in a long time that she had trusted her intuition, and it felt good.

After a brief silence, Kathryn heard what sounded like a groan. "Okay, Kath. Anything you want. I'll make the arrangements with the locksmith, but why not come home now? I'll get a motel room for you to pop into where you can feel safe and hang out for a few days. We could make a special thing of it. I can join you; we'll have picnics in the room. It can be fun until you feel it's okay to move back to the house."

Kathryn found herself shaking her head. "No, the person who wants to kill me could be watching the house or hospital and follow you to me." Even as she rejected Drew's proposal, she felt her heart sink. A small seed of hope had bloomed. Perhaps her husband wasn't interested in trading her in after all.

"I'm leaving Bobby's on Sunday and then heading to Houston to visit Sandy," she added quickly. "I would really like to see her." Kathryn added the last bit to throw Drew off her trail since she planned on staying at a hotel overnight.

Drew finally heaved a resigned sigh. "All right, Kathryn, whatever you think best. Just know, though, that I miss you and . . . want you to come home."

He sounded like a man uncertain of his course, a man caught between two loves, one for his wife and one for his mistress. At the back of her mind, she wondered if she was making a mistake. In their twenty-five years of marriage they had rarely been separated, and then only overnight, when Drew slept at the hospital on behalf of a patient. Was she reacting to a break between them, or causing one? "Believe me, I wish with all my heart it didn't have to be this way, Drew."

After hanging up, she texted Sandy.

Looking out her son's window, she sighed, feeling safer than she had in days.

If only she had noticed the man in the rental car, parked just down the street, with a clear view of Bobby's apartment.

Chapter Thirty-One

Feeling as if she had no one else to turn to, Kathryn decided it was time to call Mike McCoy the next morning before she and Bobby had left for dog rescue. Thankfully, he answered on the first ring.

"I'm glad you called," he said. "I was starting to think you took me for a lunatic."

"For a moment there I kind of did," she admitted. "I'm in Denver. Can you meet me?"

"Yes. I've learned some things, and I need to speak with you."

They agreed to meet at the Brown Palace Hotel in Denver at five o'clock on Sunday.

Bobby had known that something was troubling her, but she played into the distraction of the new puppy he had picked up on Saturday so that he would only ask the simple questions Kathryn had expected. Had she seen anything more of that stalker? Kathryn had answered truthfully: No, her stalker had disappeared. Perhaps she had been wrong about him and his intent. Was Dad okay? Yes, he was fine, just overworked as usual. Kathryn knew he'd pump his sister for information later.

The position she found herself in had created a conflict with her conscience. Every instinct within her rebelled at lying to her son, but she could not tell him that instead of flying directly to visit Sandy on Sunday, she was meeting a man, a stranger, at a hotel where she had reserved a room overnight rather than fly into Houston at such a late hour. Sandy had said: Not a problem, so long as you tell me everything when you can. My door is always open.

At the hotel in downtown Denver, shortly after Kathryn turned over her valet key to a member of the parking crew, she received a text from Drew. Sorry, honey, but the locksmith can't come until Friday. Love you and miss you.

Kathryn texted back: Love and miss you, too.

She headed for check-in before meeting Mike McCoy in the Ship Tavern, the most casual of the posh hotel's restaurants. The hotel's magnificent nine-story atrium lobby made her feel she'd stepped into a world of nineteenth-century Victorian elegance. Established in 1892 and named for its owner, Henry C. Brown, the Brown Palace had at one time been Denver's tallest building, and was certainly its most remarkable, with its triangular shape. It would be well populated should anything happen during her meeting with Mike McCoy, and should her killer be in the neighborhood.

It was a quarter to five, and the lobby was clearing of its weekend tourists and businessmen. Placards were being taken down from an insurance conference, and Kathryn noted the dismantling with dismay, having forgotten that once the hustle and bustle of the weekend was over, a Sunday lull would fall over the place, and the lobby, a cavernous space, could be as deserted as a tomb.

At the reception desk, the reservation clerk welcomed her to the Brown Palace with a practiced smile as she inquired with a striking of computer keys, "You will be with us only the one night, Mrs. Walker? Is that correct?"

Kathryn meant to respond, but a sudden loss of lung power cut off her breath. The sensation was similar to the one she'd felt years ago when an elevator in which she was alone had become stuck between floors. How in the world had she, Kathryn Turner Walker, who as far as she knew hadn't an enemy on earth, ended up in a hotel lobby, running for her life, meeting a man she had barely met, deceiving her family into believing she was with her oldest friend? The horrifying incredulity of it smacked her with such force that the clerk's eyes grew round with concern.

"Mrs. Walker, are you okay?"

Kathryn cleared her throat and forced a smile. Her heart was pumping wildly. "Yes," she answered. "Just felt a little winded there."

The clerk nodded in sympathy. "That happens at this altitude. So you will be with us only the one night, is that correct?"

Kathryn nodded and handed over her own credit card, not the Visa that Drew had access to.

Her business with the clerk finished, she considered taking her one piece of luggage, borrowed from Bobby, to her room on the fourth floor rather than dragging it into the Ship Tavern, but her throat constricted thinking about entering the empty elevator alone. She must get control of herself, she thought. She drew in a deep breath and, as she did, saw Mike McCoy walk into the lobby in his usual tailored western attire, the fawn Stetson set squarely on his head, like a well-to-do rancher in town on business.

To her surprise, she felt the telltale butterflies that she used to feel when she first met Drew. There was a part of her that still didn't trust him, but she was learning to listen to her intuition again. Everything about him made her feel comfortable and that he was genuinely trying to help.

She waved from the reservation desk, a little frantically, she realized, and greeted him with an outstretched hand when he reached her. "It's awfully good of you to take the time and trouble to come to Denver to speak with me in person, Mr. McCoy."

His hand felt like a warm glove. It made her feel safe. She was sorry when he released it.

"No trouble," he said, "and I'm relieved that you agreed to see me. Mind if I register first?"

"You're staying the night?" she asked, surprised.

"I've made a reservation."

Kathryn blushed watching him go to the registration desk. When he returned, she asked, "Are you sure staying here isn't a problem?"

"Of course not. I wanted to be here in case you have an unwanted visitor in the night."

"You are scaring me, Mr. McCoy."

"It's Mike, by the way, and I am glad you're a little scared. You're going to need it."

Chapter Thirty-Two

S auvignon blanc for you?" Mike asked.

"Something stronger. A gin and tonic." Kathryn smiled thinly. "Maybe two." She tried to laugh, but she was bracing herself for the worst.

A man in a gray suit with black hair and a goatee passed by. Kathryn watched as Mike's gaze followed him to his table. Her companion's attention had also centered for a few seconds on someone else entering the restaurant, who apparently left before coming into his line of vision. Mike McCoy must have retinas trained to mentally photograph every detail of his surroundings. Considering her circumstances, she found that comforting.

"All right, so what do you have for me?" she asked.

"First, have you run into any trouble while you were here?" Mike began.

"Well, yes and no." Kathryn told him about the debacle at the truck stop, including asking the deputy to run Golf Cap's identity. "Nobody in Little Rock, Arkansas, had ever heard of Tim Grayson. Not that I was surprised."

Mike looked impressed. "I did manage to find the guy," he said, "and have a conversation with him."

Now it was Kathryn's turn to look impressed. "How did you

learn his real name? That sleazy desk clerk must have given you the information he gave me."

"I got his license plate number from his SUV at City Market and tracked his real name and address from there. I just wanted to verify that he'd left town." Mike took a swallow of his drink and set down his glass to withdraw a notepad from his jacket pocket. "When I met with Mr. Morris in Houston, he was very forthcoming."

"You went to Houston?" Kathryn asked, surprised. "Why? I understand your motivation—even obligation—to *warn* me, but to go above and beyond as you have for—"

"Why not?" Mike interrupted, as if her question were ludicrous.

"Because you don't *know* me."

Mike leaned toward her. "Mrs. Walker, with a couple of exceptions, I didn't know any of the persons I've tried to help rescue through the years, and not all of those attempts were successful."

"But . . . weren't they"—she searched for the right words—"*official* missions?"

"Consider this a favor for a friend. I'll simply provide you as much proof as I can, proof you can take to the police." Mike raised his glass to her. "And then, tomorrow, we can be done."

Reluctantly, Kathryn picked up her glass, not sure that she wanted to be abandoned to her fate.

Mike slid a notepad across the table to her. "As I indicated, Morris shared the information he knew, which didn't include the name of the person who hired him. Except for the assumption that his client is male, he hasn't the faintest hint of the person's identity, and I believe him. But there is a log that contains every detail of your daily life, where you will be at certain times, with whom, every routine, including the information that your former maid gave him. That's why I've been trying to meet with you to warn you."

Hesitantly, she opened the book and read the pages outlining the daily activities of her life. She was shaking when she finished, her gin and tonic empty. "I *knew* whoever it is had access to our house. . . . The damper sign was deliberately set the wrong way."

Mike laid a calming hand on her arm. "Describe to me what happened," he urged quietly.

"I nearly died from monoxide poisoning Tuesday and had to be taken to the hospital." Kathryn described the series of events—the appearance of the policeman, Frank, and Jim on her doorstep. "If Jim, our neighbor across the street, hadn't seen my light on in my studio, where he knows I paint most afternoons, I would be dead." She drew air deep into her lungs and explained the scene in her studio. "Whoever is trying to kill me turned the brass fireplace plate that I have hanging from the key that turns on the gas. It wasn't a mistake. I'm very careful about things like that."

"I'm sure you are," Mike said. "How did the men get into your house?"

"Frank knew where a house key was hidden on the front porch."

Mike nodded. "And Frank Danton is your neighbor?"

Startled, Kathryn wondered briefly how he knew about Frank. The man knew everything. "That, and he is a very old friend of my husband's."

"Your husband's friend. Not yours?"

"Frank dislikes me—intensely."

"Why is that?"

She shrugged. "The age-old story of the best friend not liking the wife."

Mike had been scribbling away. The waitress appeared at their table. "Another?"

"Definitely," he said, and to Kathryn he remarked, "So that makes two times that he has tried to kill you."

Kathryn's jaw fell. "How do you know?"

"I know about the volunteer run down at the library."

"The driver thought it was me, since we look so much alike and wear similar raincoats. I was supposed to read to the kids that day, but most were away with their families for spring break, so only Janet was needed." Kathryn could feel the dizzying plunge of blood from her head. She told Mike of her suspicions and that Rosalie

Deemer had taken flight early Monday morning. "Her neighbor said she seemed afraid." Kathryn let her head drop into her hands. "I don't understand why this happening to me."

Mike leaned across the table. "I can't answer that, but this I can tell you. Morris was given a deadline to gather information about you."

Kathryn could feel the walls closing tighter.

"Going by the time constraints Morris's client held him to and the attempts on your life so far, we figure you have until the end of April."

Chapter Thirty-Three

Kathryn could not draw a breath. *The end of April.*

"I can name one possibility that would explain the necessity for that time limit," Mike said.

"What possibility?"

"The five-million-dollar term life insurance policy due to expire at the end of this month, which names your husband as beneficiary upon your death." He said it so casually that the waitress didn't even raise an eyebrow when she set down their drinks.

That shook her from her state of asphyxiation. "*No! No way!*" Kathryn's heart pounded at the ridiculousness of the notion. "Don't even consider that possibility! My husband is not behind this. He loves me."

Mike put his hand on her arm again and said in a lowered tone, "Take it easy, Kathryn. We always have to rule out those closest to you. Money does strange things to people. I know you love your husband, but is there any reason he could do this?"

The possibility, even as remote as it was, sickened her. But when Drew and Elizabeth spoke, they had said that he needed to decide before the end of April. Surely this couldn't be it.

"Give me a minute to absorb all this," Kathryn said, closing her eyes. Elbows on the table, she pushed her hair back and held her head between her hands. She could not remember the last time she'd drawn a steady breath. Mike leaned back with his scotch and water to allow Kathryn time for the shock of these new revelations to settle in. Opening her eyes, hands unsteady, she lifted her glass to her lips.

"Better?" he asked after she'd taken a shaky swallow.

"So what am I to do?" she asked.

"Is there anyone, anyone else you can think of, that would want you dead?" Mike's ballpoint was poised over his notebook. "Maybe it's your long-ago past that we should be looking at—anybody at all, Kathryn? People can carry grudges for years and seek revenge for the smallest offenses, sometimes without their targets even knowing why. And don't forget the names of women who might have reason to want you dead. They could have hired somebody to do it. The attempts on your life don't fit the profile of a professional killer."

Haltingly she said, "I . . . have reason to believe my husband is having an affair with his chief resident at the hospital, and plans to ask me for a divorce at the end of April."

Mike raised an eyebrow, but otherwise, his face revealed no judgment. "I'm sorry to hear that."

"He's not even confessed to having the affair. I . . . had suspected for some time that there was something going on with him, but never . . . this. I just happened to overhear a conversation between the two of them that leaves no doubt in my mind, if not my heart, of what they have been planning."

"But why the end of April?"

"She's told Drew that's her deadline, or she will leave him." She shrugged. "I think Drew is just buying time until he can make up his mind."

Mike shook his head, confused. "You haven't confronted him?"

"Too personal a matter to discuss, Mike. Let's move on, shall we?"

With some reluctance, Mike turned back to his notes. "We were talking about your past, anyone who might have a grudge against you."

Kathryn shook her head helplessly. "Outside of Elizabeth, the only other person I could think of was Rosalie, but she's long gone. I'm sorry, I don't recall even making someone mad at me. I stayed invisible for the most part."

"A girl as intelligent and pretty as you?" Mike asked. "Are you sure there wasn't some old boyfriend that you rejected, or a jealous girlfriend you stole him from?"

Kathryn felt herself blush. "No, there were no boyfriends and no jealous girlfriends. I was focused too much on getting a scholarship to a good college, getting a degree, securing my future. I seem to have given off an aura that said 'Get lost.' "

"Until Dr. Walker came along."

Kathryn sighed, stirring the swizzle stick in her nearly empty drink. "Yeah. Until Drew came along."

"What about the years you worked as a lab assistant? Did you cross swords with anyone during that period?"

"Not a soul." Kathryn didn't want to think about it. Though she'd occupied the lowest rung on the professional ladder in the laboratory of the bioengineering company, she'd been treated with appreciation and respect. Some of her fondest memories were of the people she'd worked with there.

"How about among your husband's associates along the way? Ever tangle with any of them?"

Kathryn shook her head. "No."

"What about relatives?" Mike's pen remained poised under the sparse list in his notebook.

"I did one of those at-home DNA tests, but there weren't any matches. We didn't have a very big family, and it would appear that they are all gone."

"What about your husband's enemies? If surgeries go wrong, doctors' families can be targets of revenge from patients and their families."

"I thought of that, but Drew declares there's nobody he's ticked off to that extent, assuming he believes my life is in danger, which he doesn't. There have been only two malpractice suits brought against him, and they came to nothing. The patients withdrew the charges when it was proved they did not follow doctor's orders."

"What about this Frank Danton?"

"Frank?" Kathryn emitted a short laugh. "You can forget him. He's a jerk, but Frank wouldn't harm me because of Drew and the kids. We're like family to him."

Nonetheless, Mike made a note of the name and information, then leaned back in his seat. "Do you have a place to go where you will be safe for the rest of the month?"

"I made arrangements to stay with a friend in Houston until the weekend. I'll grab a flight in the morning and pick up my car when I return Friday. I'll drive home and lock myself in, get the police involved." She picked up the notebook. "I'll take this as evidence."

Mike shook his head. "That won't do." He leaned forward again. "Kathryn, you must understand that the man who wants you dead knows all about you. Every aspect of your life. Morris did a thorough job of investigating you. It's all there in the log. Your potential killer knows the names of your friends, your husband's friends and colleagues, your preference in wines. Nowhere familiar to you will you be safe. He's probably already figured out that you will bunk with Mrs. Danton in Houston until you believe this has blown over. He will be on your flight and follow you to your friend's door."

"But he doesn't know I'm here."

"Yes, he does. He is sitting a few tables over, to your right."

Chapter Thirty-Four

Dumbfounded, Kathryn only barely managed to stop herself from spinning around immediately. "*What?* How do you know?"

"Don't turn your head."

What was he talking about? The only person sitting to her right was a man with shaggy black hair and a goatee. She'd never seen this person before in her life.

"Are you sure?"

"No. But my gut says that's our guy. We'll know for sure if he follows you to your room. He'll be forced to follow you to learn its number."

Kathryn felt on the verge of passing out. "Oh, God."

"Don't worry. I'll be right beside you. He won't try anything as long as there is a witness."

"But what about during the night? What if he tries to . . . to pick the lock, break into my room, or attacks me in the morning when I leave my room alone and the corridor is empty?"

"You won't be alone. We'll enter your room together, if you don't mind. And with your permission, I'll sleep there, and you can have my room if you prefer. If he tries to pick the lock, as you say, he'll have a surprise waiting, but I doubt that he will try anything if he thinks there's a man with you."

Still lightheaded, Kathryn looked at him in wonder. Why would this near stranger take such steps to protect her? "How can I ever thank you?"

Mike shook his head. "No need," he said. "As a portrait painter, you have a trained eye for faces, their structure and features, right?"

She nodded. "I'd like to think so."

Mike signaled the waitress for a menu. It was time for food. Apparently, the man at the nearby table thought so, too. He lifted a hand to beckon his server. While he stayed distracted, Mike leaned toward Kathryn and instructed in an undertone, "Now take a good look at him, but don't make it obvious."

Kathryn faked interest in a couple who was escorted to the table next to the man's, then turned back to Mike.

"Did you get a good look?"

"Good enough."

"Then when we go up to our rooms, I suggest we put our recollections together and form a composite picture of the man's face without the wig and see what we come up with. You may recognize your enemy."

Kathryn's mouth went so dry, she could hardly swallow the last of her gin and tonic. She was no profile artist, but with the addition of Mike's powers of observation, she'd be adept enough to draw a sketch of the man's features, and possibly put name and a face to the person who wanted her dead.

Menus were set before them, and they gave their order to the waitress. The man followed their lead. When their meals came—soup and salad for Kathryn; a medium-rare steak for Mike—they ate in silence, the important talking done. Kathryn's churning stomach rebelled at the food, trying instead to digest the shocking discovery of her husband's deceit and her worry over finding a safe location to ride out this April storm. If not to Sandy, where could she go? And how long would the money in her personal account last?

As if reading the tortured train of her thoughts, Mike offered quietly as their dinner dishes were cleared, "You are welcome to stay at my ranch until this guy can be defused—and we will get him, Kathryn. He could never track you there, but if you accept my offer, and I hope you will, for your own safety, you can tell no one where you are, not even your husband. If the man who is looking to kill you is desperate enough, Dr. Walker could be made to talk."

Kathryn gazed at him, astonished at the offer. It was the perfect solution, but was she leaping from one fire into another? She trusted this man, but put to the test, who knew what she'd run into at his ranch, isolated and alone, no one knowing where she was? Since they'd met, she'd been in Mike's presence for a total of little more than four hours.

But this man was the only hope she seemed to have. The police couldn't do much, not until she had solid evidence. She thought about Drew, and how much he would disapprove, but it's not as if her husband had consulted with her before bringing his chief resident into their lives. Kathryn decided, suddenly, it was time to seize her own agency. She said, "I accept your offer and its terms."

Mike grinned. "Good. Then let's play ball."

They rose, and after a few moments meant to mask his intent, the man who had been watching them did the same. Mike and Kathryn headed slowly for the elevators, deliberately giving him enough time to suggest that he was simply another hotel guest who'd decided to call it a night. The elevator doors were open to the lobby. Mike and Kathryn entered the compartment first, Mike holding the door until they all could step in. "Good evening," Kathryn said brightly. The man acknowledged her greeting and smile with a nod and immediately turned to face the door, indicating he was not inclined to make friendly elevator chatter. Mike punched the number for the fourth floor.

"What floor?" he asked the man, his finger poised to push a different button.

"Four," he said in a gruff voice.

Kathryn studied every detail of the man from behind. She guessed his age to be in the late sixties. Nothing from her limited view conjured up a recollection of anyone she'd ever met before in her life.

Chapter Thirty-Five

Mike, too, was scrutinizing their elevator companion from head to toe. At the fourth floor, the man stepped out and paused in the corridor, moving out of their way, ostensibly to hunt for his key card. Mike did not fall for the ruse. With a polite pressure, he put his arm around Kathryn's waist and pulled her close. "Let's make this look good," he said, nuzzling her ear, whispering, "He means to make us think he has a room on this floor, but I'm betting he's no guest of the hotel."

Kathryn let herself relax against his strong frame. The corridor was deserted. At Kathryn's door, the man passed by them as Mike inserted the key card, he and Kathryn appearing to be wrapped up in no one but each other. Once inside, Mike immediately dropped to his knees to peer under the door, listening for the return of the man's footsteps.

Chilled to the bone, Kathryn asked, "If you hadn't been with me, and I'd have been alone, what do you think he planned to do when he followed me to my room? Kill me on the spot?"

Mike nodded. "Possibly. If the corridor had been deserted, he could have been long gone before your body was ever found."

Kathryn's legs threatened to fold, and she dropped onto the edge of the bed. "What happens if he comes back?"

"I'll stay here." He smiled gently when Kathryn blushed, looking at the single bed. "Don't worry, you should take my room, since he doesn't know where I am registered. Or if you'd rather not be alone"—Mike headed to the desk and pulled out the complimentary notepad—"I'll sleep on the floor and then we'll head out early tomorrow. Until then, let's get to work."

The man in the gray suit and fake mustache viciously punched the lobby button in the elevator. "Damn!" he said aloud. Another attempt foiled, but how was he to know that Kathryn would meet a lover at the Brown Palace? It explained why she'd be spending the night at the Brown Palace when she could have stayed with her son. He had assumed she was headed back to Avon.

If he hadn't seen it with his own eyes, he couldn't have believed that Kathryn Frances Walker would have an affair. Not a girl of her moral disposition, still married to the handsome surgeon she'd been so crazy about when he was a medical student. But then they'd been married twenty-five years, and long marriages could grow icy. His certainly had.

What was he to do now? He couldn't dispose of Kathryn while she was in the company of her lover, a hard-nosed rancher by the looks of him, and not a man he'd want to tangle with. He imagined Kathryn would be leaving for Avon in the morning after her tryst. He could wait.

But then what? She had to be getting wary of attempts on her life, if she suspected that his failed hit on her damned lookalike at the library was meant for her. She'd avoided her habitual routines. Her hasty departure from Avon; the incident at the truck stop, when he'd luckily remained unnoticed; and the quick, nervous surveillance she gave her surroundings when she was with her children—they all left little doubt in his mind that she suspected danger. She would stay on guard, shunning her usual haunts, leaving few opportunities.

Her death had to be made to look like an accident. It was now April 11, ten days before he was to leave for Bethesda for the round of parties in his honor before his keynote speech opening the NIH convention on April 24. Less than two weeks to clear his path of her obstruction. He figured Kathryn would sleep in with her lover in the morning and not leave for Avon until much later.

He'd make sure it was *much* later. Kathryn was a loose end. There was always a witness, a bit of DNA, or a pesky camera that ruined everything.

He had plans. He would not allow this woman to ruin them.

Chapter Thirty-Six

Kathryn and Mike set straight to work making pencil drawings of their recollections of the man's face, filling in the features together before moving to an actual colored drawing of the composite. They agreed that the initial outline should include the wig, because hair can fool the untrained eye into mistaking it for a shape that it is not, and later adjust the facial contours the hairpiece might have been meant to conceal.

There were nine major face groups with which Kathryn was familiar: oblong, rectangular, circle, square, heart-shaped, diamond, oval, triangle, and inverted triangle. She was delighted when Mike showed her his outline of an inverted triangle, the type of face that is typically narrow at the chin and wide at the forehead. Her outline was the same.

Next they concentrated on the eyes, in Kathryn's view the most important detail. They then proceeded to their individual renderings of the jawline, nose, cheeks, and forehead. In comparing their outlines, they were both amazed that they were much the same. Kathryn suggested that Mike had drawn the lips a little too full, and the face should be slimmer. Mike thought Kathryn's forehead a bit too high. Both made the adjustments. They were now ready for a full, colored drawing of the face without the wig.

"Let's use your outline, and I'll referee," Mike suggested.

Kathryn agreed, and for easier communication, they sat beside each other on the bed, Mike looking over her shoulder. Using the colored pencils from her purse, Kathryn set to fleshing out a semblance of the face of the man who wished to kill her. When it was done, she stared at it. Mike was right. Originally she had drawn the forehead too high. But when she narrowed it, a memory tried to surface. Something about the symmetry of the well-shaped eyebrows and hooded eyes was familiar to her. "Let's young him up a bit," she said, explaining to Mike that if she'd known the man between college and the move to Avon, he would have been in his thirties. Carefully, she smoothed out the vestiges of aging. She plumped up the flesh between the cheeks and nose, removed the droop of the jowls, and softened the lines on the forehead and around the eyes. Her heart began to race.

"You recognize him?" Mike asked, picking up on her tension.

"I'm not sure," she said. "The hair. I need to give him hair and make a few adjustments, then I'll know." Deftly, she colored in thinning brown hair and reduced the shade of the eyebrows. Then, mentally, she inserted the smile she associated with the face. Only one person owned the smile she remembered, the engaging dimples when the lips were drawn back from the straight white teeth. The addition fit. She straightened and held out the drawing at arm's length. "My God," she said.

"Who is he?" Mike asked.

"My . . . my old college doctoral adviser, Dr. Edmund Croft."

"Your doctoral dissertation adviser?" Mike repeated incredulously. "Are you sure?"

Eyes glued to the drawing's shocking revelation, Kathryn answered shakily, "As sure as I can be of the face of any man I've ever known. This is the face of Dr. Edmond Croft, who I last saw twenty-one years ago."

"What motive would your professor have to kill you—especially after all these years?"

Kathryn thrust the drawing at Mike as if it burned her fingers.

"I have no earthly idea. None at all. I'm the one who had reason to be *his* enemy! He rejected my dissertation, preventing me from receiving my doctoral degree. It was such a betrayal, after he'd been supportive of my proposal from the beginning."

Mike studied the drawing. "Dr. Edmund Croft. Tell me about him."

"He was, and might still be, chairman of the department of bio-engineering at Rice University in Houston, my alma mater. He was the youngest person ever to make full professor at Rice, which was no mean feat. Everybody—his students, the staff, even the custodial crews—thought he walked on water."

"Did you?"

"I didn't trust him. He was brilliant, but not a good man." Kathryn thought a minute, Dr. Croft coming to life in her memory. Always so handsome, sure of himself, confident he was entitled to the respect and admiration he received, all overlaid with charm, likableness, the air of being easy to approach. This impression she conveyed to Mike.

"He wore it like a mask he put on for the day, but underneath I sensed a ruthlessness about him," she said. "Even considering his great intellect, professors as young as he did not fill the position he occupied without having stepped over a few bodies along the way. Even then I sensed that his reputation was the most important thing in his life. It was important to him to be important."

"You were that discerning at such an early age?"

Kathryn smiled wryly. "Believe me, I'd been exposed to worse in my day. Anyway"—she shrugged—"that was my perception of Dr. Croft, but there was no denying his brilliance, and I respected him for it. That's why it hurt so much when he turned down my dissertation on the heart pump as 'science fiction.' "

To that day, she remembered the put-down vividly.

"The problem I see with your finished proposal is threefold, Kathryn. One, you do not address whether the technology is currently available to produce your device. Two, there are engineering challenges to producing

it. Heart pumps have an external battery, and there is no way we can put
something inside the body that would need to be charged like that. Can it
be manufactured with biocompatible materials? Third, is this device in
line with the appropriate US Food and Drug Administration and inter-
national regulatory requirements?"

Kathryn could remember staring at him in paralytic shock. None of
the factors he listed on his manicured fingers had been brought up to her
before, and they were not relevant to her proposal. Her adviser's long,
lingering sigh added salt to her wounds when he commented, "Perhaps I
was too hasty to support you in bypassing a master's to begin your doctoral
studies in your field. I let my pity for your home and financial situation
cloud my judgment."

"But you told me that spending a year earning a master's was a waste
of time for someone of 'my brilliance,' " Kathryn had objected. "Or so you
said at the time."

"Well, yes, there was that," Dr. Croft agreed as he rose to dismiss her.
"I am genuinely sorry, Kathryn, but I have my reputation to consider, and
I cannot put my stamp of approval on this dissertation."

"For the life of me, Mike," Kathryn said now, "and I suppose
I mean that literally, I can't imagine why the man would want me
dead. And why now, after all this time?"

Mike got up from the bed and reached for his laptop. "Let's see
just what this Dr. Croft has been up to."

Google listed an impressive array of academic accolades and ac-
complishments in Dr. Edmund Croft's stellar career since Kathryn
had walked out of his office, heartbroken. He had risen to become
the youngest dean of the School of Engineering at Rice University,
going from chairman to dean in record time. After leaving the university, he accepted a position as chief technology officer at Medi-
Corp, a medical engineering corporation that mainly manufactured
devices to assist and replace the circulatory functions of the heart.

"Oh, my goodness!" Kathryn exclaimed as she and Mike read
that Dr. Croft was due to address the National Institutes of Health

on April 24 about a device that he had invented and had been working on privately for years, a device that sounded extremely familiar. The patent for the device was pending and expected to be granted this year—on *April 29*.

Kathryn turned to Mike, wide-eyed. "He was lying that whole time. He saw the potential of my invention, and he stole my dissertation! He's just been biding his time until the device was feasible. This heart pump he says he invented is mine—I laid it out plain and clear in my prototype."

Mike thought for a moment. "Did others in your program know about your work? Were there others reviewing your dissertation who might be able to corroborate that this work was originally yours?"

"No. Oh, my goodness—I protested his decision, but my dissertation never went to the review board so that I could contest his rejection of it. He must have used his influence to see to that."

"He must be worried you will expose him now that your invention has come to fruition."

"Exactly. He'll make a lot of money when that patent is granted if he sells it to a company that manufactures heart devices, most likely the one he works for now. But I'm no threat to the patent. He filed it first, so the device would remain in his name unless I was prepared to sue for rightful ownership. If I'm remembering correctly, that type of case is messy. It would take years in the courts, not to mention the fortune I'd have to pay in lawyer's fees. Dr. Croft must be banking on that. No, it's his reputation that he's worried about. If word got out that he stole the idea for the device from one of his students, it would all be ruined, everything he's worked for, the image he's created for himself. He'd lose his job at MediCorp, assuming they have a problem with the theft. You never know with some of these medical corporations."

"What about the university?"

"He would certainly be disgraced, but if he claimed that he used a private laboratory for his work, then Rice would have no financial claim. I would even have grounds to sue Rice for denying me my doctoral degree, and they wouldn't want that kind of publicity."

"But why would he believe that you could expose him? Unless . . . do you still have a copy of your dissertation?"

Kathryn nodded, despite her ears ringing. "I thought maybe one day I could go back and finish my doctorate. I kept my dissertation, just in case I wanted to build from it. A committee of three is required to read a dissertation, but the student's senior adviser decides first if it even goes to committee. I kept all the copies that I had prepared, thinking it was heading to the three, plus my notes and research material as well. I have both physical and digital copies."

"Does he know you kept your material?"

"It's a reasonable guess. Master's and doctoral candidates consider the evidence of those years of work as a badge of honor. I have a thumb drive and research materials in a box in the attic, and a printed copy in the safe in my kitchen. But what I don't understand is, since Dr. Croft has access to my house, why not just keep searching for it? Why is he trying to kill me?" *And maiming Janet for life.*

"Perhaps he ran out of options, or time. If it's in a safe, he surely hasn't found it yet. And if he was in your house when he changed the damper sign, you might have surprised him while he was looking. Perhaps he just hopes to get you into the hospital and out of the way until he's found all the evidence. But think about it: If you were gone, and nothing led back to him, would your family even know where to look? Would they even know that you had any connections to the device Croft is claiming as his own?"

Kathryn's face flushed as Mike dropped his eyes and stood up, closing his laptop. "You're not safe as long as Croft knows you've got proof to discredit him."

"You're right," she said through tightly clenched teeth. "I intend to get the bastard before he gets me."

"And how do you plan to do that?"

"I will go to Houston before his appearance at the NIH and present my dissertation and body of evidence to the dean at Rice myself."

Chapter Thirty-Seven

Monday, April 12

Here's the plan," Mike told Kathryn the next morning over room service breakfast after a sleepless night. "In case our man is still in the vicinity, bets are that he intends to follow your car when the valet returns it. We're going to let him. We know who he is now and will recognize him, especially if he's still in disguise. He'll be on your tail as soon as you pull away from the hotel, and I will be on his."

"But he'll recognize you as the man with me last night," Kathryn pointed out.

"He'll think I'm following you to our next meeting place, or even just that I happen to be behind you until we go our separate ways."

"And then what?"

"You are to drive to Boulder, as if you're going to visit your daughter again, not directly to Avon, as he will probably expect, and head straight for the Boulder County Sheriff's Office, which can be seen from the road. It's on Flatiron Parkway. Your GPS will take you there."

"Why the county sheriff's office?" Kathryn asked, reluctant to engage with a member of that law enforcement agency again.

"It's a safe choice, and you've made the acquaintance of a Boulder County deputy. Our man will wonder if you've spotted him and gone to seek protection. By now he would know that you are aware of a threat to your life. He'll hightail it out of there, and I will follow him. If I see that you are not being tailed, I'll honk from the street before you enter the police station, and you can follow me to the ranch without worry."

"Officer Dearborn told me that I could put in a report of a possible stalker, since the name I gave him didn't come up as a registered private investigator."

"That's a good idea," Mike said. "We can have a record of this for law enforcement."

While Kathryn and Mike waited for their cars to be brought round in the busy Monday morning hustle, they did not see the man of the evening before. The young man dispatched to retrieve Kathryn's Cadillac brought back a long face. "I am sorry, Mrs. Walker, but your car appears to have been vandalized. Three flat tires. This is very rare at our business, ma'am, I want to assure you. Somehow the vandals got past our security guard and damaged our security cameras."

"Show us," Mike said. The worried valet led the way to the reserved parking area, and Kathryn gasped when she saw her car sitting on its tire rims. The rubber had been thoroughly slashed.

They called the police immediately, and the chagrined valet brought them back to reception to wait until the car could be repaired.

Alarmed, Kathryn turned to Mike once they were alone again. "Why do you think he did that? Is he hoping to trap me here?"

Mike hesitated before replying, his gaze at her sure of his answer but reluctant to express it. "My guess is that he might have figured that since he can't reach you here, while I'm here and you're not alone, he might have tried to delay you here while he headed back to Avon to search your home."

In a gridlock of panic, Kathryn grabbed her handbag and removed her cell phone. "I've got to call Drew immediately," she said. She imagined Dr. Croft failing in his search and lying in wait for Drew to come home, tired after a long day, torturing him for the location of their hidden safe. On his own, Croft would not find it.

"Wait!" Mike ordered sharply, as she was about to thumb in the numbers. "Before you call, have you thought about what you'll say when your husband asks how it's going with your friend in Houston?"

"Yes," she said, "the truth."

"And that would be?"

Mike had a right to ask, Kathryn had to admit, but where to begin to explain to Drew the incredible discoveries of last night and the danger he was now in? The truth would sound like some implausible thriller, and Drew wasn't one for reading fiction.

"I can't lie to him, Mike. I'll tell him everything I can." She just hoped that he hadn't made his decision yet and taken off with Elizabeth.

Mike got up from his seat. "I'll step away so that you can have some privacy."

She determined that she would not mention Mike McCoy. Drew would have to take her word for the information she and Mike had uncovered. The safe was opened so rarely, would he even remember the combination? If he didn't answer, though it wasn't proof, she had an idea who he would be with. Could her fraught system handle that? She dialed his number anyway.

"Kathryn!" he answered on the first ring, his voice full of relief, even jubilance. "Did you make it to Houston okay? How's Sandy?"

"Drew . . ."

Kathryn could sense his spirits take a nosedive at hearing the hesitancy in his name. "What's wrong?"

That's a question more for you to answer, she thought, but answered firmly, "I'm not at Sandy's, Drew. I'm at the Brown Palace Hotel here in Denver."

She thought at first that Drew had gone off the line, but the

ID screen remained alight. "Why? Did you miss your flight? Why aren't you at Bobby's?"

"Because I'm here, Drew. I didn't miss my flight to Houston. I will not be going to Sandy's for the week, and Bobby doesn't know that I'm spending the night at the Brown Palace."

Kathryn heard him draw a deep breath. "Kathryn, honey, what the hell is going on? Why aren't you going to Sandy's?"

"It is a long story." With certain omissions and various shadings, Kathryn began her account by revealing the name of the man she had identified as her potential killer.

"You mean *the* Croft?" Drew erupted in disbelief. "Your doctoral adviser at Rice? In God's name, why would he want to kill you, Kathryn, and after all this time?"

"My dissertation," she said, and explained the trail she'd uncovered that made sense of Dr. Croft's desperation to destroy anyone who might have evidence of his fraud. "The survival of Dr. Croft's reputation is crucial to him, and he'll stop at nothing to protect it. He's even followed me here to the hotel. I discovered he's been on my tail since I left Avon. That's why I'm here at the Palace, where there are people about. I wanted to lead him away from Bobby."

Drew's silence resounded with incredulity. Kathryn continued calmly, "He doesn't know yet that I've identified him."

"Kathryn . . . ," Drew began.

"Don't interrupt, Drew. I'm not through. You must pack a bag, get out of the house for the rest of the week, and take the evidence with you. The dissertation I mailed to myself is in the safe. In the attic there is a box containing my research papers and a spare thumb drive holding my dissertation. It should be in the green trunk near the back windows. Then I suggest that when you do return to the house at the end of the week, you have the police with you. Do you know the combination of the safe?"

Sounding shaken from a nightmare, his mind in a spin to assimilate the shocking points of Kathryn's tale, Drew said vaguely, "It's around here somewhere."

Quietly, hand over her mouth in case anyone was watching, Kathryn recited the number. "Promise me that you'll remove my papers and stay away from the house. At least until you change the locks."

A tired sigh. "Don't worry, I'll stay with Frank. He can probably use the company. I've tried to get the locks at the hardware store, but they're on back order. I called a few other locksmiths, but none are available at such short notice."

"Thank you for understanding, Drew, and for trusting me."

"Of course, Kath. But I have a question. Why don't I leave the whole ball of wax on the front doorstep, and let Dr. Croft help himself? Then you are safe, I am safe, the house is safe, you can come home, and we don't have to worry about him anymore."

"Because if he knows I know, I'll always be a threat. I can expose him even if he's destroyed the evidence. Besides, the documents aren't for him. I'm not going down without a fight."

Three hours after the discovery of the vandalism, the Cadillac's original tires had been replaced. Still, though the damage was evidence enough of Croft's intention to delay her, Kathryn was not entirely convinced that she was free of his surveillance. "He could have hired someone to follow me," she said to Mike. "He could have me tailed to your ranch."

"That's why we are going to stick to our plan," Mike said.

Mike waited until Kathryn had pulled away. The only vehicles that departed behind her belonged to hotel guests. As Mike expected, he saw no other car draw away from a parking spot and head off in the same direction as Kathryn. Fixedly, he kept her white car in sight as she followed his instructions to drive toward Boulder and the county sheriff's office. No one followed her. He honked from the street as she opened her car door to get out, then saw a young deputy approach her car.

The deputy bent down to address her through the open window. "Good to see you again, Mrs. Walker. Are you taking my advice to file a report about that private investigator?"

"Yes, please."

Officer Dearborn began to explain the paperwork and then added, "I'll be sure to tell Lindsay hello when I see her this evening."

Kathryn perked up at the sound of Lindsay's name. "Lindsay, my daughter?"

"Yes, I hope you don't mind. I could get another officer to take my place if you're not comfortable with me."

"No, no, that's fine." Kathryn said, "but could you not mention anything about this? I don't want to worry her."

"Of course," Officer Dearborn said, a little too quickly.

Kathryn realized the ranch might prove not to be as secret a hideout as she and Mike had banked on. Leaving Boulder, the Range Rover flashed its lights for the Cadillac to pull over to the shoulder of the road. Mike got out and approached as Kathryn lowered the driver's window. What an awesome figure he made, she thought. It wasn't only the rancher's look, but his strong and purposeful gait.

"What was that all about back there?" he asked, a bit tersely. He'd noticed the deputy watching his car as he drove away.

Kathryn worriedly explained her brief history with the deputy and the potential consequences of this latest encounter with him. She, too, had seen David Dearborn, notebook in hand, watching Mike's immediate reverse from the parking lot when she backed out. The deputy had a date with her daughter that evening, and Kathryn couldn't trust him to keep the information to himself, not if he thought it might get him into Lindsay's good graces. The last thing Kathryn wanted was for her daughter to find out she'd been in Boulder instead of in Houston with Sandy today, especially if it was going to lead to questions about Mike, whose plates Dearborn was surely running right now.

"So am I to expect a visit from this Deputy Dearborn?" Mike had asked.

"More likely from my husband, if Lindsay finds out about the deputy's suspicions," Kathryn said, sickened at the black lie her daughter would have caught her in. But if she was honest with herself, she hoped Drew would be a little jealous, realizing that he wasn't the only one who could move on.

Mike nodded and returned to his car. If necessary, he'd be ready for any fallout.

After settling into the guest room at the MM Ranch, Kathryn headed out to the wraparound porch to drink a cup of superbly brewed coffee in the late afternoon sun. She was alone except for the company of Kirby, a graying border collie who was no longer able to keep up with the sheep. He had taken to her upon sight, and let it be known that he preferred her company to trotting after Mike and his foreman, Lonnie Taggart, as they tended to business out on the ranch. It was roundup season, the time of the year when the herd was counted and driven in for vaccinations, and pregnant cows were delivered to birthing pens.

After today, Lonnie would remain at the house with her. Quiet, a man of few words, he'd welcomed her with old-fashioned courtesy. One side of his face showed the healed ravages of a severe burn, which gave his flesh the sheen of petrified wood. Apparently the preparation of meals and the care of the house fell among his main responsibilities at the MM Ranch.

"Lonnie made up a pot of coffee for you, ready to plug in," Mike had said before heading out. "He roasts the beans himself."

"If it tastes as good as the soup and sandwiches he made us for lunch, I may be too spoiled for my Folgers when I get home."

"You'll find he's an excellent cook," Mike had assured her with a grin.

Kathryn sensed that they'd served together in the army. Pleasant and polite as he was, she could tell Lonnie Taggart was a man of mystery. Like his boss, he wore jeans and a flannel shirt under a herdsman's jacket, and both men were strapped into chaps that would protect them in the prickly brush. Lonnie explained that roundup season was "literally the thorniest time of the year for raising cattle." The MM was definitely a working ranch, not a gentleman's weekend retreat.

But then none of her mental images of the MM Ranch had turned out as she'd expected.

Kathryn had imagined a man's cluttered hangout, a mishmash setup in need of a good scrubbing, but the house was orderly and spotlessly clean, tastefully furnished with an eye to male comfort.

Coming upon the site, Kathryn had driven past a well-tended fence of barbed wire strung taut between gleaming white steel posts. Following the Range Rover, she'd entered the compound through an electronically controlled black wrought-iron gate flanked by hand-cut stone columns the color of rose quartz. No overhead arch announced the name of the place; an inscription engraved in brass on a plaque set into one of the stanchions was apparently all that was considered necessary to declare the property as the MM Ranch. A smoothly paved road bordered by neat hedges of flowering Burkwood viburnum led to the house, which didn't have the sprawling dimensions or rustic splendor of a Hollywood wealthy cattleman's ranch, but instead felt quietly, confidently prosperous.

Like the house, the porch invited calm. It faced snowcapped mountains overlooking tranquil pastures where cattle grazed in the cold but sunny afternoon. In such a serene place, with the comfort of the dog beside her, Kathryn thought she should feel at ease, but peace was not possible. Would the deputy betray her confidence? Had Dr. Croft hit their home by now?

Her cell phone rang, and Kathryn jumped, spilling her coffee. The caller was Drew.

Chapter Thirty-Eight

Where are you?" Drew asked immediately. "I called the hotel, and they said you'd checked out. I've been trying to call you all day."

"I'm sorry, the phone reception has been pretty spotty."

"Where? Maybe I can come meet you."

Kathryn's heart skipped a beat. She wasn't sure if it was because she didn't want Drew around Mike. "I'd rather not say. Just know that I am safe until we figure out our next steps."

After a short pause, in which Drew considered this refusal, he continued, "Well, Kath, the good news is, I found all the material you asked for, and it's all safe in my desk at the hospital, locked up tight. Croft will never access it there."

"Thank you," she said, relieved.

"What if he's left?" Drew asked suddenly. "Now that there's nothing more for him to get. Then you'd be safe, and you could come home."

"How would we know? And anyway, would he leave without getting what he came for?"

"Unless he slept in his car, he had to crash somewhere last night, didn't he? I can call hotels and motels to ask if a Dr. Edmund Croft registered with them. If he's checked out, we don't imagine he'll go far. He still thinks you are the only one who knows the truth; he's not going to want you to talk, especially not before the NIH conference."

"Dr. Croft wouldn't have registered in his real name, and he might be in disguise, so a description of him won't be of use," Kathryn pointed out.

"Look, the guy's no master criminal. He wouldn't have access to false credit cards and drivers' licenses, so he'd have to use his own when he registered. My bet is that the only precaution he'd take to avoid being traced in the area would be to choose a down-and-out motel outside of Avon that he'd not be likely to stay at. It's worth a go, Kath."

Kathryn thought over the idea. Drew's suggestion made sense. *Especially if he bribes the registration clerk for information.* Dr. Croft would surely assume that she'd suspect him of the theft, but she'd have no evidence to prove it. A record of his being in the area on the date in question would give her additional ammunition to use against him. "Good thinking, again, Drew," she said. "If you can locate where he stayed last night, see if you can take a look at his registration form and snap a picture of it as proof."

"I'll figure a way to get a copy," Drew said. "I'll get back to you, and if all is well, will you come home?"

"We'll see," Kathryn said.

Drew hung up dissatisfied. *We'll see.* What was there to *see* about? Kathryn never signed off with *sweetheart* or *darling* anymore, and hadn't for this whole rotten month, but how could he blame her? Drew reprimanded himself for not trusting his wife's instincts and moved quicker.

Anxiety nestled in the pit of his stomach. Kathryn had been *off* for most of the month. So much so that he wondered if she had found the accounts, or, even worse, his secret. Drew swallowed the guilt down and set about making it up to Kathryn. He thought perhaps if he did this one thing, it would be the start of all the things he intended to do to make it up to her. He started making phone calls. It wasn't until his eighth call, to a motel in Edwards, a small town east of Avon, that he found him.

"I'm sorry," the clerk replied to Drew's request, "but Dr. Croft has checked out as of this morning."

Smiling to himself, Drew got in his car and drove to the motel. The pimply-faced clerk recognized him the moment he strolled in; Dr. Walker had replaced his father's knee just a few months earlier. The boy listened respectfully as Drew explained that he was here to visit his friend Dr. Croft. Could the clerk please put him through to Croft's room? Drew pretended fury when the young man regretfully admitted that the man had checked out already.

"How could Edmund, one of my closest friends, leave town without making a move to see me?" Drew exploded. The clerk was flattered that this eminent doctor would share such strong feelings with him. "He'll try to deny that he was here," Drew declared, and asked if he could take a photo of his registration form. The clerk chewed his lip as he contemplated allowing the transgression. Finally he nodded, letting Drew take a quick snapshot before snatching the registration card away.

Drew drove away, satisfied that Croft was no longer a threat, at least not for the time being. He'd call Kathryn with the good news from his car while he was heading for Elizabeth's.

Chapter Thirty-Nine

Mike and Lonnie returned to the house as the sun was going down, Kirby running to greet them as they unsaddled their horses. It was apparently quitting time, as cowhands on horses and in chaps materialized from various directions of the ranch. From the porch, Kathryn watched them congregate in the corral with Mike and Lonnie before finishing up their end-of-the-day duties with horses and tack. The whole scene looked straight out of a western. As Mike and Lonnie started toward the house, she went to greet them, Kirby at their heels, feeling self-conscious, as if she were the woman of the house come out to meet her men at the end of the day.

"I have news," she said to Mike as each man unbuckled his chaps.

"You can speak freely," Mike said. "Lonnie knows most of the situation."

"Drew ran a check of the motels and found that Dr. Croft has left town, at least for the time being. He thinks I can return home now, but I told him no, not until I'm sure I'm completely safe."

"Let's not take any chances," Mike said. "One of us will stay with you until you make your plans to leave for Houston and your meeting with the Rice officials. You are welcome to stay here as long as that takes."

"I appreciate that, Mike," she said, "but speaking of Rice officials, and to get me out of your hair as soon as possible, would you mind if I use your computer? I regret having to ask to invade your private space, but I find it hard to do extensive research on my phone, and I want to be sure who I should be contacting."

Mike waved her apology aside. "By all means, be our guest," he said. "I can log you in whenever you need."

"Thank you. I will call the university tomorrow. I just hope that the dean will understand I'm not a crackpot."

"And if you can't make contact with him?"

"Then I'll go to Rice and storm the doors."

"I believe it," Lonnie grunted.

"Like I said, you're welcome to stay as long as it takes," Mike repeated.

Boots replaced with loafers, he stood. "We'll wash up, and then maybe you'll join us for a drink before dinner? I believe we can scare up a gin and tonic or a glass of sauvignon blanc."

"I accept with pleasure," Kathryn said, at least relieved that she appeared to be no interruption to the two bachelors' evening routine.

Lonnie headed off toward the kitchen, saying, "Count me out, boss. I have to get the meal started, and I left the table a mess after lunch." But seconds later he pulled up short, seeing surfaces cleared, leftovers put away, and the dishes and pans washed and stored.

"I took the liberty of cleaning up, Mr. Taggart," Kathryn said. "I needed something to do. Was that presumptuous of me?" She didn't want him to think it had been a violation of his domain.

"Oh, heck no," Lonnie said. "I think that was mighty kind and helpful of you, ma'am. And the name is Lonnie."

"Well, then, Lonnie, I have a proposal," Kathryn said. "To earn my keep while I am here, would you allow me to cook the evening meals? I assure you that I am a passable cook."

A grin spreading, Lonnie said, "It's a deal, ma'am."

"I saw a loin of lamb in the refrigerator. Is that dinner?"

"Sure is. And there are potatoes and carrots, too . . ."

"I'll find them," she said, shooing the men out of the kitchen. Kathryn saw Lonnie toss a glance at Mike, one of appreciation and approval. Kathryn smiled for what felt like the first time in weeks.

Chapter Forty

Despite the strain on her nerves, Kathryn found some release of her tension in the restful atmosphere of the house and genial company of the men. They switched off the evening news—focused on the collapse of the housing bubble—and conversed without awkwardness against a background of easy-listening music. Mike asked her if she'd been bored during the day.

"Kirby might have been, but I wasn't," Kathryn said. "I managed to keep myself pleasantly occupied." Unable to sit still, she'd abandoned the front porch after a while and gone on a tour of the grounds, visiting the horses in the barn, chickens in their pens, lambs in a sheepfold, and two pigs in their crib enclosure. "Now I understand better the expression 'happier than a pig in mud,'" she said with a smile.

Her most unexpected find had been the greenhouse, with neat rows of spinach, lettuce, spring onions, and greens. Eggplants and tomatoes hung from their sturdy stalks as well as climbing green beans, English peas, and yellow squash from their trellises. Beyond the greenhouse was a garden plot, already tilled to receive spring seeds. Chickens, pigs, a greenhouse, and a vegetable patch? It wasn't as if the MM had to grow its own food. So who was the farmer in the house? she asked the men over her glass of sauvignon blanc.

"That would be me," the foreman answered. "I grew up on a farm, and once a farmer, always a farmer. Mike here is the rancher."

The conversation turned toward Kathryn's field of study and why she had chosen a specialty in biomedical engineering in particular.

"And your adviser called your thoracic gizmo science fiction," Mike said.

"Knowing better," Kathryn said. "All my life I wanted my doctorate, and he stole that from me. It'd be nice to at least get some redemption."

She had put together ingredients for a hearty meal, one that Lonnie and Mike would appreciate after working outside all day. The aroma of roasting carrots, potatoes, and onions with marinated lamb—she hoped not supplied from the sheepfold—added to the cozy atmosphere. Fresh peas from last year's harvest that she found in the freezer simmered in butter.

"Sure does smell good from where I'm parked," observed Lonnie, sitting in a lounge chair with his feet on an ottoman. The men had changed into fresh clothes, their hair still damp from their showers, and as they'd entered the room, Kathryn's nose had picked up a trace of bath soap, which reminded her of Drew's fresh scent. An ache filled her chest. "Let's hope it tastes as good as it smells," she said.

Mike handed Lonnie a cigar. "Let's take a walk, Sergeant."

It was late in the evening, and Kathryn had headed to bed. Even though they were well out of earshot of the guest room and could hear the faint sound of shower water running, Mike preferred to talk outside. They slipped on jackets and lit up under a night sky as clear as black crystal. The recent rain had left a residue of its breath behind, crisp and refreshing, hinting of an early spring, but the men were well aware of the mercurial swings of April. They knew not to trust its promises of warmer weather coming.

"I'd be willing to bet we're in for another snowstorm this week," Mike said, his gaze toward the mountains.

Lonnie nodded. "Old man winter's not through with us yet. Something else on your mind besides a prediction of the weather, boss?"

"Kathryn is afraid her husband will try to find her and lead her killer straight here."

"What do you think?" Lonnie asked.

"I think he is an idiot who doesn't appreciate what he has." Mike stopped himself. "The man is cautious to the point of being a danger to everyone around him. Did you know he didn't think they should alert the police about any of this, to wait for proof? I swear, if she were my wife—"

"But she's not," Lonnie said, letting out a puff of smoke.

Mike puffed his cigar and nodded silently. "It doesn't change the fact that I am still worried about her trip to Houston."

"Why is that?"

"Dr. Walker has a five-million-dollar life insurance policy out on his wife. There sure as hell are a lot of things a man can do with that kind of money." Mike examined the cigar in his hand, turning it over in his fingers. "Who knows, this threat from Dr. Edmund Croft could present the perfect cover if the opportunity arose." He put the cigar back in his mouth.

"Is she aware of the term policy on her life?"

"She is." They had reached a corral, and both men laid their arms on the railing and looked up into the starry night. Mike explained Kathryn's intention to meet with officials at Rice University while there was time to blow the whistle on Edmund Croft. "She'll probably fly out to Houston with her husband."

"Then it's best to leave it alone," Lonnie said. "We have a nice calm life. You don't need to go poking at bears."

"Yeah, you're probably right. I don't need to go messing with a complicated woman, even a soon-to-be-divorced married one."

Lonnie's eyes widened. "No! Is her husband crazy?"

"I asked myself that very same question, but according to Kathryn, he's in love with another woman and intends to ask her for a divorce at the end of April."

"Why then?"

"The woman gave the doctor an ultimatum. Either file for divorce by then, or she's gone."

Lonnie whistled. "So the doctor has more than one motive for being rid of his wife. Does she believe he's capable of killing her?"

Mike shook his head. "She won't hear of it."

"What do you think?"

"I couldn't say. Men have killed their wives for less." They turned to walk back to the house. "Kathryn will see this trip to Houston as a way to patch things up."

They walked in silence for a while. Finally, Lonnie drew on his cigar, expelled its smoke into the air, and said, "You know, when my father left for another woman, I always resented her. I saw her as the reason why my parents split, when in reality there were probably other issues at play. If there is something between the two of you, wait. If it's meant to be, it will work itself out."

Mike looked sideways at Lonnie. "You know, you really should have been an officer."

"Nah, too much responsibility." Lonnie laughed. "But if she were to stick around, I wouldn't mind her taking over the cooking. She's a hell of a lot better than I am."

Chapter Forty-One

Tuesday, April 13

Against all her expectations, Kathryn slept soundly. She woke with a start to pawing and whining at her door, and then a hushed voice: "*Kirby, get down. Come back here!*" It was already seven o'clock. She had slept a full nine hours. Moments later, her cell rang. It was Drew.

"Hello," she said, clearing the morning fog from her throat. The reviving smell of brewed coffee drifted into the room.

"Kathryn, are you all right? You don't sound all right."

"I'm fine, Drew. I just woke up. Haven't had my coffee yet."

"At seven o'clock? You never sleep until seven!"

"Well, I did last night." *We need a new mattress*, she almost said, then remembered that after April they might not be sharing one. "How are you faring?"

"Hard to say. What are our next steps?"

Kathryn outlined her scheme. "My efforts might come to nothing, but I have to try, Drew. The only way I can guarantee my safety is by exposing him. I'm trying to get an appointment this week."

"I want to go with you to Houston, Kath, and I can't this week. I have surgeries scheduled, and I'm on call this weekend. There's no one to replace me. Can't you postpone your trip until next week?"

"That's out of the question, since the kids will be home for spring break. I want this over and done with, Drew, the sooner the better. You want me to come home, don't you?"

"You know I do, Kath. Listen, I know this is something that you feel you need to do, and I want to support you, I really do, but I am just concerned about your safety." Drew paused for a moment. "We could drive. I'd pick you up where you are. We need some time alone, Kathryn. There are . . . important issues we have to discuss—life-changing issues that are also time-sensitive."

Life-changing issues. Time-sensitive. Well, there it was. She knew what he would say—that her husband was getting ready to break her heart. "There are some things I simply have to do on my own. These 'life-changing issues' will have to wait."

"All right, if you insist, Kathryn."

Before Kathryn could respond, Drew had hung up. The abrupt disconnection seemed to be the norm between them these days.

Needing warmth and coffee, she quickly put on slippers and a robe, glancing at the dismal selection of clothes in the closet. She was going to need something suitable for her meeting in Houston.

Mike, dressed in work clothes, was in the kitchen pouring out a cup of coffee, its aroma rich and strong. She smelled biscuits baking in the oven. Kirby came toward her, wagging his tail, either in apology or greeting.

"Good morning," Mike said. "Sorry that Kirby woke you. How'd you sleep?"

"Like the dead, though I hate to use the term." She bent down to give the dog's neck an affectionate rub. "My cell phone woke me up anyway." She took the cup Mike offered her, warm to her fingers. The caffeine was a balm to her senses as she sipped. "Where is Lonnie?"

"Out on the farm. He starts every day out there before sunrise."

"Must be wonderful to be among growing things at dawn." A

weak sun was peeking through the kitchen windows, a cold beginning to the day, but it added a coziness to the warmth of the kitchen, Kathryn thought. She could get used to living in a place like this.

"He'd appreciate your saying that," Mike said. Kathryn sipped her coffee while Mike turned back to the stove, lining up slabs of bacon in a pan. Kathryn tried not to think of the cute piglets she'd seen yesterday. "Hope you like biscuits, bacon, and eggs."

Tuesdays were her oatmeal and fruit breakfast, but she would go with the flow of whatever was served from this kitchen with gratitude. "What's there not to like? Everything smells delicious."

His back to her, Mike said, "It's none of my business, and if the subject is too personal to discuss, we can drop it, but I have a question to ask, out of concern, not curiosity."

Kathryn had the feeling that Mike's focus on the stove was in part an excuse to avoid facing her. "Ask away," she said.

"What do you plan to do with the rest of your life if your husband divorces you? Have you thought about it?"

"I don't know. Finally start my career." She combed her fingers through her hair. "I've been with Drew so long, I can't imagine life without him. All I know is that when this is over, I want a fresh start—hopefully with my husband, but if I have to, I am ready to do it alone."

Chapter Forty-Two

To respect Mike's breakfast efforts, Kathryn feigned enjoyment while the men ate heartily of the bacon and creamy eggs, light-as-air biscuits slathered in butter, and homemade jam. Afterward, she asked if she could use the computer.

Mike gave her a thumbs-up. "Whatever you need. I'll be with the men rounding up the rest of the strays today, but Lonnie will be here, so have at it."

"And don't bother with the dishes," Lonnie put in when he saw Kathryn begin to pick up their plates. "I'll see to them. You just scoot along and do what you have to do."

Kathryn returned to her room to get dressed, her mind on how to get her hands on the box of evidence in Drew's office. She couldn't show up at his office to collect it, but she could arrange for him to leave it at a designated place for her to pick up.

In the ranch office, Mike's desk had been tidied. Papers were stacked neatly in bins. A writing pad and pens had been set out, bookshelves dusted. Her eye lit instantly upon two framed pho-tographs. They were pictures of a beautiful dark-haired young woman with luminous brown eyes, dark skin tone, and strong facial features. Obviously, Mike's wife.

There were two scenes. One appeared to be an engagement

photo, the kind one submits to the hometown newspaper. Kathryn took down the second picture, where the wife stood with a woman wearing a long black *abaya*. Mike's wife looked to be in her early thirties then. She was utterly gorgeous, but with a beauty comfortingly different from Kathryn's own. An inexplicable feeling of relief passed through her. She had worried Mike might be trying to save the life of a woman who looked like the wife he had lost.

Lonnie passed by the open office, pausing when he saw her with the photograph. "That's Beth," he said. "Mike's late wife."

Kathryn turned toward him. "I had assumed so. How . . . did she die, Lonnie?"

"It was three years ago," he said from the doorway. "Beth was in Iraq as a UN humanitarian relief worker. That's how she and Mike met in the first place—he was on a mission in some godforsaken place, and she was doing her best to relieve pain and suffering. Five years they were married. Used to take R&Rs together. Rest and recreation," he offered by way of explanation. "They were living together temporarily in Baghdad, and she was pregnant. Mike had just come in from a mission in Syria. Someone planted an IED—a homemade bomb—under his jeep. We'll never know if it was a direct target or not. But the next morning, when Mike was asleep, Beth got in the jeep to run an errand. Killed her instantly. Mike retired from the army not long after, but he spent a long time working to track down the man who had killed his wife."

Locked in the horror of the scene, still holding the framed photograph, Kathryn visualized Mike hearing the explosion, perhaps blown out of bed by it, rushing out to find the burning jeep, and knowing instantly what had happened. "He told me she died in an accident." She gulped. "Mike never told me the whole story."

"I'm glad you asked," Lonnie said. "It might help explain things."

"Yes, yes, it does," Kathryn said, thinking she understood what he meant. "Mike told me he couldn't save her life, and he hoped to save mine."

"Oh, well, there might be more to it than that," Lonnie said, edging back to the door. "Mike is the kind of guy who thinks of everybody else first. It's his best and worst trait."

Kathryn was left staring at the empty doorway. What did Lonnie mean by *There might be more to it than that*? Sitting back in her chair, for the first time she let herself wonder what her life would be like here on this ranch with Mike, without all the pressure of having to prove herself to anyone.

She replaced the photograph, the arch of Beth's smile suddenly appearing all the more beautiful and tragic.

She fired up Google and began her search. It was over in ten minutes. She had located the name of the dean, read his biographical sketch, and studied his photo with a stirring of having known him, though the name and face rang no immediate bells. He was fifty-five, her age, and a graduate of Rice. A classmate, maybe? He had earned his master's at Rice, but his doctorate at MIT. Impressive. Using her cell, she dialed the number given for the university and asked to speak with Dr. Arthur T. Madison. She might as well start with the head cheese. To her surprise, she was put through to his office, the phone answered by the dean's secretary. Kathryn made her request. "Who is calling, please?" she was asked.

Kathryn identified herself as a former student at the university, and included her maiden name in the hope that "Turner" triggered a flicker of recognition. She explained that it was a matter of urgency that she speak with Dr. Madison.

"Just a moment, please."

Kathryn was prepared to be told to leave a message and Dr. Madison would get back to her, a delay that might mean hours or days or her call never returned, but again to her surprise, she waited less than a minute before a male voice came on the line. "Would this be the Kathryn Turner Walker with whom I took a course in physicochemical hydrodynamics? Actually, we were in *two* courses together. The other one was Dr. Croft's structural biology class."

Kathryn faltered, and before she could answer, she heard a

chuckle. "It's okay if you don't remember me. I was pretty nondescript. A little short guy, thick glasses, thinning hair, wore tweed jackets, the nerdy type. I liked sitting in the back row. Or am I describing myself to someone who isn't *that* Kathryn Turner Walker?"

Then Kathryn remembered. *Of course!* She had forgotten his name and face, but she now remembered Arthur Madison as the geeky kid behind her in PCH who was the most driven person in their class. He was every professor's favorite student.

She laughed. "The very one and the same, Dr. Madison."

"Oh, please. Arthur it was then and is now. What can I do for you, Kathryn?"

Chapter Forty-Three

Kathryn had grappled with the best direction to take to disclose Edmund Croft's theft of her idea. Should she ask for an appointment about a serious matter too delicate to discuss over the phone, or give the dean a thumbnail sketch of her reason for needing to see him? How close was Arthur Madison to Croft? Croft had been Arthur's master's thesis adviser, Kathryn remembered now. He would have needed a letter of recommendation from him to be considered for admission into MIT. If she revealed the purpose of her call to the dean by telephone, would he forewarn Croft? Now that she knew who she was talking to, she decided it best to be direct with Arthur, trusting he wanted to preserve the integrity of his department and alma mater.

"I was hoping for an appointment to see you in person about a situation that requires your immediate attention," she said.

"What situation? Can you give me a hint over the phone?"

"It has to do with a heart device that I developed while I was working on my doctorate, the one I never received. I have reason to believe the invention was stolen by a former member of Rice's staff who will be granted the patent for it at the end of April."

Arthur responded with a grave silence. After a few breath-held seconds on Kathryn's end, he asked in a neutral voice, "Are we talking about Edmund Croft?"

"I am afraid we are."

"What does your calendar look like?"

"It's clear."

"I can see you the day after tomorrow at my office, the day after tomorrow, at ten o'clock. Will that work?"

"Perfectly."

"I'll need to see some pretty solid evidence that would support your claim. Dr. Croft is a former instructor for Rice, we can't take these accusations lightly."

"Don't worry, I have evidence."

Ending the call, Kathryn realized she was trembling. Perhaps it had been too easy. She still had no idea on whose side Arthur Madison would come down, Edmund Croft's or hers. She would walk into her old classmate's office with all she possessed to hang Croft. Would Arthur have alerted her former adviser, and would he be waiting to confiscate her evidence? After all of this, would she be walking into a trap of her own making?

Goodness, she was beginning to think like Mike, but so she should, Kathryn thought. She had to consider every angle. Arthur, for all his chummy enthusiasm, was holding his cards close to his chest.

Maybe she'd better bring someone with her to serve as a witness. Sandy came to mind, but, ever the fiery advocate in defense of her friends, she'd stroll in with a knife in her purse, metaphorically or even literally. With an instinct that had driven Frank crazy, Sandy would be sure to take charge of her proceedings with the dean as if she were Kathryn's lawyer come to represent her.

Lawyer . . . Should she give theirs a call? No—she didn't want to think of the bill on their tight budget, and it was unlikely she'd be free on such short notice.

Mike would accompany her in a heartbeat, but what would

Arthur Madison make of her walking into his office accompanied by a man who was neither her husband nor her lawyer?

That left Drew. He was the most logical and uncomplicated choice. They could meet at the airport, and Drew could bring her a change of clothes and the box of evidence against Croft. It would be natural and to her advantage to have her husband, an eminent physician, by her side.

Mind made up, Kathryn booked two tickets to Houston and dialed Drew's office number, since it was lunchtime.

To her relief, he answered immediately. "Kathryn!" he said, his voice tight, wary, full of concern.

"The dean of Rice's engineering school has agreed to see me this Thursday at ten o'clock, Drew, and I want you with me when we meet," she began in the voice of someone who would accept no argument. "I need you to serve as a witness and to help me safekeep the evidence I bring to the meeting. The dean turns out to be an old classmate, but he was also a favorite of Croft's. I don't know what's about to happen, and I want to be prepared for anything. If Dr. Madison tries to push this whole thing under the rug, and my proof of fraud with it, I'll need your help. So even though you're busy this week, you'll just have to arrange your obligations to be with me on Thursday. I've made flight reservations for us tomorrow. We're booked on United Airlines for a nonstop flight to Houston leaving at eleven. Can I trust you to make it?"

She was speaking hurriedly, but after a brief pause Drew said, "Of course you can trust me to make it! To hell with my obligations and with Hensley. I'll have to move some irons around in the fire, of course, but I can do it. What time and where do you want me to pick you up?"

"I—I'll meet you at the airport," she stammered. She wanted to keep Mike McCoy and his ranch out of this. "That will be much easier for both of us and give you more time to arrange those irons in the fire. Please bring me my dissertation and evidence box and some clothes to wear. I'll send you a text describing the clothes I need."

"I'm happy that you want me along. I can't pick you up where you are?"

"The airport is easiest. I'll make reservations for us at the Holiday Inn Express nearest the airport," Kathryn added, "and we can rent a car."

"And so you know, I was able to get the locksmith out Thursday, so the house will be ready for your safe return. I'll ask Jim to make sure he does the job correctly."

"Good."

"It will be good to have you home, Kath. See you tomorrow at the airport. Let's get there in time to have breakfast together. Nine thirty?"

"For that life-changing discussion?" she couldn't resist asking.

"Not the place or time. Like you said, it will have to wait. And Kath?" Drew interjected quickly before she could break the connection. "I . . . want this to work out for you . . . if you want to try again for your doctorate. I just want you to know I support you on that."

For after the divorce? So that she would have a job to fall back on as a consolation prize for her failed marriage? "Thank you for your blessing, Drew," she said on a formal note, and hung up before sorrow closed her throat.

Chapter Forty-Four

The landline rang in the ranch house as Kathryn was packing the last of her things for the airport. She would not be coming back to the MM Ranch if all worked out in Houston. As long as Rice took immediate action against Croft, she could go home without fear. Her heart swelled with hope that the crisis would be over. A few moments later, she heard a knuckle tap on her door. "Soup's on!" Lonnie called out.

"Be there in a second!" she called back as Lonnie moved on down the hall, Kirby padding after him.

"Mike just called to say he was tied up out with the cattle and won't be joining us until suppertime," Lonnie explained over steaming bowls of beef vegetable soup and fresh salads from the garden. Kathryn had worried things might be awkward between them after their conversation about Beth, but Lonnie was happy to just discuss dinner. "Feel free to serve whatever you can find in freezer and pantry," he said. "Surprise us."

Companionably, they washed up the lunch dishes together, Kirby standing by for handouts, and eventually Lonnie headed out back to repair tack with instructions to "holler if you need me, and I mean that literally."

Kathryn found herself reluctant to inform Lonnie and Mike

that she wouldn't be returning after tonight, now that things were being resolved. It felt like admitting to a misdeed. Mike would be disappointed to hear that Drew was accompanying her to Houston.

Kirby chose to keep her company while she planned dinner—rainbow trout, fished from a freshwater tributary on MM land, and vegetables from this season's harvest, which made her wonder what Mike had been doing shopping in City Market with all the bounty from ranch and farm available. Kirby eventually lay down for a nap, now and then popping an eye open to watch her movements, and at one point, prompted by a sudden doleful feeling, she stopped in her preparations to give his head a pat. "I am going to miss you, Kirby," she said.

When she had all in order, she poured two cups of coffee and, Kirby pattering after her, brought one to Lonnie and took a seat beside him on the porch. All was quiet and peaceful, the sun bright, the skies a cloudless blue. The calm before the storm.

Beside Lonnie's chair was a box filled with an assortment of leather tack items in need of repairing, a glovers needle between his fingers. "Hand-sewing leather gives a fellow appreciation of the huge amount of work that goes into the average piece of horse gear," he mused.

"I would imagine so," Kathryn said, wondering at all this man was capable of. She would miss him, too. How could she feel so much loss at the idea of leaving a place where, by her calculations, she'd spent less than forty-eight hours, and with two men and a dog she barely knew? She'd always considered herself a girl who preferred city noise and traffic, accessibility to shopping, theaters, restaurants—indicators of people living! After all these years, she still found Avon dull, despite the hordes of skiers who descended upon the town almost year-round now. Her malaise she'd kept from Drew; what husband wanted to hear of his wife's lukewarm feelings for the locale he'd chosen to live out his career? Were it not for her house that she loved and her daughter's interment here, would she miss Avon at all? But this place . . . She pushed the thought from her mind.

"Not for me to intrude on anybody else's thoughts, but you're doing some mighty heavy thinking over there, miss," Lonnie commented.

Kathryn chuckled. "I was just thinking how peaceful it is here and . . . how surprised I am to find it so agreeable to me. I've always thought of myself as a city girl."

"Circumstances change our perception of ourselves," he said, patiently drawing the needle through the leather.

"I was also thinking that I will miss you all when I am gone."

"Well, now, we'll miss you, too. And Kirby"—the dog had plopped down where he could keep an eye on both of them— "Kirby hates goodbyes. He gets enough of that when Mike leaves on a mission."

"He does that often?" Kathryn asked.

"Too often, for Kirby and me."

"But I thought he was retired."

"He is, but now he works as an independent contractor. He's gone for months at a time." The job finished, Lonnie snipped off the thread, dropped it into the box, and retrieved another bridle. His tone was grim when he spoke. "One of these days he won't make it back."

Kathryn's heart pitched. "Why not?"

"Let's just say, his assignments aren't always in the safest locations. He'd quit, settle down, if he could meet the right woman."

Kathryn did not instantly reply. Good Lord. Had Mike told him about her pending divorce? "Well, then," she said for something to say. "Let's hope the right woman comes along."

Lonnie's eyes stayed glued to his task, hands patiently pulling the thread through the leather, but Kathryn could read his unspoken thoughts: *She already has.*

Kathryn had no idea how she felt about that.

Chapter Forty-Five

That evening, Kathryn was on her second glass of wine when she casually mentioned that she'd booked a flight to Houston at eleven the next day, so she would be leaving for the airport at nine.

"So you were able to get everything lined up with the people you need to see that quickly," Mike said, sounding pleased. "Good for you."

"It was easier than I thought. As it turns out, the dean of the department of engineering and I shared a class together, and he remembers me—with affection, if I didn't misread him. He agreed to see me right on the spot when I explained the purpose of our meeting and the person it involves."

"Where will you be staying?" Mike asked.

"At the Holiday Inn Express near the airport."

"Then we can expect you to be back with us until this bad business is behind you end of April, right?" Lonnie said.

Kathryn shifted position in her chair. "No, if my business is successfully concluded in Houston, and I expect it will be, I won't have to impose on you further. I'll drive home from the airport Friday and should be safe enough in my own home. My husband has arranged for the locks and security code to be changed Thursday.

Our children arrive Saturday for a few days of their spring break, so it's essential that I get home."

"So this is your last night with us?" Lonnie's rueful laugh seemed to cover a deeper regret. "Damn, we'll miss your cooking," he joked.

"I don't like the idea of your going alone," Mike said. "What if things don't go as you hope, and Croft remains an active threat?"

Kathryn swallowed. "I . . . won't be alone," she said. "My husband is going with me. He'll meet me at the airport tomorrow."

A heavy silence fell, chilled by disapproval from both men. Mike studied her over his glass of scotch and water, his expression grave. She could guess at his thoughts. *Stubborn, stubborn woman.* After a moment he said, "I'm sure you've thought this through."

"I have, Mike. It's the most practical decision. Drew will bring the proof I will need to dethrone Edmund Croft." Kathryn attempted a smile. "Seriously, Mike, I believe your fears for my safety in the company of my husband are unfounded."

"If your decision is made, it's made," Mike said, getting up abruptly to go to the bar for a refill. "But in case we haven't made the invitation clear," he added, splashing water into his scotch, "if your expectations don't work out in your favor, you are welcome to return here if you feel the need."

"Amen to that," Lonnie said, raising his glass.

Chapter Forty-Six

Wednesday, April 14

The next morning, before sunup, Tessie Kittredge watched Drew drive out of his garage from her wide living room window.

"Jim!" she called loudly into the kitchen. "Come here!"

Jim reluctantly got up from his morning paper and coffee. "What is it this time, Tess?"

Tessie nodded out the window. "Drew is not wearing scrubs."

Jim peered across the street. "No, he's not. What of it?"

"Well, where is he going this early, dressed like that?" While the garage door was creaking down, Drew had gotten out to retrieve the morning newspaper, dressed in a sport coat and slacks, loafers, and an open-necked shirt. "Something is definitely going on over there," Tessie pronounced. "Where has Kathryn been since last Thursday? She's been gone nearly a week."

"To see the kids, maybe? She sees little enough of Drew, with his backbreaking schedule."

"For almost a week, with no sign of her coming home? And after that health scare she had? She's never been away from Drew that long. She's never left Drew, period. And then there's Rosalie Deemer disappearing in the middle of the night. I went by to see

Rosalie yesterday because I hadn't heard from her, and a neighbor told me Rosalie had just up and left without saying a word to anybody, but that she'd seemed frightened of something. And get this: the morning after Rosalie took off, guess who drove up and talked to the same neighbor, and he mentioned that even she looked frightened."

"First you tell me to 'get this,' then you tell me to 'guess who.' Which is it, Tess? And what *she* are you referring to?"

"The *get this* and the *guess who* and the *she* was Kathryn Walker, and nobody has seen her since. I have a feeling Drew is going on a trip. Otherwise, why would he ask you to meet the locksmith tomorrow to change out the locks?"

Jim scratched his head. "Want me to run over and ask Drew where he's going before he gets back in his car?"

"Would you, hon? I need to know if he's going out of town. Hurry now."

But he was too late. Drew saw Jim coming and hopped back in his car, waving to him and pointing to his wristwatch to indicate he was out of time for a chat as he accelerated rapidly away.

"Missed him," Jim reported breathlessly to Tessie.

"I'm going to call Frank Danton. He'll know," his wife announced, putting down her knitting to make the call. "With all the mysterious goings-on over there, I need to know if Drew has left town so I can keep an eye on the place."

Drew was convinced that Croft was long gone from Avon. He'd kept a lookout for an unfamiliar vehicle on his tail, a strange face behind the wheel, and identified none. Also, since the man had a key to the house until the locksmith came, he would have had free rein to search the place from top to bottom while Drew was at the hospital and during the two nights he'd stayed over at Elizabeth's. Drew had been able to find no evidence of a disturbance.

As Drew headed to the airport, determined to arrive in time to be seated before Kathryn made her appearance, he kept wondering about her mysterious friend, and where she might be staying. He had to admit that he might never know. She might refuse to tell him after his confessions.

But this short trip to Houston did not offer the time or place to lay bare to Kathryn all the secrets he'd been keeping from her. He had to concentrate his energies on helping her, and nothing else; his support was the least he owed her now.

Chapter Forty-Seven

Kirby followed Mike and Kathryn out to her car, whining. Experience had taught the collie the significance of a traveling bag, and he looked up from one to the other as if to ask which one of them was leaving. Kathryn reached down and patted his head, and immediately the dog dropped belly down to the ground, head on paws, eyes sorrowful.

"He knows you are leaving and doesn't want you to go," Mike said as he opened her car door.

"He's a hard fellow to say goodbye to," Kathryn said.

"You can always come back here," Mike said for the third time. "You will let us know the outcome, won't you?"

"You can depend on it," Kathryn promised, and turned to wave goodbye to Lonnie. Hands in his jeans pockets, the foreman responded with a grim-faced nod. It was time for Kathryn to be on her way, but she hesitated as she started the motor and Mike closed the door. The window was down, his hand on the frame. She pressed hers over it. "Don't go get yourself killed, Mike. You've earned the right to the rest of your future, and I can't imagine a better place to spend it than here on this peaceful ranch, where Lonnie and Kirby need you."

She removed her hand, hopeful that he heard no implication, no promise in her simply expressed desire that he take care of himself. He acknowledged her statement with a short salute. "I'll keep that in mind," he said.

Joining Lonnie on the porch, the men watched the Cadillac drive away. "You're just going to stand by and let her go off to Houston alone with her husband, boss?" his foreman asked.

"Not a chance," Mike said. "I've booked a two o'clock flight to Houston."

Kathryn drove into the airport's parking facility and saw Drew's car already there. The familiar car and the anticipation of seeing her husband again after what seemed like months set her heart to thumping. She willed it to calm.

Drew had watched her approach through the window of the small café, and he rose from their table to wave at her when she entered. He cut a dapper figure in his blazer and dress slacks, but she was shocked at and moved by the pronounced creases in his thinner face. Her first impulse was to smooth her fingers over those worry lines, but she reminded herself that it was no longer her hand he wished to soothe his brow. He hurried to meet her at the door and pulled her into a tight embrace. "Kathryn, honey, it's so good to see you," he said in a voice throaty with emotion.

"You too," Kathryn said, feeling melancholy. She could see the consequences playing before her like a movie. The children would never forgive him if he left her for another woman. He might have happy moments with Elizabeth at first, but she could picture her husband sad and alone in the end. The sorrow of those images made her hug him even tighter.

"Thanks for letting me tag along," he said, still holding her.

"Thanks for agreeing to it," she answered. He released her after a final short squeeze that manifested again how pleased he was to see her, and Kathryn felt the flicker of her hope billow. "Let's sit down," she said.

They took a booth. Kathryn had worried that she wasn't sure how to speak with her husband anymore, but thankfully they fell into a rhythm, like two old friends.

Chapter Forty-Eight

After seeing Kathryn off, Mike began immediately to pack a bag.
"You'll see that Kathryn's all right, boss?" Lonnie said.

"She'll never be out of my sight."

"I have a feeling this operation ain't going to go as smooth as she'd like to think."

"They never do," Mike said.

The man who caught the two o'clock flight to Houston looked nothing like the well-to-do local rancher who was a familiar face around town.

Drew and Kathryn spoke little on the plane, having run out of topics safe to discuss over breakfast after their warm reception of each other. "What will you do if Arthur Madison isn't sympathetic?" Drew had wanted to know.

"If Arthur doesn't believe my evidence, or wants to avoid a scandal, I'm planning to make a deal: give me the doctorate that's my due, and I won't expose Croft. If he doesn't agree, I'll threaten to go to the press with my evidence."

"You'd do that?" Drew asked, eyebrows raised.

"No, but Arthur won't know it's a bluff. I've had enough, and I've done all I can do. But I can't help but believe that when Arthur hears the whole story I have to tell about our former graduate adviser, he'll do right by me."

They had limited their conversation to Drew's dissatisfaction with his work, memories evoked by the beat-up old briefcase he had bought secondhand as a medical student, packed now with Kathryn's research work, and their plans to occupy the children when they were home for spring break.

"They're worried about you, Kath," Drew said.

"By the time we're home, this nightmare of their mother's will be over, and we can tell them all about it. Then at least those worries will be off their minds."

Drew's eyes had narrowed slightly. "*Those* worries? What other worries?"

Kathryn guessed he was wondering if she knew about him and Elizabeth. "Aren't there always other worries, Drew?" she hedged, sipping her coffee. Subjects for conversation exhausted, she kept her nose stuck in *Horizons*, the United Airlines magazine, while Drew stared out the window, the space between them filled with unspoken issues as palpable as the presence of another passenger.

"I thought it would be nice to invite Sandy to join us for dinner," Kathryn said to Drew after they'd checked into the Holiday Inn Express. "It's been so long since we've seen her, and I'd love to catch up. I could ask her to meet us at Pappadeaux Seafood Kitchen. I'm hungry for creole food. Aren't you?" The long-established restaurant had been their favorite place to splurge on special occasions.

"Sure. Why not?" Drew said, but Kathryn could tell he was disappointed by the suggestion. "But promise me you won't discuss the meeting with Madison. Let's just tell Sandy that I'm here for a few days at the behest of Houston Memorial to discuss a case. No need to bring her in on all this yet."

"I agree," Kathryn said. "Good thinking." She smiled at him.

He smiled back and tenderly tucked her hair behind her ear. "Then let's go down to the bar and drink on it," he said.

They had just been seated at a table in the lobby with their drinks when another hotel guest strolled in. The man headed toward the registration desk, having checked the couple out to his satisfaction in his peripheral vision. "Your name, sir?" the reservation clerk asked.

"Michael McCoy," he said.

Chapter Forty-Nine

That evening, Mike followed the couple to Pappadeaux Seafood Kitchen, where they met another guest. Mike worried that Kathryn would notice him, wary that she might notice another man in her vision too often to be a coincidence, but her attention was on her chatty friend, and the restaurant was a well-known eatery for out-of-town visitors. He chose a table where he could see the doctor across the table from her. He was adept at seeing beyond the surface of a man, and his observations of the husband answered a number of questions. By the time he'd finished his seafood platter, he'd made up his mind about Dr. Drew Walker.

Before leaving the ranch, Mike had received a call from his case officer at the CIA, asking if he was ready to take on another assignment "tailor-made" for his expertise and experience.

"Where?" he'd asked.

"Pakistan. A black bag. I can't say more about it over the phone. Grab a plane and meet me Monday the nineteenth at Langley?"

Mike had hesitated. A black bag assignment was another name for illegal acts ordered by officials from the highest rungs of authority. They were highly dangerous missions, usually undercover and among enemies.

"I'm thinking of retiring, Sam. For real, this time. I've got a ranch to run." In the silence from Sam that followed, Mike could picture his case officer's pink face seizing in shock.

"Retiring?" Sam echoed. "You?"

"It has to happen sometime."

"You'd go nuts too long out of the field."

"Not if I have something to live for."

Sam said grudgingly, "Don't tell me there's a woman involved."

"Could be. In any event, I am tied up with other critical matters right now. I'll have to get back to you."

"I'll need to know by Friday at the latest. This mission can't wait."

"By Friday at the latest," Mike had promised.

That telephone conversation occurred shortly after Kathryn drove away from the ranch, just before one of his men reported seeing a black Mercedes outside the gates earlier that morning. Sitting across from the Walkers now in the creole restaurant, working through his glass of scotch, Mike decided on his answer to Sam. He would call him tomorrow.

Once the Walkers were safely in their hotel room, Mike went on a reconnaissance mission. One destination was the university building housing the office of the dean of bioengineering, and the other was the residence of Edmund Croft. He intended to follow the Walkers to their meeting in the morning, but he could lose sight of them in the heavy Houston traffic, so it was necessary to know where they were going. His other objective was to get a good look at the man who'd made Kathryn Walker's April a living hell. Kathryn's composite drawing of him wasn't enough, and his disguise at the Brown Palace had prevented Mike from getting a good physical read of him. Every instinct in him warned that Croft wasn't through with Kathryn Walker yet.

It was ten o'clock. Locating the dean's building was secondary to getting a visual of Croft. The former professor lived in an apartment complex close to the campus. The sober appearance of the place and a sign announcing that the wrought-iron gate would automatically be locked at 11:00 p.m. would not have appealed to students, but he suspected there were several other university staff living there. A carport was attached to each unit, the open invitation to petty theft or worse that Mike had been counting on. Lights were on in several rooms of the former professor's apartment. Mike parked the rented Lincoln Aviator on the street and walked through the wrought-iron gate directly to Croft's carport. Croft drove a late-model, square-bodied dark-blue Nissan Cube, the vehicle that had run down Janet Foster, confirmed when Mike checked the shockingly minor damage to the front fender. The arrogant bastard had used his own vehicle as the murder weapon rather than return a damaged car to its rental company, confident that it could not be tracked to him.

After a quick reconnaissance to make sure that no one was around, Mike proceeded to thrust the blade of a specially designed retractable box cutter straight into the rubber of three of the car's tires one inch from the tread's beginning. He pocketed the knife and, while waiting to hear the slow hiss of deflation before ringing the doorbell of the owner's apartment, snapped pictures on his phone of the Nissan's license plate and damaged front bumper.

An eye appeared at the peephole, then the door opened the width of the security chain. "Yes? May I help you?" Croft inquired.

"Excuse the interruption, sir," Mike said, "but I thought you ought to know that I just saw a man running from your carport. I can't help but think he was up to no good. I got part of a license plate number, and I can give you the description of him and his car."

Croft's eyes widened at the information, then narrowed in suspicion. "And who are you?"

"James Crawford. I was just leaving after visiting one of your neighbors."

"I am afraid I can't open my door to just anyone at this time of night. Can you show some form of identification?"

"Don't blame you." Mike took out his wallet to produce a driver's license that showed his picture and confirmed his name as James Crawford. He held it to the crack of the door.

Croft squinted at it. "And the name of my neighbor?"

Mike looked uncomfortable, replacing the card in his wallet. "I'd rather not say. Look, I just thought I'd do the right thing, but I don't want to become involved."

The security chain fell with a clang. "No, wait!" Croft called, standing fully visible to Mike in the room's glow. His trained eye took in every detail of Croft's features. His disguise at the Brown Palace had been an impressive work of deception. Croft stepped out of his apartment and went to investigate his car.

Mike, disguised himself, stood a good distance back to show that he presented no threat. After tonight, Croft would never see the man standing before him as he was now. "Young guy. Ran like he was in his late twenties. Medium height, straight black hair. He drove a gray Honda Civic. Here's the license plate number. Sorry I couldn't get it all." He handed Croft a slip of paper.

Croft took it, frowning. "I don't know of anyone of that description."

"Well, maybe it was nothing, but he came from your carport. Just thought you'd want to know. Good night."

"Uh, well, yes, indeed. Thank you for taking the trouble, Mr. . . . uh, Crawford."

"No problem," Mike said.

"I think I'll just go take a look," Croft said, closing the door quickly behind him before Mike could get too far away. It was obvious that he did not wish to be without assistance should he need it. "Mind hanging around just a bit?"

"Not at all," Mike said.

"Oh, my God!" Croft exclaimed when he saw the damage to his tires, Mike holding a distance back. "I know exactly the little shit who did this. He's an intern at the medical lab where I work. How could I not have recalled him from your description? I threatened to have him dismissed last week."

"Seems to me that he'd be too smart for this kind of vandalism, since he'd be the first suspected," Mike said in defense of the hapless intern.

"He's not the brightest bulb on the Christmas tree, one of the reasons I threated to fire him. It could only be him." Croft's face was red with fury. "If he drives a Honda Civic, and the partial of this license plate matches it, his ass is grass."

"He not only slashed your tires, he put a dent in your fender."

"Oh, that's old. Hit one of those guard poles at a drive-through—they make those spaces so dang tight."

"Seems like a simple thing to get fixed."

"I know," Croft said, looking sheepish. "I've been distracted, and money has been short as of late, but hopefully that will change soon."

Mike hoped the kid had a good alibi. "I'm sorry, but I have to be somewhere," he said, stepping away. "Sorry about your trouble."

"You're going to unit twenty-three, am I right?" Croft said suddenly, a knowing glint in his eye. "Watch out for her. She has men friends coming and going all the time. She came on to me right after I moved in. I wouldn't have any part of her. You shouldn't either."

"Thanks for the advice," Mike said and walked away.

Chapter Fifty

Mike hoped Croft didn't ask the woman in apartment 23 about the man he suspected had called on her earlier. Not that it mattered—Croft would never recognize him again if he stepped on his foot—but a check on James Crawford with the woman might raise his suspicions about the person who had reported the vandalism. Mike thought the risk negligible, though, and he'd accomplished his two goals. He'd gotten a good look at Edmund Croft, and he'd temporarily crippled his mode of transportation, which would require hours to repair. If Croft had gotten wind of Kathryn's appointment the next day, it would take precise dovetailing to intercept her. Taxi or hired car would be clumsy and unreliable, and could be traced back to him.

Mike was gambling that by the time Croft's Nissan was up and running again, the dean would have heard Kathryn's case, and it would be all over for the boy, with more trouble to come. Before steering the Aviator toward the Holiday Inn Express, where he had a room booked a couple of doors down from the Walkers, he put in a call to the chief of police in Avon.

✳

His fury growing, Edmund Croft slammed back into his apartment and consulted a directory listing the names and contact numbers of the permanent personnel at MediCorp. The names of all the temporary underlings, of which Jonathan Delaney was one, were on file at the office. But, precise man that he was, Croft liked to have contact information for everyone he worked with, even the lowest, like Delaney, on hand at his apartment in case a need arose, like tonight. He hoped he'd bothered to make a note of Jonathan Delaney's. Sure enough, to his relief there was the little bastard responsible for tonight's vindictive destruction to his tires. He dialed the number.

A voice answered amid a blare of hard rock music and loud party noises. "Yeah?" came the inquiry, slightly slurred.

"Is this Jonathan Delaney?"

"Who wants to know?"

"Dr. Edmund Croft."

There was a second's shocked silence. "Oh, yes, sir!" The voice snapped to attention. Croft got the impression that Delaney was moving to another room. The background din grew fainter. "What can I do for you, Dr. Croft?"

Croft felt the sway of a few seconds' confusion. "Sounds like you have a party going on there," he said, grasping for a reason for the call.

"Uh . . . yes, sir. Just a few of my pals and their girlfriends thought we'd get together."

"Then you've been there all night?"

"Yes, sir. I'm the host. I mean, sort of. Everybody brings something. Do you . . . need me for something?"

"I must say I'm relieved," Croft improvised, gathering his wits. "I heard on the news that the car of a young man fitting your description was struck by a hit-and-run driver tonight. I . . . was just checking to make sure it wasn't you. The victim . . . was driving a gray Honda Civic. He is yet to be identified."

Jonathan's voice brightened. "Well, sir, I'm glad to report it wasn't me. I drive a Bug—that is, a Volkswagen—but it sure was good of you to check on me. Frankly, I'm . . . surprised, sir, and feel honored."

Honored. This kid was a menace. "Have a good night, then," Croft said, and hung up. He realized he was sweating, yet he felt in the grip of a chill. He believed the imbecile. He couldn't have stolen away from his party and returned in the short time the stranger had reported seeing him run from his carport. If it wasn't Delaney who had put a knife to his tires, then who the hell was it, and for what reason? Who hated him enough to do such a vicious thing? And what might be next?

Maybe the vandal had gotten the wrong carport. That was a possibility, wasn't it?

And then, like the sudden flash of a floodlight, he knew. *Kathryn Walker.* She would hate him enough to hire somebody to deflate his car tires, as he had her Cadillac's in the garage of the Brown Palace. He thought he'd destroyed the cameras at the parking structure. Cursing, he realized he must have missed one, and now Kathryn knew. An eye for an eye. There was a world of meaning in the act. A statement. Three tires, not four. In the same way, the punctures had gone through the rubber to the inner tubes, to make sure his car was totally disabled. He scanned the area, just in case she was still there, watching.

His stomach beginning to churn, Croft sat down thoughtfully. This swing in events required some clear analytical deductions. Why would Kathryn incapacitate his car? That is, if she or her husband was behind this. Suddenly the image of James Crawford flashed in his mind. Was his the hand that had inflicted the damage? Croft had never seen him before. He threaded his fingers through his still-abundant hair to rub his head. How much did she know? Had he left any tracks behind?

Finally, he got up and poured himself a stiff drink for courage. He loathed having to resort to this, but he'd telephone the widow in apartment 23 to check on James Crawford.

"*Ed!*" Valerie Hanson of unit 23 with the glaringly red lipstick and dyed black hair sang out before Croft could identify himself, alerted by the ID screen. Croft winced. From first introductions at the apartment complex's mailbox, she had taken such a liberty with his name. He had *never* been known as Ed. "To what do I owe the pleasure of hearing from you at this time of night?"

"Another time, Valerie," Croft replied. "I am inquiring if you know a fellow by the name of James Crawford."

"Can't say as I do. Name doesn't set any bells to ringing. Why are you asking?"

"You, er, didn't have him as a visitor tonight?"

Valerie's tone sharpened. "I've been alone all evening. What's going on?"

Croft decided to tell her the truth, with the small insertion of a lie. "Somebody slashed my tires tonight, Valerie, and a conservatively dressed man—walked with a slight limp, nothing suspicious about him—rang my doorbell to report that he saw someone running from my carport. He stayed with me when I went to check and made the awful discovery. He told me his name was James Crawford, and that he'd been visiting you."

"Well, that's a damn lie!" Valerie said hotly. "I don't know any James Crawford, and there's been no one here tonight."

"That's why I'm checking with you," Croft said in his most placating tone. "I had begun to have my suspicions. Thank you, Valerie. I will call the police."

"You want me to stay with you until they come—to verify that I don't know a James Crawford?"

"Thank you, but that won't be necessary. Sorry to have disturbed you. Good night."

"But—" Valerie started to say, but Croft had broken the connection.

Croft poured another gin, nerves shaken. He would not call the police. He hardly needed them examining his car. To calm himself, he recalled that James Crawford had neither denied nor confirmed that he'd been with Valerie. He could have been visiting another neighbor, but Croft wasn't about to call each one to check. Now he was convinced that the vandal was a university student, out to state his grievance against a professor who had wounded him in some way, and had mistakenly slashed the tires of the wrong occupant. There was no other explanation for it.

Chapter Fifty-One

Kathryn and Drew arrived back at the hotel late and prepared for bed in almost total silence, drained by their reunion with Sandy Danton, whose chatter had flowed nonstop.

"My ears are throbbing. How about yours?" Drew had asked as he swiped their key card into the door slot of their room.

"What did you say?" Kathryn had joked, cupping a hand around her ear.

Now she crawled into bed first, on the side she occupied at home, and had settled with a novel when Drew came out of the bathroom. "Good book?" he asked, getting in on the other side.

She had not read a page. "I'm not really into it yet," she said. The space between them on the king-size bed lay like a no-man's-land that each appeared careful not to invade.

Drew arranged his pillows to prop himself up against the headboard. Kathryn had thought he would turn out the light. They both needed sleep. He looked dead tired, drained, and she needed her wits about her tomorrow. But with his long arm he reached across the gulf between them and took her book away, set it on his bedside table, and folded his hand around hers. The familiar warmth of his flesh shot up her arm like an arrow straight to her heart. She fought back tears.

"You weren't reading," he pronounced.

"No."

"Want to tell me what's happening? Something has created a distance between us, Kath, and it isn't just that I was a louse in not trusting your judgment. You're not one to hold a grudge, even against your husband for not being there when you needed him. So what is it? Is there anything you wish to share?"

Is there anything you wish to share? The question annoyed her. *How about you going first?* she wanted to hurl back at him. There was no use denying his charge—the fissure between them was as plain as a crevice in a dry creek bed—but how like Drew, to ask her to explain herself when the situation was his to confess. His intent was clear. He wanted to draw out how much she knew of his backstairs activities.

"I'd think the reason for my preoccupation was clear, so no," she said. "Is there anything you want to share that would explain *your* preoccupation lately?"

He sighed. "I know I haven't been as present as I should be." His grip on her hand tightened. "Please trust me on that. I just have a few things to work out, and then . . ."

"And then what?"

"Our lives may be different . . . from the way we've lived them. I think it will be a good idea for you to work on your doctorate." Drew squeezed her hand again. "Give me until the end of April to work through some things. I have to do this on my own, as I know you'll understand. I just ask you to be patient until then, and trust me."

She removed her hand. "Yes, I understand doing things by yourself," she said, and turned over to switch off the light.

Chapter Fifty-Two

Thursday, April 15

Kathryn had stopped by a mall earlier and picked up a black suit, a hot-pink blouse, and black pumps. In their hotel room Drew had surprised her with the string of pearls and matching earrings he'd presented to her on their fifteenth wedding anniversary. "The salesgirl told me that crystal is the symbol for the fifteenth year of marriage, but I thought crystal beads might break, and these will last forever," he'd said when he fastened the strand proudly around her neck. "She told me that pearls are the traditional symbol for thirty years of marriage," he'd added, nibbling her ear, "so now I've got that anniversary covered."

Kathryn wondered if she'd ever wear them again after today. As she removed them from the velvet jewelry bag, Drew said, "Here, let me," and took them from her hand to drape them around her neck. The strand fastened, she refrained from touching them. Her pride would not allow her to ask if he remembered the day he gave them to her. She would strike no chords that created more second thoughts in his mind about ending their marriage. And did she want him to remain with her, if his heart still yearned for Elizabeth? If the woman shared space with her in his memories? No,

Kathryn decided with a sudden clarity as bright as the Houston sun streaming through the window. She would not live with a man of a divided heart.

The cold realization struck the breath from her, as if she'd been punched in the stomach.

"Kathryn?" Drew said, his voice concerned. "Listen," he ordered, turning her to face him from the mirror, where she'd been staring at him in this new light. "It will be all right. I will be right beside you to verify every word you say. If nothing comes from this, at least Edmund Croft will be put on notice that if anything happens to you, he'll be the first the police will grab. Motive, opportunity, means, and witnesses—all there. He'd be a fool to try anything now. So you are safe."

At her blank look, Drew tried again. "Look, honey," he said, "no matter what happens, take satisfaction that you've done your best to discredit a scoundrel and prove you deserved that doctorate back in '89. You know, in high school, when we were going for the state championship, one of the players asked the coach, 'Sir, are we going to win this game?' A dumb question to ask in the locker room just before we hauled our asses out to the field for the toughest game we'd ever played, but the coach looked at him and said, "Son, if you give it your best, give it all you've got, then no matter the score, you have won the game.' " He studied her face with a hopeful smile. "Now, let's go get 'em and win this game. What do you say?"

Kathryn reached for her jacket. "I'm hungry. I need something in my stomach before we leave," was all she said.

They had a quick breakfast in the hotel dining room, Kathryn careful not to smear her lipstick. Only a few tables were occupied that early, one by the man who had passed them in the corridor last night, going to his room a few doors down from theirs. Kathryn had noticed he walked with a slight limp.

With Drew carrying the satchel containing Kathryn's body of evidence against Edmund Croft, they arrived at the dean's office ten minutes early. As soon as they introduced themselves, the secretary smiled. "You can go right in. Dr. Madison is waiting for you."

Arthur Madison rose immediately from his desk in the library-paneled room, showing every one of his straight white teeth. Kathryn remembered his engaging smile. "Kathryn, it is a pleasure to see you again."

"It is so good to see you again. God, it's been years," Kathryn said with a smile.

He gave Kathryn a hug. This was not the welcome she'd expected of a distinguished dean, but then there were no pretensions about Arthur.

The dean stood back to look at her. "I'm not lying when I say you have hardly changed, Kathryn Turner." He held out his hand to Drew. "Nor have you, Dr. Walker."

"We went to different universities. I didn't expect you to remember me?"

"I saw you often enough at Rice, visiting Kathryn," Arthur said, with a laugh, and indicated they take seats.

So Arthur had kept an eye on her at their old alma mater. It was a good beginning, and Edmund Croft was nowhere to be seen.

"Okay, Kathryn Turner Walker, what do you have for me?" Arthur Madison said.

Kathryn unsnapped the satchel.

Having forgotten to set his alarm, Edmund Croft awoke later than intended. He shot up out of bed to the agony of a pounding headache and a nauseous stomach, all as a result of only two gin and tonics—or was it three? He ground his temples with the palms of his hands. *What a time to be hungover*, he chastised himself. He was always prompt—none of this "fashionably late" business for him—and he had two hours for a couple of aspirin to take effect, to shower, shave, dress, make coffee, and get a taxi to the 11:30

luncheon in his honor at MediCorp. It was to be a catered affair, and the whole place would be shut down for it—at least for a couple of hours. Arthur Madison and the president of Rice University were to be in attendance, along with other eminent scientists from around the state, as well as the company's CEO and financial officer. Croft had to look his sharpest.

The taxi arrived and deposited him with a few minutes to spare, to his relief, and he managed to greet the crowd that applauded his entrance with a smile and deep bow without feeling as if his head were about to bop off. The CEO, dollar signs in his eyes, was the first to offer his hand. "Blessed be the day you came to us," he said.

"Blessed be the day you *stole* him from Rice, you mean," said the financial officer genially.

Excellent champagne and food were served by a cadre of waiters of the first class. Croft was assigned to the head table, flanked by the CEO on his right. Conspicuously empty was the chair to his left. It was to have been occupied by the president of Rice University, who would introduce him at the National Institutes of Health in Bethesda, Maryland. Croft learned that he had sent his apologies, but without explanation. Disappointingly absent also was the university's dean of engineering.

As his colleagues began to filter back to their workstations at the end of the lunch and the caterers restored the room to normal, he received a telephone call from his old secretary, now Dr. Arthur Madison's. Would Dr. Croft be able to meet with the dean at his office this afternoon? Well, yes, he could be there within the hour, Croft assured her. Clearly the dean and president, unable to attend the luncheon, were making it up to him by having a private ceremony of their own to offer congratulations, no slight intended at all.

Chapter Fifty-Three

Dr. Croft has arrived," the secretary reported to Arthur Madison. "Shall I show him in?"

"Yes, indeed," Arthur Madison said.

Actually, Croft had arrived at the George R. Brown School of Engineering ten minutes earlier to chat a bit with his former secretary. On the pretense of showing interest in her family members, especially her grandchildren, he thought he might get some idea of the lay of the land beyond Madison's closed door. A trace of his unease was back, niggling and annoying, diluting the euphoric mood in which he'd left the luncheon. When she got up from her chair with a big smile at the pleasure of seeing him again and hugged him warmly, he felt confident his reception inside the doors would be the same.

But then he was ushered into Madison's office. There, along with the president of the university, were Kathryn Turner Walker and her husband, seated in overstuffed chairs, staring at him coldly. A quick glance at Madison's desk confirmed his worst fears—there was the old dissertation he'd tried so hard to find and destroy. There was no statute of limitations for criminal cases involving theft of inventions. For the first time in decades, his golden tongue failed him.

"Edmund, good of you to join us," said his former student without rising as he gestured toward an empty chair.

"We thought we might discuss your . . . invention," Madison said. "It appears, from the proof provided by Ms. Walker, that the device we are soon to celebrate was actually developed *by her* when she was a student here. Were there any thoughts on the matter you might like to add?"

Croft pulled at his collar. "No, no. This has to be a mistake."

"I've looked over all the plans. There are no substantive differences."

"N-no," Croft stuttered. "The tube . . . I use a different material than she does."

Madison smiled slightly. "Ah, and would you like to tell us more about the material she describes in these plans?"

Edmund grimaced—of course that had been a trap. They hadn't shown him the plans.

Dr. Walker spoke up. "Dr. Croft, there is no way you could have known about her design."

"This is ridiculous." Croft looked at the president. "You know me."

"That's the thing, Mr. Croft." The president leaned forward, resting his elbows on the table. "It seems to me this is just the sort of thing you might be capable of."

Edmund started to protest, but the president cut him off. "You won't be attending the Bethesda event at the National Institutes of Health. And the director of the NIH's speakers' committee will be informed of the grounds for your withdrawal."

"But, but," Croft sputtered, "I'm the keynote speaker." He turned to Kathryn. "This is all your fault. I can't believe you did this to me."

"You tried to murder my wife," Drew began, eyes shooting daggers, but Kathryn put a hand on his arm and gave him a little shake of her head. Throughout the entire thrashing, Croft had stolidly taken no notice of the intensity of Kathryn's cold silence, but at her husband's accusation, his tongue sprang into action, and he wheeled around to face Drew.

"That's a damn lie," he disputed hotly. "All of it. Ridiculous allegations to besmirch my reputation." Croft glared at Kathryn. "I would think before you accuse me, you should look to your own affairs." He slammed the door behind him as he stormed out.

"Well," Arthur Madison said, with a note of finality. "Now I'd like to talk to you about making things right."

"I'm just happy to have my name associated with this device."

"Well, we were thinking more than that," Arthur began. "With your name being associated with the patent, you will get all of the profits."

"Dr. Croft already filed for the patent," Kathryn reminded them.

Arthur shook his head. "The university is prepared to dispute that, and I think, with all this evidence, we would win."

"Even so, I'm not sure those rights truly belong to me."

"Kathryn," Drew hissed, "what are you doing? We need this money."

"Jonas Salk didn't profit from the polio vaccine because he wanted to maximize the vaccine's ability to get out into the world. We can save more lives this way."

"As honorable as that is, we live in a different time," Arthur said. "Someone else like Edmund will come in and file the patent, and all your honorable ideas will go out the window."

"What if you file the patent but set up a foundation for those who need it?" the president said. "Mrs. Walker, you deserve to have some financial compensation, even if it is a small amount."

"Honestly"—Kathryn turned to him—"what I really want is my doctorate."

The president and Arthur exchanged a look. "Why don't we check the university records to see where you left off in the program," Arthur said. "Between your heart pump and the work you have already done for your degree, I am sure we can work something out."

✳

The image Croft had worked a lifetime for was stripped from him in a little over an hour. Stepping from the dean's office, he walked past his onetime secretary's desk without a word or glance, leaving the woman staring after him. It would be the last time the former head of the engineering department of Rice University—a favorite son of the university—would set foot on its campus.

Sitting partially hidden by a student's design poster in the reception hall of the building, Mike watched Dr. Croft step from the dean's office. That hangdog look must mean that Kathryn had won her battle. He hoped she would call to report the news before he left for his new assignment on Saturday. Mike folded his newspaper and followed the man out.

Feeling like the victim of a lightning strike, Edmund Croft pushed through the doors of the George R. Brown Building in a daze. He was halfway to the visitors' parking lot before he remembered he had no car. He'd expected the university to have him driven home as a courtesy.

Several realities were clear in the rubble of his despair. He would lose his job at MediCorp. Image was everything to them. *Everything!* The usual duration of a patent was twenty years, but he'd already signed a contract releasing the patent to the company for a lifetime, thinking that in twenty years the device might be extinct.

A wave of nausea overtook him, buckling his arthritic knee, and he would have fallen if a man who'd been walking behind him had not caught his arm. He started to say thank you before his benumbed brain registered that he'd seen the man before.

"Hello, Dr. Croft, remember me?" the man said, his smile, a mere twist of his lips, as sinister as a switchblade.

Edmund blinked. It was the man who'd alerted him of the vandal running from his carport. For a moment, he couldn't remember the name.

"James Crawford." Alarm shot through Edmund. "Wha-what are you doing here?"

"To give you a warning, Dr. Croft. Listen to it carefully. If you ever, by word or deed, try to harm Kathryn Turner Walker or a member of her family in any way, I will kill you. You must trust me on that. You will never see me coming. Do you understand?"

Edmund nodded numbly. His face, already pasty, bleached to the shade of uncooked dough.

Mike saw that he had made his point. The professor's cowardice exuded from him like stench from an armpit. Kathryn Walker and her family were safe. "Good," he said and walked away without any limp at all.

Chapter Fifty-Four

In the rental car on the way back to the hotel, Drew said, "Well, Kath, how do you feel, now that you achieved what you came for?"

"Like I can breathe again. Since this nightmare began, I've been holding my breath, and now I can let it all out, at least over this issue."

"Over *this* issue? Are there any others?"

She could tell he was wondering if she knew about his affair, his debts. She shrugged. "My doctorate is not in the bag."

"You'll do great on the orals."

"I can't count on that. I'm going to have to do a lot of studying, and on top of that, Arthur is going to give me feedback on the paper so that I can update it before my thesis is published. And then I will do my orals. I have a lot of work ahead of me."

"Then why did you insist on doing it so soon?" Drew asked. He forced down his exasperation at her arbitrary time crunch, especially when the kids were going to come home for spring break.

"I want a new beginning for me."

"For us," Drew corrected.

"Right," she said. "For us."

Eyes intent on the road, Drew asked, "Kathryn, why did you

stop me from confronting that bastard? I wanted to see how he'd squirm himself out of that before the dean and the president."

"And give him grounds to sue us for slander? We're rid of him, Drew. He's been exposed for what he is, and we have nothing more to fear from him. Let's let sleeping dogs lie."

Drew glanced at her. There was that terse edge to her voice again, which frightened him. But how could she have learned all that he must confess to her? He changed the subject.

"The kids don't have to be entertained," he said. "They'll understand how important this is to you and support you. So will I."

"But you'll be working next week," Kathryn reminded him.

"Not Monday or Tuesday. I've made arrangements to be off those two days. I've held off telling you until I was sure that Hensley would go for it, but Elizabeth texted me a while ago that everything is all set." Drew glanced at her. "I want to spend time with the kids, but mainly I had an idea that you might want me around for a few days, no matter what."

Surprised, Kathryn wondered if Drew was saying he would stick with her until the worst was over, then be gone.

"That . . . was considerate of you," she said. "I appreciate it."

He reached over and squeezed her hand. "The least I could do."

His cell phone rang. It was lying on the console between them.

"Want me to take it?" Kathryn asked. "It's Jim Kittredge."

"Put it on speaker. He's calling about the locksmith. You talk to him. I've got to concentrate on getting us through this traffic to catch our plane."

The locksmith had come and gone, and Jim would hang on to the keys until they came home.

Kathryn began thinking of all the preparations for the kids at home. There were beds to make, groceries to buy, food to prepare. The cupboards were bare, Drew told her, and the refrigerator, too. He had cleaned them out while she was gone. They would divvy the chores. He would see to the shopping while she prepared the children's rooms.

Chapter Fifty-Five

Saturday, April 17

On Saturday, before the pancake batter was stirred for brunch, the house was already full of laughter. Bobby was thrilled to introduce everyone to his new dog, who swaggered confidently into the house on his short legs, and Lindsay squealed in delight. Drew, never particularly an animal lover, gave the dog's ear a gingerly scratch and asked his name.

"Hannibal," Bobby said.

Lindsay looked horrified. "You'd call this adorable dog *Hannibal,* as in Hannibal Lecter?"

"No, silly, like Hannibal the Great, the Carthaginian general who defeated the largest army Rome ever put together."

"Oh, right," said Lindsay. Given her brother's penchant for ancient history, she should have known.

Brother and sister felt the warmth of their parents' joy at their homecoming. Kathryn and Drew explained the full chronicle of the month's events, all the way to the showdown in Houston. The pancakes devoured over a fresh pot of coffee, the family sat around the breakfast table, and Lindsay's and Bobby's eyes grew rounder as they listened to the story that had begun with "the man with the slanted shoulder" their mother had warned them to watch out for. The only thing they left out was the location where Kathryn had hidden. At the end of the tale, Drew looked at Kathryn proudly and announced that they were to have two doctors in the family.

They had accepted that Kathryn would be brushing up on her orals most of their visit and would see little of them during the day. "Not to worry, Mom," Lindsay said. "You do what you've got to do. We've got this. I'll help Dad cook."

"And I'll clean up," Bobby said.

"And I believe I can take care of unloading the dishwasher," Drew threw in.

Activities were lined up. To Kathryn's surprise, Drew suggested they drag out home movies to watch that night. Sunday, the kids would visit with their surrogate grandmother, Natalie, and on Monday evening Uncle Frank was coming for dinner. Drew would be grilling steak and corn on the cob.

Kathryn was left with no responsibilities but to get on with her studying. That afternoon she could hear the children and Drew in the family room having a grand time playing gin rummy. She surveyed the daunting spread of research notes, data charts, graphs, and the final version of her dissertation on her desk and floor for review, but her mind was locked on Mike McCoy. She was surprised that he had not returned her call, but it was just as well. Like a guardian angel, he had looked after her through the whole trip. He had been the occupant of the hotel room only a couple of doors down from hers and Drew's, and now that she thought about it, she was sure she had glimpsed him at Pappadeaux Seafood Kitchen the night they met Sandy there. And though she had not seen him, she had no doubt that he'd been on the premises during her meeting with Arthur Madison.

She owed him so much. The review of her notes could wait. She picked up her cell and called the MM Ranch. Lonnie answered. "Yeah, sure, come on out," he said. "The gates will be open."

Next, she walked into the family room and said, "Kids, I have to borrow your dad for a while in my office."

✳

Kathryn was not surprised to see Mike's Range Rover in the open garage as she parked in front of the house. She'd presumed that since the ranch was on the way to Avon from the airport, he would not return to the Park Hyatt but would steer for this place of mountain grandeur and meadow tranquility after the racket of the city.

It was Lonnie, accompanied by Kirby leaping in welcome, who greeted her at the door. "Got a fresh pot on. Come on in and have a cup," he invited. "Mike's not here, I'm afraid."

"Oh? Out on the range, is he?" Kathryn said, disappointed, wondering if Mike had his cell on him and could be summoned. It was important that she see him today; she'd have no other opportunity before leaving again for Houston. She followed the foreman into the kitchen. He looked washed-out today, depleted. He shuffled as if some symptom of an old injury had cropped up.

Lonnie made a racket of withdrawing the coffeepot from its burner. "I wish."

Kathryn felt a ripple of unease. She pulled back a chair and sat down. "Good Lord, Lonnie, what is it? Where is he?"

"On a mission. Left this morning before daylight." Lonnie plunked their mugs down before them.

"What kind of mission?"

"One of *those* kinds of missions, only worse. Black bag operation, they're called. Has to do with intelligence gathering." He sat down heavily and blew on his coffee. "He got a call yesterday and was out the door, leaving only a note."

Black bag operation. The term made her skin crawl. "Oh, God, Lonnie, why? I thought he was about to retire from . . . all that."

"He was, but he wanted to clear his head, he said." His lips quivered on the rim of his cup as he drank. After a swallow, he said, "He was there, you know, watching over you, making sure you were okay."

"Yes, I know," she said softly, her scalp tingling.

Lonnie's brow moved upward. "You recognized him?"

"Of course I did." Lonnie lifted a shoulder and didn't meet her eyes. She had the sense that she was somehow responsible for his boss putting himself in harm's way.

"How long will he be gone?"

"Supposed to be in and out by the end of the month. We'll see. He has something on him to take before . . . this happens to him, if he's captured." Lonnie pointed to the scarred side of his face.

Cyanide to avoid torture. Kathryn's mouth went dry. The rich aroma of the coffee suddenly had the smell of burnt ashes. "Will you let me know, Lonnie? I must know."

"I'll call the moment I hear, one way or the other. I'll be right by the phone, Kirby and me. Night and day."

"And so we wait," Kathryn said, in the clutch of a new terror.

"And so we wait."

"Oh, Lonnie . . ." Too agitated to stay seated, eyes glimmering with tears, Kathryn stood abruptly. Lonnie scraped back his chair to meet her at the end of the table. "And you, Lonnie?" she asked. "What about you if . . . he doesn't make it home."

"This is my home for as long as I need it. Mike made sure of that. We got to keep the faith."

"Call me night or day on my cell, any hour," Kathryn said.

"I promise," Lonnie said.

That night the family trooped down to the game room in the basement with bowls of popcorn to watch home movies that had Bobby and Lindsay all but falling out of their chairs with laughter.

"Dad," Lindsay said at the last reel, "you need to get these preserved. Take them to a professional who can digitalize them."

"Yeah," Bobby concurred. "A copy of these would be the perfect Christmas gift for Lindsay and me. Right, sis?"

"Perfect," Lindsay agreed.

Chapter Fifty-Six

As the week progressed, Kathryn attempted to throw all her energy into preparing for her orals. Whatever else the tail end of April would spew out, it would not derail her pursuit of the doctorate. Drew surprised her by offering to go with her to Houston. She shook her head.

"You've taken off enough days from the hospital. You'll have old Hensley spitting bullets if you ask for more time off," she said, assuring him it was for the best that she go alone. She would have her own set of wheels available at the airport, in case he was tied up at the hospital when she got back. Secretly, she preferred to drive herself to the airport, to be spared the effort of making conversation with her disloyal husband. She had already reserved a room at the airport Hilton for two nights and booked a Friday-morning flight for one that would get her into Houston in plenty of time to meet the dissertation committee in the afternoon.

Saturday, before she left for the MM Ranch, Drew had listened to her clarification of her extraordinary association with Mike McCoy without interruption. If he was jealous or had doubt of her fidelity, he showed no signs of it, even when she explained that she must see Mike to thank him personally for all he had done for her. Drew seemed to accept the truth: that she'd had a chance encounter with a man possessing the expertise and resources to save her life, which she had readily received when no one else was available. His motive for offering his assistance was pure and simple. He had hoped to protect a wife and mother from possible death, having been unable to save his own wife and unborn child. Mike McCoy had been like an unknown passerby who pulled her to safety and disappeared in the crowd.

"Sounds like a good man, and I am grateful to him," Drew said when she'd finished. "I hope to meet him someday."

"I hope you'll have that opportunity, too," Kathryn said with fervor.

"How long will you be in Houston?"

"Two nights."

"Why two?" he asked, when she told him of her flight schedule. "I thought you'd be returning Saturday! I'd hoped we could celebrate, pop a bottle of champagne? Why not skip the hotel and stay with Sandy?"

"Sandy would be a distraction," she said, thinking that he'd hardly disguised his concern over the Visa bill. "And I couldn't get a Saturday flight. I'll be back on Sunday. We can pop the cork then."

"What will you do with yourself all day Saturday?" he'd asked.

She smiled to allay the trace of annoyance in his eyes. "Rest, maybe go to a spa." She shrugged. Saturday, she planned to look at apartments.

But try as she might to focus on her upcoming dissertation defense, the dread of her divorce and worry over Mike's fate invaded her brain like a drumbeat.

On Wednesday morning, the children left and Drew returned to work, his face stripped of the jolly mask he'd worn for the family's benefit, sagging under the weight of his inner turmoil. She longed to cry to him, *I know about Elizabeth, Drew. I know you're going to ask me for a divorce. I know you will have to sell the house to settle your debts, inevitable anyway once we part, so get us out of this limbo already.*

Hoping for another opening for him to confess, she couldn't

resist asking when he came home Wednesday evening, "How did your visit to the gym go? After all the family activity, I thought you might be too tired for barbells."

"Endorphins are not called peptides for nothing," he said, evading the question. He planted a kiss on top of her head and left her with a take-out meal that she forced down at her desk while Drew ate his on a tray before the TV. That night they fell into bed exhausted, with barely breath enough to wish each other the courtesy of a good night's sleep.

On Thursday, Drew left their home for the hospital with the same distracted air, but that evening he returned determined to give her all his attention, the last night before she left to take her orals. "Let's make an evening of it and go to Vin48," he said, and handed her a fancy bottle of sauvignon blanc. "From Elizabeth, to wish you luck on your orals," he said. "Awfully thoughtful of her."

"And how does Elizabeth know my preference in wines?" Kathryn asked.

"She asked me your wine of choice at Barbara's birthday party. Remember?"

"I do," Kathryn said. "I'm just surprised that she does."

"If I've learned anything about Elizabeth, it's that she never forgets anything." He watched her slip the bottle into the wine rack. "Aren't you going to open it?" he asked, surprised.

"Let's save it for another occasion," Kathryn said. *Like when I hear that Mike McCoy has made it home safely.* She withdrew a bottle of a cheaper vintage from the refrigerator and poured herself a glass.

"To celebrate your homecoming, doctorate granted," Drew agreed. "More appropriate."

Chapter Fifty-Seven

Friday, April 23–Saturday, April 24

"They are ready for you now," Arthur Madison's secretary informed Kathryn. In the conference room a committee of three, Arthur Madison included, waited to hear the presentation of her defense and rationale for her doctoral dissertation. All rose at her entrance, Arthur smiling, wiggling his eyebrows at Kathryn like a conspiratorial schoolboy. As she took her seat, a bottle of champagne was cooling in an ice bucket in the corner. After all her arduous preparation, was this proceeding to be nothing but a rubber-stamped apology?

But no, the committee had come prepared. Quite ignoring the obvious fact that her invention had been stolen from her, the patent for it to be granted to the thief on that day, the members listened intently to Kathryn as she presented her analysis and prototype. To put a credible finish to the proceeding, the committee asked well-prepared and challenging questions. Then Kathryn was excused to wait in the hall while the committee called for the final vote.

"Congratulations, Dr. Walker," Arthur announced, beaming,

when he came to fetch her from the hall. Each member of the committee had signed the front page of her dissertation in full support of awarding the degree. All had agreed on the quality of her research, the soundness of her logic, the originality of her ideas, and the lucidity of her prose—the body of elements that Dr. Croft had nixed in his evaluation of her work.

"It's a shame your husband is not practicing here in Houston so you could put that degree to work with us, Kathryn," Arthur said when the others had left after a round of champagne. "I don't imagine Avon, Colorado, offers much of a chance at that. Just today several biotech companies reached out, looking for recruits to fill positions in their labs."

"Do you happen to have their contacts?" Kathryn asked.

Arthur looked surprised. "Are you interested?"

"I might be."

He searched her face. "Follow me to my office, and I'll get them for you," he said. "And then I hope you will agree to be our guest for dinner tonight? I'd like you to meet my wife. Fridays we eat at Houston's Steak House. We'll pick you up."

Back in her rental car, before starting the motor, Kathryn first called her children to impart the news of her victory, then dialed Drew. His phone rang and rang, surprising her, since his last words before leaving the house that morning were that he'd be standing by to receive her call. Chagrined, she left a clipped voicemail, then settled back against the car seat and drew in a deep, satisfied breath. *Dr. Kathryn Turner Walker.* The bells of a cathedral to her ears. Not only would she now be able to earn a living for herself, but the degree that she had dreamed of since she was a child was finally hers.

Drew finally called just as she was leaving to meet the Madisons, full of apologies for missing her earlier. "I was called into a meeting with Hensley that didn't go well," he said, sounding upset. "I'll tell you about it when I see you Sunday. We have to talk, Kathryn."

"There you go, sounding ominous again." His reaction to her achievement felt like a puncture to her triumph over Edmund Croft.

"I know," he said apologetically. "Congratulations, Kath. Enjoy your evening with the Madisons."

The next morning, Kathryn called the numbers of the bioengineering firms Arthur had given her, on the chance that someone in the know might be working on Saturday. It was the type of vocation notorious for luring dedicated scientists back to their labs on a Saturday morning to pursue what they'd begun during the week, or catch up on paperwork when the rest of the working world was enjoying their weekends.

Her first two calls reached recordings that the offices were closed, but a private phone number had been scribbled on the back of the third card belonging to the Carleton Corporation. Kathryn dialed it, and to her surprise, someone answered. From his annoyed "Yeah!" Kathryn could tell she'd caught him in the middle of something. Scientists did not suffer fools gladly, so in an unwavering voice, she made sure she did not sound like one. She introduced herself, explained the reason for the call and how she'd come by the number, and asked if the speaker could assist her with information.

The man identified himself as Dr. Clark, vice president of research and development. "I appreciate Dr. Madison getting back to me. How about we set you up for an interview Monday morning at ten?"

Monday morning? Her return flight was booked for Sunday. It didn't matter. She would cancel it and take another Monday afternoon. "I'll be there," she said.

She spent the rest of the day preparing the groundwork for a life without her husband. She had googled the Carleton Corporation, and seen that there were a few apartments available for rent in the area. All good news, should she need it. She called United Airlines to rebook her flight, and the reservationist informed her that her Sunday flight would possibly have had to be canceled anyway. A severe thunderstorm was headed into Colorado, and the Eagle River Valley would get the brunt of it.

Relieved to have a good explanation to give Drew about the canceled flight, Kathryn texted him not to expect her until late Monday afternoon. She'd be back on April 26, with four more dreaded days to go before the end of April.

Chapter Fifty-Eight

Sunday, April 25–Monday, April 26

Drew telephoned as Kathryn was on her way to breakfast in the hotel's coffee shop on Sunday morning. Disappointment, even desperation, was thick in his voice. "You were right about the canceled flight, Kath. It's raining buckets here, and parts of I-70 are closed because of flooding. What lousy timing."

"Call Frank to keep you company."

"I'm not in the mood for his company. I want yours. I had hoped we could have this evening to talk."

"It will keep until tomorrow. I'll get a flight and should be at the house by the time you get home from the gym."

"I'm not going to the gym. I'll be here when you arrive. Book the flight as early as you can, Kathryn. I need to see you."

He hung up before Kathryn could offer another word. Once Drew would have said, *I need to* be with *you*.

Next she telephoned Arthur Madison with news of her Monday appointment at the Carleton Corporation and to ask for advice. Without a résumé or work experience, she worried that she might be laughed out of Dr. Benjamin Harris's office—if he was capable of laughter, she thought.

Without a trace of surprise at her interest in the job, Arthur asked for the number on the back of the card. "Have no fear," he said. "Biomedical engineers are in demand. Houston is steadily becoming a mecca for life sciences corporations, and laboratory positions are hard to fill. Leave it to me."

The next morning, Kathryn set out for her interview. Not to her surprise, she found Dr. Benjamin Harris much as she'd pictured him in her mind, a cross between a curmudgeon and a teddy bear. Arthur had paved the way, and Harris received her with a sympathetic ear. He warmed to her quickly, and at the conclusion of the interview, Kathryn left his office with a job, with the title of assistant to the scientific director, and a commensurate salary based on a probationary period. She would begin her new duties May 11. That would give her time to settle into the apartment she leased on her way back to her hotel.

The storm proved to be a hit-and-run affair, and Kathryn's Monday United Airlines flight arrived on time at the Eagle County Regional Airport in the late afternoon. She decided to collect her car and get on the highway before notifying Drew that she had arrived, but before she could make the call, her cell rang. The caller was Lonnie. She pulled over to the side of the road to take the call, her eardrums so deafened by her heartbeat that she wondered if she'd be able to hear him.

The moment she said hello, Lonnie said, "He's on his way home. His plane landed at JFK at sixteen hundred hours. He'll have to report to Langley for a debriefing."

"Will I be able to talk to him?" Kathryn said. She did and always would love her husband, a fact that had been as obvious to Mike as it had become crystal clear to her. She could never give her heart wholly to another man, not in the way that a man like Mike deserved. But he had figured that out for himself in Houston.

"I think he knows where you stand," Lonnie said, "and he understands. We both do."

It was pointless now to meet Mike face-to-face. He had the full picture. She would probably never see him again, but he would remain in her memory as the man to whom she owed the rest of her life. For his sake, she would make the best of it.

"Then give him my best, with thanks to you both for everything," she said simply to Lonnie, with the lump in her throat that always forms at permanent goodbyes.

"I will, and it was our pleasure," the foreman said, and hung up.

Next, Kathryn dialed Drew's cell. "I'm on my way," she said.

"I'll have a martini waiting," he said. "You may need it."

Chapter Fifty-Nine

Drew came out into the garage before she'd cut the motor and embraced her in a hug that cut off her breath. Then he led her into the family room and to her recliner, as if she were a stranger unfamiliar with the layout of her own house. He handed her a martini and cleared his throat, cutting right to the chase, as if he might lose courage if he delayed a moment longer.

"Kath, I have some confessions that I hope won't make you hate me."

Kathryn sipped her martini, outwardly calm. She'd thought she was ready for this, but the familiar pressure was mounting in her chest. "I could never hate you, Drew." With some sorrow she saw that, whereas before he could have passed for a man years younger, his age had caught up with him.

"You say that now, but you may change your mind." Drew took a deep breath. In a voice filled with anguish, he said, "Kathryn, honey, I have been a fool. From the beginning of our marriage, I was determined never to let you down, never give you reason to think less of the man you married because I had failed you. Even if I faltered behind the scenes, in my lone-wolf style I have always managed to pull through without involving you." He waited for some reaction from her, but when not even a flicker of emotion gave a clue to her thoughts, he pulled in another breath and plowed on. "But I have failed you, Kathryn. We are in serious debt. I should never have invested in that ski resort. It's now gone defunct, and the investors are out every nickel. I owe the bank five hundred thousand. I let you assume we had the full capital from our savings to buy in, but we now owe hundreds of thousands in credit card debt. I've been having the credit card statements sent to my office so that you wouldn't see them."

Drew paused for some display of shock, rage, or disgust as the impact of his deceit struck, but Kathleen merely sipped her drink as if none of this were new information and waited patiently for him to continue. Puzzled at her lack of response, he swept on to deliver the next blow. "And . . . I can't pay it back unless . . . unless we sell the house."

"It's just a house, Drew," she said, shaking her head as if the matter was insignificant.

Drew stared at her in astonishment. "But you *love* this house!"

"I do. I really do. But sometimes a situation forces us to give up what we love," she said, and decided to offer a crumb of comfort. "At least we have an asset that should more than cover your expenses, with money left over."

At this, there followed the habitual squeeze of his eyes. "Well, you see, that's the thing." He plunked himself down on a nearby ottoman, the hangdog shame in his eyes preparing her for more to come. "We're broke, Kath. There won't be any money left over once the bills are paid, bills that I and I alone ran up. I've tried to economize, cut out spending, some of which made me, well . . . lie to you, again. I . . . no longer belong to the Argyle. I haven't been a member for at least six months. I've been working out in Elizabeth's basement instead."

"That must have been handy," she said. "It's so close to the hospital."

"Did you hear what I just told you? We are broke, Kathryn."

"Well, we've been broke before."

Her serenity seemed to unnerve him. He put his hands on her knees. "I must say, you are taking this better than I thought you would."

"Anything else you wish to confess?" she asked placidly.

"Yes." He hunched forward, took the glass from her hand, and set it on the table beside her chair, a sign that the worst was yet to come. The table was an expensive inlaid pecan piece, but Kathryn no longer cared about water marks. She would not be taking much from the house to her apartment anyway. The rest would remain for Drew and Elizabeth to deal with.

Drew was talking again. "I won't be getting the job as the Nuggets' team physician. It went to a surgeon in Denver. . . ."

Drew's voice trailed off. He peered at his wife closely. "Kathryn, are you okay?"

"I know about you and Elizabeth," Kathryn admitted finally, unable to wait any longer.

"Elizabeth?"

"I heard the two of you in your office. She kept saying that she just wanted to be married. She gave you an ultimatum, to be married by the end of April."

Drew paused, studying her face, then let out a laugh. "Kath, Elizabeth's gay. She and Barbara are living together. Elizabeth took a job in California, and she wants Barbara to move with her—"

"And the commitment she was talking about. . . ."

"I've been trying to help them. Barbara is a bit commitment phobic, and to make matters worse, Hensley was panicking about possibly losing three of her best surgeons. She made Barbara a really big job offer, just to keep her here."

"Barbara had this silly notion that they could do something long distance." Drew shrugged. "It was a whole mess."

Kathryn sat in silence, shocked, trying to make sense of the past month. She felt terrible for all of the hurtful things she had said and thought about Elizabeth. "I can't believe I thought she and you were having an affair, and this whole time she was going through something so dreadful."

"Oh, Kathryn, honey, I am so very sorry for all of this. Please forgive me for not trusting you with my failures, for believing that you would think less of me. I know it's hurt you, that barrier. It's been my shield since I was a kid, even against you, the woman I trust with all of my heart, and whose trust in me I've betrayed."

"Let's start over," Kathryn said, grasping Drew's knees. "I have a confession, too. This morning I had an interview with a biotech company in Houston. There are hospitals and sports teams there. It's the fresh start you and I need."

"That's a good idea." He paused. "The children will be happy to come visit every chance they get. Kathryn, I love you. I can't live without you. You know that Willie Nelson song? 'There is no me without you. We shall be forever two.' "

He was babbling, tears welling in his own eyes, beginning to leak into the drawn lines of his face.

"Drew," Kathryn said, laughing, "will you just stop talking and hold me?"

He didn't get a chance to reply. Kathryn threw herself into his arms.

Epilogue

Elizabeth and Barbara held a commitment ceremony on the afternoon of April 30. Winston General's doctors and support staff were invited and, surprisingly, turned out in large numbers. Drew served as best man and Kathryn as maid of honor.

Kathryn and Drew's uprooting from Avon and their mountain home was accomplished smoothly and painlessly. Within days, in a quiet transfer of titles, their house was sold to a doctor from Winston General, who was delighted to pick up such a luxurious house at such a discount. Still, the Walkers' equity in the property covered Drew's financial obligations; they were broke, but debt-free. To accommodate the children's visits, they arranged for a larger apartment in the complex Kathryn had leased in Houston, the distance halfway between their respective jobs. They took their return to an apartment to begin the rest of their married life in stride, and even in excitement. In keeping with their new minimalist lifestyle, together they chose the furniture and treasured items that would go with them to their new home, and sold or gave away the rest.

The month held other sterling moments. On Monday, April 19, ten days before the US Patent and Trademark Office was to grant Edmund Croft property rights to Kathryn's invention, Edmund answered his apartment door to a body of officers from the Avon,

Colorado, and Houston Police Departments, unshaven and bleary-eyed from a night of excessive alcohol consumption. Acting on a photograph and a reliable tip that his Nissan was the vehicle that had run down Janet Foster, the law officers presented him with a warrant to conduct a preliminary forensic check on his car, which he had been too distracted to repair. Ordinarily, they would not have found him home, but MediCorp had fired him the Friday before. The forensic team made short work of matching paint from the Nissan to Janet's Burberry. The Houston Police Department turned the disgraced professor over to the custody of the Avon police for arraignment in their jurisdiction.

Only Frank injected a sour note into the Walkers' happy new lives. When Drew explained to him their plans, from the seamless sale of the house to his new position at Houston Memorial, Kathryn's long-overdue launch of a biomedical career, and the arrest of Edmund Croft for the hit-and-run of Janet Foster, Frank carefully set down his drink. "What about Abby Gale?" he asked. "What do you intend to do with her body?"

"We've decided to leave her here, where she has lain for fifteen years. We will never forget her, Frank. But she's gone. She's no longer in her grave, and we must get on with living our lives."

"In an apartment?" Frank scoffed. "How's that going to look as the digs of an orthopedic surgeon when word gets out? Don't you care about appearances?'

Drew shrugged. He no longer had to prove anything to anybody.

So Drew and Kathryn began their new lives in Houston. At the end of their shifts they returned to their cozy apartment, tired but relaxed, eager for the quiet of their evenings together. Bobby had passed his school administrator's exam with flying colors and was now being considered for an assistant principal's position in Lake Charles, Louisiana, three hours from Houston. In Boulder,

Lindsay found out that she had been accepted to medical school at Texas A&M. To Kathryn and Drew's delight, each of their offspring would be only a half day's drive away. And now every night they went to sleep in each other's arms, contented that the April storm they'd weathered was finally over.

Acknowledgments

As Leila's loving partner for fifty-five years, it falls to me to recognize those who were so important to the creation of *April Storm*.

My everlasting thanks go to all her readers, fans, and friends for their support throughout her writing journey, particularly during the writing of this book. It was your interest and encouragement that helped her power through the obstacles she faced.

Thank you to Dr. John Rouse and wife, Susan—true friends—who spent numerous evenings helping with the academic issues that were necessary for the accuracy of the story.

Thank you to one of her former students who provided insight into the character of Mike McCoy.

My gratitude goes to her agent, Johanna Costillo, and to Millicent Bennett of HarperCollins for getting the book published under unusual circumstances.

I am indebted to Diane Giovinazzo, who acted in Leila's stead in putting the editorial finishes to her work.

Finally, I consider myself to be the luckiest of all men to have experienced the caring spirit of such a gentle soul.

—*Richard Meacham*

About the Author

LEILA MEACHAM (1938–2021), a writer and former teacher who lived in San Antonio, Texas, came to writing later in life. Her many successful novels include the bestselling *Roses, Somerset, Tumbleweeds,* and *Dragonfly.*